AN OLD BETRAYAL

Center Point
Large Print

Also by Charles Finch and available from Center Point Large Print:

A Death in the Small Hours
A Burial at Sea

AN OLD BETRAYAL

Charles Finch

CENTER POINT LARGE PRINT
THORNDIKE, MAINE

This Center Point Large Print edition
is published in the year 2014 by arrangement with
St. Martin's Press.

The text of this Large Print edition is unabridged.
In other aspects, this book may vary
from the original edition.
Printed in the United States of America
on permanent paper.
Set in 16-point Times New Roman type.

ISBN: 978-1-61173-961-9

Library of Congress Cataloging-in-Publication Data

Finch, Charles (Charles B.)
    An Old Betrayal : A Charles Lenox Mystery / Charles Finch. — Center Point
Large Print edition.
    pages cm
    ISBN 978-1-61173-961-9 (Library binding : alk. paper)
    1. Lenox, Charles (Fictitious character)—Fiction.
        2. Private investigators—England—London—Fiction.
        3. Murder—Investigation—Fiction. 4. London (England)—Fiction. I. Title.
PS3606.I526A83 2014
813'.6—dc23
                                                        2013030069

This book is for the three people who have meant the most to me in this life:

Anne Truitt, Mary Truitt, Emily Popp

Love is the voice under all silences

Acknowledgments

As I have prepared *An Old Betrayal* for publication, I have also been finalizing the text of my first non-mystery novel, *The Last Enchantments*, which will be published by St. Martin's Press in January. These two projects have made for a very busy year, and the effort and commitment that they've demanded of my editor, Charles Spicer, and his assistant, April Osborn, has been enormous.

Yet Charlie and April have not simply maintained their high standards in the face of this challenge, but handled my work with even more grace, patience, creativity, and kindness than before. It's made me realize what an uncommonly fortunate author I am. My most sincere thanks to both of them.

That gratitude also extends to the other people who have made 2013 easier than it might have been: Sally Richardson, Andy Martin, Sarah Melnyk, Hector DeJean, Paul Hochman, Dori Weintraub, Erin Cox, Courtney Sanks, and my terrific agents, Jennifer Joel and Kari Stuart.

Finally, I want to single out for particular thanks the people who have made my Facebook author page such a warm and interesting community. For a long time I was skeptical about writers on social media, but I've been proven wrong. Interacting with Charles Lenox's readers has been an unexpected and rich pleasure, so relatively far along in his story.

CHAPTER ONE

The long green benches of the House of Commons were half-deserted as the evening session began, scattered with perhaps a few dozen men. It was only six o'clock. As the hours moved toward midnight these rows would fill, and the voices speaking would grow louder to be heard, but for now many of the Members of Parliament were still attending to the chops, the pints of porter, and the ceaseless gossip of the House's private dining room.

In the front bench to the left side of the chamber sat a man with a short beard and kind, intelligent eyes, rather thinner than most gentlemen who were just beyond, as he was, the age of forty. He wore a quiet gray evening suit, and though by now many along the benches had begun to lounge backward and even, in some instances, close their eyes, his face and posture evinced no rebellion against the more or less limitless boredom that the House was capable of inflicting upon its observers. His name was Charles Lenox: Once upon a time he had been a practicing detective, and though he still kept a careful eye upon the criminal world, for some years he had been the Member of Parliament for Stirrington, and politics now comprised the chief work of his life.

"Lenox?" whispered a voice behind him.

He turned and saw that it was the Prime Minister. In his early days in Parliament an informal address from such a figure would have awed Lenox, but now, having moved by his own industry from the back benches to the front, he was accustomed to Disraeli's presence—if perhaps not his company. Rising to an inconspicuous stoop, he said, "Good evening, Prime Minister."

Disraeli motioned him down and sat beside him, then went on, still in a low voice, "I cannot imagine why you have brought yourself here so early in the evening. Not to hear Swick?"

Across the aisle, several rows up, a gentleman was speaking. He was Augustus Swick, a notorious crank. His speech had begun several minutes before, with the comforting assertion that in his view England had never been in a worse position. Now he had moved on to more personal issues. As he spoke, his enormous white mustache shook at its fringes.

"It is 1875, gentlemen, and still I cannot walk across St. James's Street to the Carlton Club without being harassed by every variety of vehicle, your omnibus, your reckless hansom cab, your landau, your rapid, far too rapid, clarence—"

"Pierpont!" called out a lazy voice from a back bench.

"I am delighted to hear that name, sir!" cried Swick, reddening, his brow set so grimly that this profession of delight seemed less than sincere.

"Yes, Pierpont! I had hoped his name might arise, because I must inquire of this chamber, are we all to go to private expense, as Colonel Pierpont did, to install islands in the middle of every road we wish to cross? Do every man's means extend so far? Can private citizens be expected to bear such a burden? I ask you, gentlemen, where will it end? Will it take a horse trampling me to death in Jermyn Street before the attention of this chamber is drawn to the problem of London's traffic?"

"May as well try it and find out," called out the same voice, to mild laughter.

Swick, outraged, drew himself up further, and Disraeli, with a wink, took the opportunity to move to the front bench across the aisle—for he was a Conservative, though he liked to stop in among his foes for a friendly word when the chamber was empty. He was sharp, this fellow. He had turned out Lenox's own party's leader, William Gladstone, the year before, but since then he had very carefully won around both sides of the House by tempering his imperial ambitions for England with an unexpected social conscience. Just that evening they were going to discuss the Artisans' and Labourers' Dwellings Improvement Act—a bill that sounded as if it might have come from Gladstone himself.

In fact, this was why Lenox had come to the chamber early. He had a word to get in.

By the time Swick had finished speaking, ten or

fifteen more men had filed into the Commons, and the serious business of the evening was near its commencement. The Speaker recognized the only man to stand after Swick—Edward Twinkleton, a midlands glue baron. He began to address Disraeli's act.

The housing of the poor was a serious issue, perhaps the one to which Lenox had, in recent months, devoted more time than to any other. Only that morning he had driven to the slums of Hungerford to see the problem firsthand.

Despite its origin in his own Conservative benches, Twinkleton stood firmly against the bill and was now making a long-winded argument about the idle poor. When he had concluded, Lenox stood up and, after recognition from the Speaker, began his response.

"The chief issue is not, as my honorable friend presumes, one of the comfort of our poorer citizens, but of their health. May I ask whether he is familiar with the usual, and vile, practice of the builders in these neighborhoods? Commissioned by Her Majesty's government to construct new edifices, they take the very fine gravel we, the taxpayers, have purchased—for the construction of the foundation—and they sell it on the black market. Then they replace it with something called 'dry core,' gentlemen, a mixture of trash, dead animals, and vegetables. It is only March, but in the summer, I am informed, the smell is beyond belief. Can we rightly call this England, if Parliament gives its endorsement, this evening, to such practices?"

Lenox sat down and thought he saw Disraeli incline his head slightly across the aisle in thanks—though perhaps not.

Twinkleton rose. "I commend my honorable friend's insight into the issue, and yet it cannot be lost on him that these people have always lived in the city, always in suchlike conditions, and that there seem to be more of them than ever! No amount of dry core reduces their number!"

Lenox stood to respond. "The honorable gentleman from Edgbaston neglects to consider, perhaps, the historical context of our time. During the period of the honorable gentleman's childhood—"

"As I did not receive a card from my honorable friend upon the recent occasion of my birthday, I do not see how he can be so certain of my age."

This drew a laugh, but Lenox bore onward. "During the period of the honorable gentleman's childhood," he said, "or thereabouts, one in five Britons lived in a city. Now it is edging toward four in five. Even to a very dim intellect that must be acknowledged a change."

There was laughter on Lenox's own side now, and a diffident round of hissing and catcalling on the other, all very usual, at this slight, and as Lenox sat down upon the green baize bench, smiling faintly, Twinkleton rose up, his face also traced with amusement, clearly raring for battle. Instead the Speaker, chary perhaps of any further devolution of courtesy in the chamber, chose to call for rebuttal on Montague, a Member from Liverpool. Twinkleton would have his chance again in a moment. In the meanwhile, Montague, who had all the charisma and verve of a dying houseplant, returned the tone of the House's discourse to its proper tedium.

When Montague had been speaking for ten minutes or so, Lenox saw that a red-haired boy was approaching him, having darted down one of the aisles. This was Frabbs, his clerk, a bright and attentive lad. He handed Lenox a note. "Just came to the office, sir," he said.

"Thank you," said Lenox.

He tore the envelope and read the short note inside. Interesting. "Any reply, sir?" asked Frabbs.

"No, but find Graham and ask him whether the vote on this bill will come in this evening, or if he thinks there will be another day of debate. You can signal me from the door, I shall keep an eye on it."

"Yes, sir."

Graham was Lenox's political secretary, his most important ally; it was a position in most instances occupied by some ambitious son of the upper classes, fresh from Charterhouse or Eton, but Graham was, unusually—perhaps even uniquely—a former servant. For many years he had been Lenox's butler. A compact, sandy-haired, and shrewd fellow, he had taken to his new position without faltering, and now had more to do with the running of Parliament than fully half of the body's own Members.

As Montague bore onward, down into the depths of his prepared remarks, Lenox's eyes kept flitting to the side door where Frabbs would appear. Catching himself at it once too often, he smiled: It was the old internal debate, the mild pleasures of Parliament, the sense of duty he felt to be there, laid against the thrill of being out on the hunt. Detective work.

Lenox's father had been a great man in the Commons, and now his older brother, Sir Edmund Lenox, stood among the two or three chiefs of the party. For his part, Charles had always taken a great interest in politics, too—had sometimes wished that the seat in the family's bestowal, which of course Edmund took upon reaching maturity, might have been his—and had been thrilled when he won his own. It felt like an ascent, for in truth many of his class looked upon Lenox's previous career as a folly, even an embarrassment.

How he missed the old life! Twice in the past two years he had emerged briefly from retirement, on both occasions in singular circumstances, and now he often thought of those cases, their particular details, with a longing to be back in the middle of them. No morning passed in which he did not pore over the crime columns of the newspapers, coffee growing cold in its cup.

He thought of all this because of the note Frabbs had passed him: It had come from his former protégé in detection, Lord John Dallington, asking for help on a case. Having read it ten minutes before, Lenox itched with irritation at his position already, eager to be gone from the Commons.

It was true that he had promised Disraeli, and several other men, that he would be an assiduous participant in these debates. Still, he had already exchanged words with Twinkleton once, and for an hour or two's absence anyway he would hardly be missed. Particularly if the vote was to be delayed beyond that evening.

Ah! There was Frabbs's head, popping around the doorjamb—and yes, there was the thumb in the air. With a murmured good-bye to the men on his bench, and a promise that he would return just after the break, Lenox stood and made for the exit, happier than he had been since he left the house that morning. A strange circumstance, Dallington's note had promised. Lenox smiled. Who knew what might await him out there in the great fervid rousing muddle of London?

CHAPTER TWO

A stroll up and across Green Park took Lenox to Half Moon Street, where Dallington lived. The address was a fashionable one, popular especially among the young and idle rich, lying as it did close by both their clubs and Hyde Park, where they might ride their horses in the morning. Dallington lived toward the Curzon Street end, almost precisely halfway between Parliament and Lenox's own house in Hampden Lane, which was situated in the leafy, more sedate precincts of Grosvenor Square.

John Dallington, the youngest son of a very kindly duke and duchess, must have been twenty-seven or -eight by now—but he was fixed in many London minds as a disreputable cad of twenty, who had been sent down from Cambridge in sordid circumstances, then spent the subsequent years making the acquaintance of every gin hall and debauched aristocrat in Mayfair.

This image might have been just once, but by now it was unfair. Lenox knew as much firsthand. Several years before, Dallington had, to the older man's very great astonishment, expressed an interest in detective work, and though the lad was still prone, in times of boredom, to relapse, visiting with friends from that less seemly era of his life, by and large he had settled into adulthood. His apprenticeship to Lenox had been profitable to both men. Indeed, through his own intelligence and industry he had now succeeded Lenox as the premier private detective in the city—or at the very least trailing just behind one or two other men who followed the same calling.

Dallington inhabited a chalk-colored building of four floors, taking the large second story for himself. At the front door now was the neighborhood's postman, in his familiar uniform, the scarlet tunic and high black hat. Dallington's landlady—a redoubtable and highly proper personage in her twenty-fifth month of mourning for her husband, only a little black crepe around her shoulders—answered the door and took the post, then saw Lenox farther down the steps.

"Mr. Lenox?" she said, as the postman touched his hat and retreated.

"How do you do, Mrs. Lucas?" Lenox asked, climbing the steps.

"Are you here to see Lord John, sir?"

"If I might."

"Perhaps you can convince him to take his toast and water."

"Has he been ill?" Toast and water was the food considered most suitable for convalescents, at least for those who belonged to the generation of Lenox, of Mrs. Lucas, of Twinkleton—boiling water poured over burnt toast, and mashed into something like gruel. Personally Lenox had never found it palatable.

This made sense of the note, at any rate, which had contained a postscript apologizing that the young lord couldn't come to him.

"You shall see for yourself," she said, turning and leading him into the dim hallway.

"Not contagious, is he?"

"Only his mood, sir."

"I see."

She lifted a candle from the table in the front hall and led him up the stairs. A boy was sweeping them but made way.

"Mr. Lenox, here to see you," called the landlady when they reached Dallington's door, tapping it chidingly with her nails.

"Push him in!" called out the young lord. "Unless he doesn't like to get consumption."

"Ignore him," she whispered. "Good evening, Mr. Lenox."

"Good evening, Mrs. Lucas."

By contrast to the shadowy stairwell, Dallington's rooms were a riot of light, candles and lamps everywhere. Such was his preference. Because of that the air was always tolerably warm there, especially now, in the spring. The sitting room one entered from the hall was pleasant and comfortable, with dog-eared books in piles upon the mantel and one of the sofas, watercolors of Scotland upon the wall, and a cottage piano in the corner,

"How do you do, Dallington?" asked Lenox, smiling.

The young man lay upon a divan, surrounded by discarded newspapers and letters stuffed back into their envelopes. He wore—the privilege of the ill—comfortable clothes, a soft jacket of blue merino and gray woolen trousers, with scarlet slippers on his feet. "Oh, not very badly."

"I'm glad to hear it. Now—"

"Though if I die I would like you to have my collection of neckties."

"They're too colorful for me. It might be that an especially garish meat-pie seller would agree to take possession of the quieter ones."

Dallington laughed. "In truth it's only a head cold, but I must keep Lucas on her toes, or she's liable to come it pretty high. Toast and water, indeed."

His appearance made a lie of this deprecation, however. Despite his years of drink he was usually healthy-looking, face unlined, hair sleek and black. At the moment, by contrast, his skin was pallid, his eyes red, his person disheveled, and on top of that he had a nearly continuous cough, though he managed mostly to stifle it in a handkerchief. It seemed no wonder that he didn't feel equal to venturing out upon a case.

"I can't stay long," Lenox said.

"Of course, and thank you for coming—I thought perhaps you might not be able to get away from the Commons at all. It's only that I'm due out to meet a client at eight in the morning, and finally decided two hours ago that I don't think I can go."

"You couldn't reschedule?"

"That's the damnable bit, I—" Here Dallington broke into a fit of coughing, before finally going on in a hoarse voice. "I have no way of reaching the person who sent the note. An enigmatic missive, too. You can pick it out from the birdcage, if you like, the red envelope."

This brass birdcage, absent of avian life, was where Dallington kept his professional correspondence. It hung near the window. Lenox went to it and found the letter Dallington meant, tucked between two bars. It was undated.

Mr. Dallington,
The police cannot possibly help me; perhaps you might. If you are amenable to meeting, I will be at Gilbert's Restaurant in Charing Cross Station from eight o'clock Wednesday morning, for a space of thirty-five minutes. If you cannot contrive to meet me then I will write to you again soon, God willing. You will know me because I am dining alone, and by my light-colored hair and the striped black umbrella I always carry.
Please please come.

"Well, what do you make of that?" Dallington asked. "It is unsigned, of course, which tells us that he desires anonymity."

"Yes."

"Moreover, he cannot know me very well, to address me as Mr. Dallington. I don't stand upon much titled formality but I generally receive it anyhow."

"What else?"

Dallington shrugged. "I cannot see much farther into it."

"There are one or two telling details," said Lenox. "Here, for instance, where he says he'll wait for thirty-five minutes."

"Why is that odd?"

"Such a specific length of time? Given that he proposes meeting at a train station, it suggests, to me, that he will catch a train shortly after 8:35. Do you have a Bradshaw?"

"On the shelf there," said Dallington.

Lenox pulled the railway guide down and browsed through it, frowning, until he found the listings for Charing Cross. "There is an 8:38 for Canterbury. The following train doesn't leave until 8:49. I think we may presume that your correspondent is traveling to Kent."

"Bravo," said Dallington. "Is there anything else?"

"Yes," said Lenox. He paused, trying to define his reaction in his own mind before he told it to Dallington; for the letter had unsettled him.

"Well?"

"It is something in the tone. I don't know that I can identify it precisely." He gestured toward the page. "Its despairing scorn for the police, for instance. His carefully generic description of himself."

"He is being cautious, you mean?"

Lenox shook his head. "More than that. This phrase, 'God willing,' and then this rather desperate final line. All of it together makes me believe that the man who wrote this letter is living in a state of mortal fear."

CHAPTER THREE

Just before ten that evening Lenox's carriage pulled to a slow stop in front of his house in Hampden Lane.

"A great many lights on downstairs for the hour," he murmured to Graham, who was sitting beside him. "Yet Jane must be done with supper by now."

Graham, who was reading the minutes of an electoral meeting in Durham, didn't look up. "Mm."

Lenox glanced over at him. "Do you never tire of politics?"

Now Graham did pull his eyes away from the paper, lifting his gaze toward his employer. He smiled. "I find that I do not, sir."

"I sometimes think you're better suited to all of this than I am."

"As for the lights, I would hazard that Lady Jane is waiting for you to arrive home. Not Sophia, hopefully. Well past her bedtime."

Lenox clicked his tongue in disapproval at the idea, though in truth he would have been selfishly pleased to find the child awake. Sophia was his daughter, now nearly two years of age, a plump, pink creature. All of the mundane achievements of her time of life—stumbling around in a mildly convincing impression of upright mobility, speaking fragmentary sentences—were an unceasing enchantment to her parents, and even to hear her name in passing, as he just had, still made Lenox happy. After a lifetime of polite boredom when confronted with children, he had finally found one whose companionship seemed a delight.

Lenox stepped onto the pavement from the carriage, Graham behind him, and started up the steps toward the house. It was a wide one for a London street; before they had married, Lady Jane and Lenox had been next-door neighbors, and by knocking down a few walls strategically they had merged their houses. It had only taken two or three hundred arguments (between two generally mild people) before it was finished to their satisfaction. It was done at last, at any rate, and thank the Lord for it.

With a nod good night, Graham opened Lady Jane's old door, on his way to his rooms there, while Lenox took the front door to the left, the one that had been his own for so many years.

As he came in, the house's butler, Kirk, greeted him and took his coat. "Good evening, sir. Have you eaten?"

"Hours ago. Why the hullabaloo?"

"Lady Victoria McConnell is visiting, sir."

Ah, that explained it. Toto often visited at unusual hours. She was Jane's cousin and also closest friend, a vibrant, sometimes flighty woman, good-humored, even in her thirtieth year now exceedingly youthful. She was married to an older man, a friend of Charles's, Thomas McConnell; he was a doctor, though he didn't practice any longer, such work being conceived as below the dignity of Toto's great, very great, family.

"Are they in the drawing room?"

"Yes, sir."

This was down the front hall and toward the left, and it was here that Lenox turned his footsteps, walking briskly past the flickering lamps in their recessed sconces along the wall. It was good to be out of the Commons. The debate was still going, and he had spoken several times more after returning from his visit to Dallington, but it had become apparent quickly that there would be no immediate vote—many men had much to say upon the merits and imperfections of the bill—and that the truly consequential speeches, from the frontbenchers, would be delayed until the next evening.

He came in and found Lady Jane and Toto side by side on the rose-colored sofa, speaking in low voices.

"Charles, there you are," said Jane, rising to give him a swift kiss on the cheek.

"Hello, my dear. Toto, I fear you look distressed."

She ran a hand through her blond hair. "Oh, not especially."

He went to the sideboard to pour a glass of Scotch. "Did you have money on Scheherazade in the fourth at Epsom? Dallington lost his shirt."

It was then, to his surprise, that Toto burst into tears, burying her face in Jane's quickly encircling arms.

In a woman of slightly lower birth it would have been a distasteful spectacle. Rules soften toward the top, however. It was not the first time Toto had cried in Hampden Lane, usually because of a mislaid necklace or a serial novel without a happy ending, and it wouldn't be the last.

"Don't be beastly, Charles," said Jane. "Toto, you and I shall go to my dressing room—come along."

Toto, wiping her eyes, said, "Oh, who gives a

fig whether Charles sees me cry. I cried in front of Princess Victoria when I was a child after my aunt pinched my neck—to keep me quiet—and had a square of chocolate as a prize, so who knows what good may come of crying in front of people, I say. Charles, come and set yourself upon that couch, if you like. You can hear it all, the whole truth about your horrid friend."

As he sat Toto gave a fresh sob, and Lenox, having believed it to be another trifle, saw that Toto, whom he loved, was truly upset. Alarmed, he asked, "What has happened?"

There was a long pause. At last, softly, Lady Jane said, "She is worried about Thomas."

Immediately Lenox's thoughts flew to drink, and he felt a lurch of worry. There had been a time when McConnell was lost to that vice, in the earlier years of his married life with Toto, when she had been perhaps too callow to support him, he perhaps too weak to handle the disappointment of abandoning his vocation, finding himself lost in so many empty hours.

Matters had improved since that time, especially after the birth of their child, Georgianna—or George, as she was called—but not to the degree that bad news would ever come entirely unexpected.

As it happened, however, his fears were misdirected. Toto, steadying herself, said, "I believe he has taken up with another woman."

Lenox narrowed his eyes. "McConnell? I can't credit that."

"It's Polly Buchanan, the shrew."

Lenox lifted his eyebrows. "Ah."

"I don't believe she'll rest until she's turned Sydenham into Gomorrah, Charles," said Toto— her voice imploring, as if she wished it to be true, and then for him to believe it. Her doubts about her suspicion stood in the way of her anger, he could tell. Her face was anguished.

Polly Buchanan was a woman of twenty-five, the relict of a dashing and red-cheeked young soldier named Alfred Buchanan, who had married her in the year '71. The week after their wedding breakfast he had gone out on a hunt in Middlesex wearing neither a coat nor a hat, contracted pneumonia, and almost immediately, with an appalling lack of consideration for his new wife, died.

With the sympathy of the world wholly hers, Polly had used the subsequent three years to flirt with every married gentleman in London, until she had a terrible reputation among their wives and rather a fond one in the clubs of Pall Mall. ("She turns a fine leg" was the sort of thing one portly gentleman at the Oxford and Cambridge might say to another.) Since she had never positively trespassed upon conventional morality and had excellent connections, she was still widely received—though rarely, any longer, much pitied.

"But Toto, dear," said Lenox, "what cause can you have to suspect Thomas of seeing this woman?"

"They rode together across Hyde Park two mornings ago, three turns, and again, I am reported, this morning, three turns."

"You were not there?"

"No. I was taking care of Georgianna while he complimented her hideous green eyes, I don't doubt, the swine."

There was a moment's silence, into which Toto sobbed. When he spoke, Lenox's voice was skeptical. "So based solely upon this rumor you have concluded—"

Toto looked up at him with furious eyes, but before she could reply Jane did. "No, Charles, you have come into the conversation halfway through. Thomas has been a different man for some weeks now."

"*Six* weeks," said Toto with profound emphasis upon the number, as if it were dispositive proof of an unspecified crime. Then she added, miserably, "He's never seemed so happy in all the time I've known him."

"Toto, dear, it must be something else. His work, for instance."

"He's working less than ever." McConnell had a variety of scientific interests and an extensive chemical laboratory. "He goes two days sometimes without entering his study."

That looked bad. "How does he occupy his time?"

"At his club," said Toto. "Or so he says. I cannot face him tonight, Jane. I cannot face a lie from my own husband."

"You may stay here," said Charles.

Jane scoffed at that notion. "No, don't say that, Charles. Toto, we would be pleased to have you, always, but you cannot run from your husband at the drop of a hat. Think, what if he is innocent of these trespasses and you stay away from home? Imagine his bewilderment. And then, is it good for George? You must rein in your imagination, Toto. It is for the best that way. Believe me, I only want you to be happy."

But Toto, however, determined to deny her cousin this gratification, burst into a fresh sob, and for the next fifteen or twenty minutes said very little and would take no refreshment or consolation. Finally, with only a meager attempt at appearing reassured, she left, promising to call in again the next evening. She might have more information then, she thought.

It was bad, no doubt of that. When they had closed the door behind her, Charles and Jane looked at each other with tight-lipped sympathy, sighed at the same time, and without needing to speak about it to understand what each felt—the sorrow, the doubt, the faint tincture of intrigue—began to walk toward the stairs leading up to their bedroom.

CHAPTER FOUR

Just before noon each Tuesday, Arthur, a footman belonging to the staff of Lenox's house, took the London underground to Paddington Station, carrying two pocket watches. Usually with a minute or two to spare he arrived at the terminal and watched, with a feeling of stale drama, as the large railway station clock ticked toward the hour. When it finally struck twelve o'clock, he reset both watches, one in each hand, to the same time.

This accomplished, he returned to Hampden Lane and wound all the clocks to match the hour upon the pocket watches, or at any rate an average thereof, which usually put the house within five seconds or so of British railway time.

So it had been for many years; it was a quirk of Lenox's, from the days when he had used the rail system at every odd hour of the day, several times each week on occasion, in his detective work, and needed to be absolutely sure of where he stood in relation to the timetables the railways printed. Like the copies of Bradshaw handily situated in half a dozen rooms of his house, it was an essential professional advantage.

When the clock chimed for half past seven the next morning, therefore, Lenox, sitting over a cup of coffee and a plate of toast and eggs, the *Times* kinked just inward in his hands to give it a firm spine, knew that it was precisely 7:30—that he was not, like most London houses, three or four or twelve minutes out, in who-knew-which direction.

He rose, buttoned his jacket, took a final sip of coffee, and went outside, where the horses, warmed ten minutes before, were waiting with his carriage.

It was a crisp, white-skied spring morning, with a firm breeze minutely rearranging the world every few seconds as it gusted, a collar flicked up before it settled again, weak new petals scattered from their branches into the streets. When he was settled on the blue velvet bench of the carriage and the horses had begun to pull, he gazed out of his window at the day. He wondered about the man who had written to Dallington—what troubled him, why he was seeking help.

The horses carried Lenox with tolerable briskness down the Strand, and soon the new Eleanor Cross came into view. This tall, thin gray monument was only ten years old—or nearly six hundred, if you accepted the spirit of the thing. In 1290, when Eleanor of Castile had died, her grieving husband, King Edward the First, had ordered a cross to be erected at twelve locations between Lincoln and London: each place where the retinue had slept for the night during the procession that bore her body to Westminster

Abbey. Cierring, a name that denoted a specific turn of the Thames, had been the final stop, and in time, the vicissitudes of spelling having finally settled, it became the Charing Cross. During the English Civil War it had been taken down and lost; now Victoria had installed its replacement.

In practice it was now most often a meeting point rather than one of reflection or piety, for of course Charing Cross was also the site of one of the busiest rail stations in London. As they pulled into the drive outside of it, Lenox could see the blue and white striped awning of Gilbert's Restaurant.

He pulled out his pocket watch. Six minutes shy of eight. "Thank you," he called up to the coachman. "Wait here, if you please."

Gilbert's was a place for a quick meal, with a simple menu, fish in the morning, chops at noon and night. It was also small. There were three mirrored walls and one glass one, looking out at the carriages and hansoms in front of the station.

As he came in, his eyes worked over the room. There were a handful of solitary diners, all men, but all were dark-haired, and none had a striped umbrella. The author of the letter to Dallington had yet to arrive.

Lenox took a seat in the corner farthest from the door, where he could see anyone who entered the establishment. A waiter, whom Lenox had overheard at another table speaking in an Italian accent, approached him. "Sir?" he said.

"Bring me a cup of coffee and a copy of the *Telegraph*, if you would."

"Yes, sir. Anything to eat, sir?"

"In a moment perhaps."

In a rack near the bar at Gilbert's were all the day's newspapers, hanging over wooden dowels. The waiter fetched the *Telegraph*—at a penny a bit further down-market than the fourpenny *Times*, but Lenox had already read that this morning—and soon after it a silver pot of coffee. In past years Lenox had read nearly every newspaper published in London, the very yellowest rags, in a hungry pursuit of information about the previous day's crimes, but now he restricted himself. There was so much reading to be done for Parliament—blue books, those slim, blue-bound parliamentary reports, on nearly any subject you could conceive—that he had little choice. To belong on the front benches it was necessary to feign what nature had made impossible, which was a comprehensive knowledge of the world's ills and fortunes. What was the price of tea in Siam? Why was the union leader of Newcastle's ironworkers divorcing? How well kitted-out was the 9th Regiment of Foot for the coming summer? Every man in politics claimed he knew the answer to every question. Only Disraeli, the sharpest mind in every room he entered, might have been telling the truth.

Lenox read the news in the *Telegraph* with mild interest, always aware of the door as it opened and closed. First it brought in a rough-looking man with a long beard, delivering three dozen loaves of bread in oversized wax paper bags, then a woman who took a table not far from Lenox and, seated, began to pore over her diary, biting her lip, scribbling out old appointments and replacing them with new. (What a mystery these women's appointment books were to Lenox. Even Jane's always looked like it bore a madman's private philosophies, scratched and cross-written over and over.) Soon thereafter a gentleman came in, going directly to the bar to order a glass of negus and a hot muffin. Dark hair, no umbrella.

Lenox checked his pocket watch frequently, so often that it would have been conspicuous in any other setting, though it was more natural in a rail station. It passed 8:10 and there was no sign of Dallington's correspondent. Lenox forced himself to read the paper. It was dreary work, until he noticed, with a smile of surprise, a certain advertisement. It was a quarter page and lay just below a half-page advertisement for Carter's Little Liver Pills. It read:

Miss Strickland's Detective Agency
No problem insoluble to our dogged staff
Former bobbies and military men

References provided. Satisfaction guaranteed.
Strictest Confidence.
Thefts Mysteries Puzzles Missing Persons
Live in doubt no longer
119 High Holborn WC1V

He would have to show Dallington. A competitor! It was time someone set up just such a business. He could picture Miss Strickland, too—she was probably a shade over six feet, with a barrel chest, a seaman's tattoo on her forearm, and a black, bristly beard. When inquired for she would have stepped briefly out of the office, leaving her capable assistant, Mr. Smith, or Johnson, or Wells, in charge. It was an old ruse. Customers, especially men, felt they were getting a better bargain when a woman was in charge of a business.

The line that made him smile was second to last: "Live in doubt no longer." Nearly every person of his acquaintance ought to avail him- or herself of Miss Strickland's services, he thought, if she was capable of such conclusive deliverance.

He did wonder what kind of cases such an ad might draw. Many petty ones, no doubt, but perhaps, here and there, something of more serious moment. The agency would have to consult with Scotland Yard if it wished to pursue a murderer, that much Lenox knew with certainty, from long experience.

The waiter looped back to him at 8:18. "Will there be anything else?" he asked. "We have a fine tart, sir."

"I'll take toast and jam," said Lenox.

"Very good, sir."

He was losing hope that the man who had written Dallington would arrive. A loss of nerve, perhaps. A fellow who wouldn't sign a letter no doubt had trepidations about meeting in person. Or perhaps he had looked in the window, failed to see Dallington's face, and gone on his way.

Just as he had this thought, the door opened and a man came in. This was more promising—at any rate he was fair, with light hair.

To Lenox's astonishment, however, it wasn't he who reacted to the newcomer's entrance first. The woman sitting near him—the one who had been sitting and scrutinizing her diary—looked up and started. Then, without saying a word, she dropped a coin on the table, stood up, and, gathering her things haphazardly in her arms, fled through a side door, just as the newcomer spotted her. With a flare of recognition he called out, "Wait!"

Only as she was leaving did Lenox notice, cursing himself for his narrow-mindedness, that she, too, was light-haired—and then, more telling still, that she was carrying hooked upon her forearm a black-and-white striped umbrella.

CHAPTER FIVE

The gentleman in the door of Gilbert's—dressed well, with a recent shave that had left his blond mustache in fine trim—made no movement to pursue the woman. He stood and stared after her for a moment and then sighed and turned back through the door.

Lenox stood up and, just as the woman had, dropped a few distracted coins on the table. "Sir," he called out.

He might have given chase to the woman, but in all likelihood he wouldn't have caught up to her, and if he had it might have frightened her. If only she had left a return address with Dallington.

"Yes?" said the man, who had paused in the doorway upon hearing Lenox's voice.

"May I impose upon you to ask that young woman's name, sir?"

"You may not," said the man coldly.

"Is it too much trouble?"

"I do not believe we are acquainted, and I cannot imagine that she would wish her identity trusted to a stranger. Plainly, since you were seated only a table apart from each other and therefore had the opportunity to speak, she did not desire conversation with you."

Nor you, thought Lenox. Time to pantomime harmlessness, however; after all, this man might be the danger of which the young woman was afraid. "I thought her exceptionally pretty."

"You are not the first."

"But then, perhaps it was some lovers' quarrel that drove her away at the sight of you."

"You are impertinent, sir. Good day."

"Will you take my card?" asked Lenox.

The man hesitated. He was well bred, clearly, his voice aristocratic, his features even and strong, his watch chain and shoes both finely made, and as clearly as Lenox could perceive these small signs in him, he could no doubt perceive them in Lenox. The rules were the rules. "Very well," he said, taking Lenox's without looking at it, then reaching into his own pocket. He couldn't find a card, checked another pocket with no more success, and then, his face puzzled, searched all of his pockets, pulling out a billfold, until at last he gave up the task as a bad job and said, "My name is Archie Godwin. You may find me at White's."

This was a gentleman's club. "As you can see, letters to the Commons will reach me," said Lenox. "Whatever your relation to the young woman, I would like to meet her again."

The man nodded curtly and stalked away.

Lenox could have cursed. It had been a blundering performance all around—first in missing the young woman, then in the faintly ridiculous pretense that he, a man past forty, would pursue a young woman of twenty. To be sure, such marriages existed, but they rarely began at Gilbert's. She would never have condescended to meet him—no matter that he was a Junior Lord of the Treasury now, as his card said—if the introduction did not come through her friends or family. Beyond that, even the most cursory investigation into his background would reveal that he was a married man. Men had affairs, it was true, but to initiate one after such a fashion would have been bizarrely indiscreet for a man of his position.

He returned to the table. The whole situation left him deeply uneasy: He had revealed himself to this Godwin out of a misplaced sense that he must act. In fact, it would in all likelihood have been better had he remained quiet. Dallington would have handled it more adroitly. Or even Miss Strickland, with her agency for detectives. Damn it all.

As he tore moodily at his toast, Lenox thought the encounter over. Was it suspicious that Godwin had been unable to find a card? Was it a name that he ought to have known? He would have to check in at White's.

At least he could do the intelligent thing now. He remained at his table and sat for another ten minutes. He was impatient to leave for every second of them, but if he had returned to his carriage too quickly, and Godwin had stayed to watch, it might have given away that his presence in the restaurant where the young woman took her breakfast was not accidental.

Finally he went out to his waiting carriage. "Half Moon Street," he said. "Quickly if you can."

The driver did his work well, and soon Lenox was at Dallington's flat. The young lord looked even worse than the day before, pale and perspiring, with a white film around his lips. For the first time Lenox felt half-worried, and for a moment forgot Gilbert's. Perhaps he ought to consult with McConnell. It would be best to chase down the doctor anyway, to see what might be found out—discreetly.

Despite his condition Dallington rose when Lenox arrived. "How was it?"

"Disastrous, I'm afraid."

Lenox took five minutes to describe the sequence of events, careful to be very specific about the dress and appearance of both the man and the woman. At the end of the story Dallington, who had been closely attentive, smiled ruefully. "The first pretty girl to light along in all the years I've been doing this, and I have the galloping consumption. What rotten luck."

"I'm sorry I mishandled it, John."

"It can't be helped. I don't doubt I would have done as you did."

"No, you're in better practice than I am."

Dallington waved a hand. "These situations are unpredictable."

"It was particularly foolish of me because a woman is so much more likely than a man to carry an umbrella of such a description. Can you think of a man who possesses an umbrella in any color other than black?"

He admitted that he could not. "I would have made the same assumption, however. You cannot let it prey upon your mind."

"Tell me, do you recognize the name Archie Godwin?"

"No. Or perhaps just, some minor echo—but I couldn't tell you a single detail about him."

"Do you have your *Who's Who* handy?"

Dallington brightened. "I do! Look on the mantel above the fireplace there."

Lenox went and fetched the book, thumbing through it to the *G* section. "Here it is," he said, then read out loud.

Godwin, Archibald Paget, b. May 19, 1846, s. of Hon. Winthrop Godwin and Abigail Paget, educ. Tonbridge School and Wadham College, Oxford. Wadham Cricket Club vice-captain, past president. Dir. Chepstow and Ely, Ltd. Recreation: Angling; cricket. Bugler, Hampshire Hunt. Clubs: White's, Clinkard Meon

> Valley Beagles (Hants). Add. Raburn
> Lodge, Farnborough, Hants.

Lenox looked up. "An address in Hampshire, and none but his club in London. Perhaps we know why he frequents train station restaurants."

"Hm. Do you know Chepstow and Ely?" asked Dallington.

"No, but it shouldn't be difficult to find out what it is."

"Nine to one Graham will know."

"No doubt about it." Lenox looked down at the book he was holding and glanced over the entry again. "Well, what do you make of Godwin?"

Dallington shrugged. "He seems quite ordinary, I suppose. I've yet to have the pleasure of meeting the beaglers of Clinkard Meon Valley, but I don't question their general character. Their intelligence, perhaps, to go chasing about with dogs on cold mornings."

"It's really too bad that Hampshire is on the opposite end of England from Kent, where we suspected your correspondent might be going by train. It would have been tidier if Raburn Lodge were near Canterbury."

"Quite."

"No London address, either," said Lenox again, looking at the book still. "I have a school friend who lives not far from Farnborough, Peter Hughes. Huge medieval castle and not a penny to

43

his name to pay for its upkeep—they live in three of the rooms and keep the rest dark. Perhaps I'll write and ask him about Godwin."

"I would guess that he's up in town briefly, and this girl felt some threat from him—that's why she wanted to meet me."

"Mm."

"You say he didn't give you a card?"

"He didn't. I thought it rather odd."

"I've been caught without mine often enough. It may be that this is merely, as you suggested to him, a quarrel between two estranged lovers." Dallington took a sip of water, looking exhausted. Lenox realized he ought to leave. "It would explain why she felt she could not go to the police."

"Yes, true," said Lenox. "But lie down, would you, John—I will look into White's this afternoon. Make sure you drink a great deal of water. It makes me uneasy to see you so ill. I think I had better send around a doctor."

Dallington looked ready to object but then weakened. "You might as well, I suppose. Mrs. Lucas will fetch him if you tell her."

"I will."

A few minutes later, Lenox walked out into Half Moon Street and climbed into his carriage again. Dallington's explanation was the most likely. A lovers' tiff. Still, he wondered at the vagueness and fear of that initial letter, its strange tone, its enigmatic origin. Before getting into his carriage he paused on the pavement and smiled. What if Archie Godwin and the young woman who didn't want to see him had nothing to do with the letter? The metropolis had offered forth stranger coincidences in its time, many of them.

CHAPTER SIX

G raham knew, of course.
"The Chepstow and Ely is a partnership that manufactures health tonics and scented soaps. They are based in the Ely River valley, sir, in Wales."

"Scented soaps. We are confronted with the classic criminal mastermind, then," said Lenox.

"Sir?"

"Only a joke. Do they do well, Chepstow and Ely?"

"Very well, sir. There are only one or two larger such manufacturers."

They were in Lenox's office in Parliament. It was a substantial, airy room with a view of the Thames. As the two men contemplated the Chepstow and Ely, the pen of young Frabbs was audible, scratching in the anteroom. "If he is listed as a director, I take it he has no express participation in the day-to-day operations of the place?"

"Oh, none, sir. Given Mr. Godwin's youth I

would suppose that he is no more than a city name, appended to their rolls to drum up interest in shares. Did you look up his father, sir?"

"Dead."

"Some familial or personal connection, I would speculate. It is not uncommon for young men who possess position without wealth to exchange a quantity of the former for the promise of the latter."

"How delicately you put it, Graham. In essence you mean that Godwin provides the lineage and some drunken Chepstow or Ely son is permitted to lose money to him at cards?"

"Chepstow is a town in Wales, sir."

"I was being humorous."

Graham smiled wryly. "Ah—no doubt, sir."

"What do I have between now and lunch?"

"You are meeting with Lord Cabot, sir."

"Push him till tomorrow if you could."

"Of course, sir."

"You think there will be a vote tonight?"

"At any rate I shouldn't miss the session, in case there is."

Lenox sighed. "Thank you, Graham."

"Sir."

Lenox did three hours of hard work then, focused intently on drafting a memorandum about the mining bill that was to come before the House the next week. There were also visitors every fifteen or twenty minutes. Once he had

46

made such pilgrimages himself, to the upstairs offices, but as he had grown more senior he found that it was the junior members who called upon him. They wanted any variety of thing; some came to him with ideas, others with requests. Often enough they only wanted to see Graham. In league with the other front-bench secretaries, he controlled the schedule of important meetings, and all of them brokered their masters' votes like experienced men of the turf.

Just after one o'clock Lenox took his hat and cloak and went down to his carriage, which was waiting in the lane outside, alongside a dozen similar ones; nearby was the beautiful pale rise of Westminster Abbey, a whiter shade of stone than the golden Parliament buildings, its intricate details somehow reminiscent of the folds and multiplicities of the world, indeed of God. Lenox stopped and looked for a moment, then got into the carriage and tapped its side. He intended to have his luncheon at home, because he needed some of the papers from his desk. Of course, he might have sent Frabbs or one of the other clerks to fetch them, but it would give him a chance also to look in on Jane and Sophia.

When he arrived home Lady Jane was busy in the long dining room, which she had decided to decorate anew; as far as he could recall she had been engaged in this activity roughly since the dawn of time, when men first stirred forth upon the plain. It had been the subject of one of their many stylistic disagreements upon joining households, though he always immediately ceded to her taste. ("Sideboard jammed stiff with dishes," she had said, teasing him, "and the same red flocked wallpaper the gentleman who sold you the house assured you was fashionable twenty years ago.") She had changed the curtains out for lighter ones, the dark carpet for a pale blue one, and the smoky mahogany cabinets for plain shelves of fresh rosewood. Lenox had to admit it made the room seem cheerier. At the moment workmen were painting the walls a plain Regency white.

"Hello, my dear," said Lenox, as she came halfway down the front hall to meet him. "How has your morning been?"

They kissed and sat down upon a small blue sofa in an alcove near the door.

She was in a cross mood. "Oh, it was wonderful, except for the six gallons of tea. Really, I call it absurd. If you so much as look in upon someone to wish her good day you are forced, by convention, to sit to a cup of tea, no matter how urgent your business elsewhere is— six teas an hour—the Chinamen may take it back, for all I care. No Englishman ever died of drinking water."

Lenox smiled. "In point of fact, that is false. We are nearly certain that cholera is waterborne. Tell me, though, did you see Toto?"

"No. I thought it best to leave her alone for the morning. I'll stop in this afternoon."

"What did Duch think of it all?"

"How did you know I went to her?"

"There was never a greater tea giver. Besides, you see her nearly every day. Does she know Dallington is sick?"

The Duchess of Marchmain was Dallington's mother. "Yes, and she's worried sick over it herself. I can't think how she found out, for I know that he wouldn't have told her himself."

"Mrs. Lucas, I don't doubt," said Lenox.

"As for Toto, Duch predicts it will pass. I told her that it seemed more serious than usual to me."

They chatted on for a few moments, a husband and wife fluent with each other's minor concerns and minor errands, and then Lenox pressed her hand and said he had better do a bit of work. She said she would go make sure that there was something for him to eat.

"I'll be in my study," he said, kissing her on the cheek before heading up the hallway toward the front of the house. His study was the closest room to the front door. Before he entered, he paused and called out, "Will you have a cup of tea with me before I begin work?" He leaned back to see her reaction.

For an instant her face darkened, and she seemed about to curse him—but then she smiled, realizing that it was a joke, and rolled her eyes.

A few minutes later, as he was shuffling through the papers on his desk, Jane knocked on the door and came in without waiting for a response. "Your lunch will be up soon."

"Thank you," he said.

She hesitated in the doorway. "I've just had a letter from Sylvia Humphrey. Word has spread all over London about Thomas and Polly Buchanan, it would appear. She writes to warn me on Toto's behalf."

Lenox looked up, eyes wide, the papers in his hands momentarily forgotten. "No, has it really?"

"I'm afraid so."

"I had thought of trying to see him this afternoon, if for no other reason than to push him around to Dallington's for a look-in."

"Is John that poorly?"

"He'll live. What are they saying about McConnell?"

"Oh, you can imagine. Leave it, for now." She came farther into the room, near his desk. "Speaking of Dallington—how was your meeting at Charing Cross?"

Lenox told her about it, attending again to his papers as he did. She made sympathetic noises at the right moments. In due course a footman arrived with Lenox's food—he often took meals at his desk—and Jane kept him company as he ate, stealing a green pea with her fingers now and again.

"Is Sophia asleep?" he asked when he had finished eating.

Lady Jane glanced at the clock on the mantel. "She ought to be awake. It is nearly two, after all. Shall I fetch her down?"

Lenox looked up at the clock. "I ought to leave soon, but if she's awake I could visit her in the nursery."

Sophia was awake, in fact, and entertaining herself as the house's cook, Ellie, sat in the corner knitting. The child turned, face open with expectation, when they came through the door, and then beamed and clapped her fat hands together with surprised delight at the sight of both of her parents in her nursery. She toddled toward them happily, cooing half phrases, a small bundle of person in a pink dress with a white pinafore and navy woolen stockings.

Lenox lifted her high up into the air, kissed her, and then set her down again. She patted her cheek where his bristles had scratched her. "Where is Miss Emanuel?" Lenox asked Ellie, who was long-enough tenured in Hampden Lane—and cross-grained enough—that she had remained seated after they arrived, though she did pay them the deference of lowering her knitting needles to her lap.

"She is downstairs fetching the little miss a snack, sir."

"You can't say fairer than that," said Lenox.

Lady Jane, who was more at home in the room than her husband, began to tidy, as he stood rather awkwardly near the doorway. Few men could love their child more than he did; yet he saw less of her than he would have wished, because it was not quite right that he should moon around her nursery. It irritated him, to contemplate this stubborn adherence to propriety, and as Sophia crowded his legs, examining his bootlaces, he decided he ought to come upstairs more.

After a few moments Miss Emanuel appeared, greeting them sunnily. This was Sophia's new nurse, a sweet, fair-complexioned young woman with straight black hair, a product of the very fine free Jewish schools in the eastern part of the city. She knelt down to give Sophia a point of toast with marmalade, which Sophia immediately dropped to the floor, sticky-side down, and then, face serious, biting her lip with concentration, set about attempting to pick up.

"No, dear," said Lady Jane gently, stopping her with a hand.

Lenox picked the toast up from the floor and wiped the spot with a cloth that was close to hand. "I observe that our daughter is rather clumsy, Miss Emanuel," he said with a smile. "Jane, perhaps we oughtn't to apprentice her to the seamstress quite yet, as we had planned."

Ellie clucked disapprovingly from the corner.

"To think of making such a joke, the poor darling."

"At any rate we might wait until her fourth birthday, I suppose."

Jane laughed. "Four? Shall she remain indolent as long as that?"

"I had planned to take her outside now," said Miss Emanuel. "Unless you would prefer we stay here in the nursery a while longer?"

Lenox looked at his pocket watch. He should by rights leave for his office again now; Graham would be expecting him. Instead he said, "I think I can find time to take her for a walk," and then, to assuage his guilt—or his lack of guilt, for which in fact he felt guilty—he said he would go downstairs and find ten minutes of work to do in his study, until Miss Emanuel had readied the child to leave.

CHAPTER SEVEN

Later that evening Lenox was glad of the roast chicken, potatoes, and peas he had eaten at home that afternoon, because during the debate there was only time for a biscuit and a glass of port in the Members' Bar, during a ten-minute recess. It was a heated session. In the end it was nearly two o'clock in the morning when the Artisans' and Labourers' Dwellings Improvement Act passed, a strange hybrid object that belonged in the affection of neither party wholly but had enough disjointed support between the two that it became the law of England. When the tide had finally turned, Disraeli gave Lenox, his chief ally among the liberals, a grave nod from across the aisle. It was a gesture few saw but that seemed to Lenox to imply much: thanks, future favors asked and given, even friendship. Compromise received a bad character from some men in the House, the look had said; but not from either of them.

He went to bed utterly spent and permitted himself the luxury of sleeping until nine. When he woke he put on his warm dressing gown—there was a chill outside that morning, the sunlight hard and frosty—and took his cup of coffee in the armchair near the high windows in their bedroom, where he could watch from three stories up the hum of Hampden Lane. Across the street at the booksellers was the oysterman, selling three for a farthing, or six with bread and butter for two farthings, and passing him on the street were any variety of urgent gentlemen. It was a peaceful thing to watch them from a still place, warm and rested.

Kirk came in with a note at twenty past the hour. It was from McConnell. The evening before, Lenox had found a moment to invite the doctor to lunch the next day, but it appeared that his friend had to decline.

Dear Charles,

Unfortunately I'm committed to lunch at the Surgeons' this afternoon, but what do you say to our meeting tomorrow instead? I can come to the Athenaeum at one o'clock if you're free then. Best to Jane and Sophia.

Thos. McConnell

Even a detective so far out of practice as Lenox was capable of stopping into the Surgeons' Club and asking at the front desk whether Dr. McConnell was there. At two o'clock, after a leisurely morning of work at Parliament, that was what he did, though he felt rather shabby for it.

"He is not in at the moment, sir," said the dignified gatekeeper of the place. Portraits lined the walls of this entranceway, where in one corner a man struggled into a pair of galoshes.

"Was he in earlier this afternoon?"

"No, sir. We have not seen him this week past, sir."

"Ah. I must have misread his message."

"Would you like to leave a note for him, sir?"

"Thank you, no," said Lenox.

So. McConnell had deceived him.

He hadn't liked to involve his carriage driver in this expedition, and so as he came out again onto Portugal Street—the club was just near the Royal College of Surgeons—he hailed a passing omnibus, its driver, in his accustomed white top hat, deigning to pull his horses very nearly to a stop. (Some drivers refused to stop for anything less than a marquess. Their discrimination against the working class was what had made the underground so popular.) It was westbound, at any rate. He stepped into the small, airless chamber and sat upon one of its two benches, which was lined with indigo velvet. Opposite him were two women discussing the bill Parliament had passed.

"Shameful how they coddle them."

"Mm."

"I had thought more highly of Disraeli."

Lenox smiled faintly, avoiding their eyes. You couldn't please everyone, he supposed. When the omnibus had traveled two miles down the Strand he got off, leaving them with an amicable nod.

At the end of the Strand was Pall Mall, of course—and that was just a turning away from White's. He hadn't planned to look in for Archie Godwin, but he decided now that Graham could spare him for another twenty minutes.

White's was a club Lenox rather disliked, the playground of young lords who made outlandish bets and drank themselves to foolishness. (In 1816 the Regency buck Lord Alvanley had bet a friend three thousand pounds that one raindrop would reach the bottom of a bow window before another. By 1823 he had been forced to sell his family's ancient lands, a surprise to nobody.) It was a beautiful building nevertheless, alabaster and intricately carved, a less hieratically inclined cousin to Westminster Abbey, with a black wrought-iron fence in front.

"I'm looking for Archibald Godwin," Lenox said to the bowler-hatted porter at the front door.

"Not in," said the porter, not unkindly.

"Was he here earlier this morning, or yesterday afternoon?"

The porter laughed. "Not unless you count December last. That was when I saw him most recent."

"Not since then?" Lenox asked, with raised eyebrows.

"No, sir."

"Hm. Strange."

"Not particular, if you consider he lives in Hampshire."

"Does he, though?"

"Has since I've known him," said the porter. He touched his hat. "Good day."

Of course, *Who's Who* had said that Godwin lived in Hampshire. Why was he in London? If he hadn't so much as visited his club, why would Godwin give his address as White's?

The last question at least had an answer, perhaps—he might have been hoping to put Lenox off. The young man was plainly a member, and correspondence sent to the club would reach him, eventually but not too quickly. By giving Lenox this address Godwin had discharged his minimal responsibility to another gentleman while managing to discourage further contact.

Lenox walked down Cleveland Row and into Green Park, until he was in sight of the brick face of Buckingham Palace. The flag was up, which meant the Queen was in residence. A bobby passed by with his usual equipment, a truncheon, a rattle, and a lamp. That rattle had come in handy to Lenox many times, when he and a bobby on the trail of a murderer or thief had found themselves in an unpleasant situation, for its noise brought every constable on a neighboring beat instantly to hand.

Once a clever criminal he had known, Jonathan Spender, had put the fact to his own use; he had obtained one of the rattles and paid a street boy a shilling to shake it on a crowded corner. As the bobbies came flying toward the boy, Spender was calmly robbing the suddenly unwatched row houses of Eaton Square.

The thought of Spender's subterfuge drew Lenox to a stop. He frowned, realizing he should have asked the porter one further question. Was it worth turning back? He consulted his pocket watch and found that it was already past three o'clock. Really he ought to have been down at the Commons, but he couldn't resist.

The porter didn't seem especially surprised to

see him again. "Still no sign of Mr. Godwin," he reported with a smile.

"May I ask you a question about him?"

For the first time the friendliness left the porter's face. It was well enough to say whether or not a member was in, and perhaps to let slip the last time he *had* been in—but to offer any more would encroach upon the privacy of a selective establishment's members. "Well?" he asked.

"This Godwin, I only met him once. He is a tall, fair-haired gentlemen, rather slim, no?"

The porter shook his head. "Are you after some mischief, sir?"

Lenox handed over his card. It was like all gentlemen's cards—his name in the center, address in the lower left, the club he frequented most often in the lower right—but it happened to say that he was a Junior Lord of the Treasury and give his address as Parliament. "We share a mutual acquaintance, a young woman," he said.

"I'm not sure you do, respectfully, sir," said the porter, handing the card back with a slight and reverent incline of his head. "Mr. Godwin is a round gentleman a shade under five foot, and by every account I've heard he has been bald since he was seventeen."

CHAPTER EIGHT

H e does not sound like a prepossessing personage," Dallington observed, chuckling, when Lenox repeated this description to him. "The hearts of the ladies of the Clinkard Meon Valley are safe, unto the most devoted beagler's daughter."

"Do you think the fellow at Gilbert's was having a joke at my expense?" asked Lenox. "Or at Godwin's?"

"Perhaps both."

"For my part, I do not." The Member of Parliament was leaning against the windowsill above Half Moon Street, smoking a small cigar and gazing out at the tree-lined walk below. It was early evening, the light weakening away toward night. He had done his work at the Commons through the late afternoon, and then stolen twenty minutes for himself to tell Dallington of his exertions; he was due back for a debate shortly.

"Why?"

"The woman's reaction, the impostor's face. There was something sinister in it. Then, too, the note was so unsettling."

Dallington shrugged. "Then what do we make of him?"

"He seemed wellborn, and knew enough to use

the name of a person not likely to appear at White's, to embarrass his alibi, in case I should search for him there. He did not count on my making more than a cursory effort."

"But what if you had written to him, and the letter had gone to this fellow in the country?"

"I'm not sure. Perhaps it was a hoax. Based upon his appearance, he was a gentleman, but the gentlemen of White's have their own rules. Not many people outside of the club like them."

Dallington himself was a member at White's. He smiled. "What more can we do?"

Lenox sighed. "I cannot see what course we have other than to wait. I fear the young woman will not write to you again, because she suspects you to have betrayed her. Although perhaps she will know otherwise and send for you a second time."

"What about Godwin, the false Godwin?"

"I asked the chap at White's whether he could identify a taller fair-haired gentleman with a silver-handled cane. Only two or three dozen, he said."

Dallington laughed hoarsely. He was still ill, but well enough now to have propped himself up by the warmth of the fireplace, lit though it was spring. "It's no matter. Two more cases have come in, and when I am well enough I shall move on to other matters."

This reminded Lenox. "Did you know,

incidentally, that there is a woman advertising a detective agency in the newspapers?"

"Miss Strickland? Yes, I've seen her notices and wish her joy in her undertaking. She can't guess how many cranks she'll have knocking at her door. Which means perhaps that fewer will knock at mine."

"You are not anxious to be bullied off your turf?" asked Lenox.

"I have Jenkins bringing me cases." This was an inspector from the Yard, who had first been one of Lenox's allies and now was Dallington's. "And there seems to have been no abatement in the number of private references I receive."

"It is true that London is adequately supplied with crime."

"No sign of a shortage to come, either."

"Unfortunately, from a civic perspective— fortunately, to someone in your line of work."

Dallington smiled. "Just so."

They parted then, agreeing to be in contact if anything fresh came to light. The younger man guessed that he would be well enough to participate in their dinner the next Tuesday; ever since Lenox had passed his practice on, the two had met weekly to discuss Dallington's work, Lenox bringing his greater experience and knowledge of the history of crime to bear on new cases. Several years before, when Dallington had still been naive, albeit enthusiastic and acute,

Lenox had nearly every week managed to shed light on some detail of a case, occasionally solving the thing in a single burst of instinct and reasoning. Now, however, it was more common for them to reach the same conclusions at the same pace—Dallington slightly faster, if anything, though Lenox still had, to his advantage, a native brilliance for causation and motivation. It made this Godwin all the more frustrating to contemplate: The impulse behind his actions was so unclear.

The next day Lenox and McConnell had lunch at the Athenaeum. Funny that the doctor's jovial mood and healthy face—sometimes so wan and pulled at, by drink or anxiety, now, like the rest of him, fighting fit—should plummet Lenox into sadness.

McConnell seemed to perceive that Lenox's spirits were low. "Are you quite well?" he asked, just as their soup arrived. Then, hurrying to make a personal question lighter, he added, "Long hours in Parliament, I mean to say?"

"Quite long at the moment, yes."

"Be sure to get a tolerable amount of daylight, now that there's some sun again. It will perk you up no end."

"Ah, have you been out riding?" asked Lenox.

"Oh, yes, every morning," answered McConnell blithely. "I find the exercise sets up the day wonderfully."

"How is the old crowd in Hyde Park?"

"Motley, as usual." To gain admission to the park one had to be dressed like a gentleman and riding a horse; some thieves hired the requisite suit of clothes and animal for four hours, and practiced upon young gentle ladies who had just arrived for their first season from the country, or the young gentlemen who would make any unscrupulous wager you pushed in their direction. One foolish young baronet, Sir Felix Carbury, had ridden into the park one morning and walked out an hour later, having been gambled off of his horse. "I generally keep to myself."

"Good," said Lenox, perhaps rather too sharply.

The next two or three days were exceptionally busy ones for Lenox, who spent most of them on the benches of the House or closeted with Graham and a small host of important politicians. Disraeli's unexpected willingness to compromise had changed their plans for the new session, and at the same time they were plotting out the map to see where they could gain seats in the next election. They also had to select candidates—or grant approval to those who had selected themselves—for a handful of by-elections, out-of-season contests that occurred when a Member died or, on occasion, inherited a title that pushed him up to the House of Lords. Lenox himself had first won Stirrington at a by-election, though by now he and his old friend Brick had handily won several regular contests.

He told Jane about his lunch with McConnell, but something held him back from informing her, quite yet, of his trip to the Surgeons' Club and his discovery there that the doctor had deceived him. Perhaps it was because Lady Jane was already so loyal to Toto that he didn't want to finalize her bias.

"When you look him in the eye it is difficult to imagine him straying," said Lenox.

It was rather late at night, and Lady Jane had been writing letters at a small table in his study, keeping him company as he sat and worked. Now they were together upon the sofa.

"Everyone I see now mentions it to me." Her voice was terribly sad.

"What does Toto say?" he asked.

"The fight has gone out of her."

"Out of Toto?" he asked, skeptical.

"For the moment anyhow. She scarcely leaves the house, I believe. At least George is some consolation to her—but she is redder-eyed than I ever saw her before, that much is certain."

Gradually the conversation shifted to more cheerful topics. Lady Jane was planning a supper in two weeks, at which Disraeli was to be among the guests, along with James Hilary, Lord Cabot, and several other political figures. Mixed in would be some of her particular friends, selected because they had no political interest whatsoever, and therefore could lift the party beyond the threat of workplace boredom, fizzy as yeast in a loaf of bread. For a long while they debated which of these friends might sit where.

"I cannot see the Prime Minister sitting next to Jemima Faringdon," said Lady Jane, pursing her lips.

"Is it because she could not tell you whether he was a Tory or a brand of face powder?"

She laughed. "I don't think she's as foolish as that. Certainly there is no face powder she could not identify by name, for beginners. But perhaps she would be better going in with Lord Cabot. He admires a lovely woman, and she enjoys flattery."

"True enough—and yet Disraeli himself is known as an admirer of young women."

They talked on like this for a while longer, until at last, yawning, she said she thought she would retire. "Can you come up?" she asked.

He sighed and stood up, walking back toward his desk. "No, I must stay awake and review a memorandum Graham has written, I'm afraid, about the Irish question, blast it to hell. Oh, and if you would tell the housemaid I need more candles—I find I've run out."

"Already?" she asked from the sofa. "Have you been eating them?"

"It has been many nights of work," he said.

Her face turned sympathetic, and she came

across the room on soft footsteps, embracing him when she reached him and kissing his cheek. "You poor dear," she said. "Yes, I'll have them sent in right now. But don't be too long coming up to rest."

"No, I won't," he said: just as capable of misleading his wife as McConnell, apparently.

CHAPTER NINE

Two mornings later Sophia was having a friend to visit her nursery, a young gentleman, not grown far above two feet, by the name of William Dean. He was the son of the vicar of Hampden Lane's small church, St. Paul's. Lenox—as he had promised himself he would—went to visit his daughter.

It was a clear morning, a breeze coming through the cracked windows. Sophia was intent upon a small wooden horse, while Master Dean, unaccustomed perhaps to the strict demands of a London social call, was staring at the wall and drooling.

"How old is this child?" Lenox asked Miss Emanuel.

"Nearly eighteen months," she said.

"I have never understood this strange tradition that has us dress our small boys in martial clothing. This one seems to be wearing a regimental jacket."

"I think he is very fine," said Miss Emanuel.

"Yes, as if he could lead a battalion into Waterloo on horseback."

The nurse laughed. "Leave the poor child alone."

Lenox smiled and tousled the boy's hair, then bent down to give Sophia a kiss, catching as he did the clean, sharp scent of Pears soap on her skin. "Good-bye, Miss Emanuel. I shall be rather late this evening, I expect, but I will visit you again in the morning."

He had found when he woke up that morning that he was not quite ready to consign Archie Godwin—the false Archie Godwin—to the past. On his way to Parliament after visiting the nursery, Lenox asked his carriage driver to stop in at Charing Cross. When they arrived he went into Gilbert's. The owner, a small, harassed, efficient Italian, granted him a few seconds of time. His answers were terse. He did not remember a tall, light-haired gentleman; he did not remember Lenox; on the other hand he did remember the lady. When Lenox heard this his hopes surged.

"The one with the black-and-white striped umbrella?"

"Yes. She comes in every month."

"Curious."

"It is not curious at all," said the Italian indignantly. His English was excellent, though accented. "In fact, the majority of our customers stop in upon strict schedules, clockwork regular."

"She comes upon the same date every month?"

"No, but always a Wednesday, and always the same time, morning."

"And she always leaves in time to catch the 8:38?"

The owner shrugged. "She does not confide to me where she is traveling, Mr. Lenox. She asks for tea and toast, sometimes for an egg."

"How long has she been coming to sit here?"

"Fifteen months, maybe eighteen."

"Do you know her name, or her occupation?"

"I do not."

"Has she ever been in the company of—"

"Never in any company at all."

"When she comes in again, would you give her my card?" asked Lenox, pressing an additional one—he had already presented it upon his arrival—upon the owner.

"Yes, if you wish. Though it won't be for three weeks."

It was a promising clue to the woman's identity that she had a schedule at Gilbert's. A monthly visit by train from Charing Cross—parents in the country, or perhaps a beau?

After visiting Gilbert's Lenox went into Charing Cross Station itself and straight up to the ticket booth, to ask if there was a woman who bought the same ticket every month, possibly on the 8:38 to Canterbury, at around the same date.

This, however, was a bridge too far. None of the several men he met, nor the stationmaster, could help him. He did manage to get the name of the 8:38's usual conductor. This gentleman was commonly to be found in the engineers' and conductors' tearoom until 8:15 each morning. Lenox decided he would come back to see the man, who might much more easily remember a regular passenger than a ticket broker would.

It would be so much better should she write to Dallington again, their mystery subject—but he held out very little hope for that.

That evening Lenox went to Dallington's rooms for their weekly supper. In general they traded meals at their respective clubs, but the young lord was still ill, though well enough for conversation, he assured Lenox in his note.

In person he had a cough, and still little enough color in his cheeks, but he did look marginally better—at least, he had contrived to stand up and put himself into a suit of clothes. (At their lunch Lenox had asked McConnell to look in on Dallington, and apparently the doctor had prescribed nothing more than rest when he came by two mornings before.) On the sideboard was a meal, ordered up by Mrs. Lucas from the chophouse, beef broth and crackers for Dallington, a beefsteak for Lenox. After they ate they shared a pot of strong tea.

The new cases Dallington had received were

dull, and after dismissing them the two gentlemen began to discuss past cases instead.

"The cleverest murder I ever saw was in '61," said Lenox. "A gentleman named Harper murdered the tax inspector—or collector, I can't recall which it was—for assessing a tax upon him for the keeping of a dog."

"Where was the cleverness in that?"

"Harper did the inspector's job for the next month. Claimed to be the victim's brother-in-law, said that the inspector had fallen ill. They swallowed it entirely at the office and let him take the man's round. Only instead of turning in the money he collected at the end of the month, he kept it all and fled on a Friday evening, a much richer man than he had before the whole thing started. And with his dog. It was Tuesday morning before anyone thought to look for him. He had even collected his victim's wages."

"Nobody in that whole month noticed the inspector was missing? A wife? A friend?"

"He was unmarried—a young man—and Harper went to his lodgings, posing as his brother-in-law again, and said the inspector had been called back to Manchester to care for his ill father. He paid the landlady out till the end of the week, and she found a new lodger immediately. She kept the inspector's possessions in her basement, thinking he would call round for them, though as you can imagine he never did."

Dallington shook his head. "Ingenious. What became of Harper?"

"We spent months searching for him. At first we thought he must have returned to Devon, where his people lived, and then we thought he might have gone overseas."

"And?"

"We never found him."

Dallington whistled. "He got away with it."

"He's survived fourteen years somewhere upon the face of the earth. Personally I imagine that he settled somewhere with the money and built a new life. By all accounts he was a stable person, no outward signs of madness. It's often the way. I still have hopes we might catch him, though everyone concerned has become old and gray."

Dallington sighed. "Even the best in our profession cannot hope for total success," he said. "Outside of the yellowbacks at any rate." These were the crime books, often based on true stories, that sold on the street for a penny or two, bound in loud yellow cloth. "I have never known Mary Elizabeth Braddon's detectives to fail."

"Nor Inspector Bucket," said Lenox, smiling. "Though he never received a sequel to test his wits a second time, as in my opinion he ought to have done."

"Perhaps all of us ought to cosign a letter to Miss Strickland, informing her that popular fiction may have misled her."

"All of us?" asked Lenox.

"Oh, you know, the usual crowd of investigators: Audley, LeMaire."

Lenox knew the names, though both men had popped up only after he had left the profession. Hearing them gave him an idea. "Do you think our mysterious young woman might have gone to one of them, after she came to us?"

Dallington frowned. "She might have done."

"She seemed desperate for help, certainly. Though perhaps our meeting gave her enough of a fright to silence her."

"There are more than a few private investigators, though."

Lenox nodded. "Well, there are scores of cheap and dubious ones. There are only a very few with any reputation among the upper classes, however. Think of her writing paper, the hand in which she wrote, her diction. Clearly she is a woman of some position. That she approached you is perhaps proof enough of that."

Dallington laughed weakly. "I cannot say that a woman spending time in my company has always vouchsafed her good breeding."

"But really," Lenox said, "to whom might she have gone, if she could not go to the police? You, Audley, LeMaire. That is the list, is it not?"

"Even Audley has a very middle-class clientele," said Dallington. "They go to LeMaire if they want

73

the old Vidocq touch. He's not especially skillful, but for some the accent makes them feel they're getting a bargain."

"I'll go around to both tomorrow," said Lenox.

"Why should they tell you anything?"

"I've no wish to poach a client, only to get one back—and the information about Godwin, the man calling himself Godwin, could be of use to them."

CHAPTER TEN

The engineers' and conductors' tearoom at Charing Cross lay toward the back of the station, far from the crowds of travelers queuing near the platforms. Its door was made of frosted glass and had the word PRIVATE stenciled in large black letters upon it. The roving ticket salesman who had pointed it out to Lenox hadn't wanted to at first, until a coin persuaded him; evidently these engineers and conductors valued their solitude. Well, too bad.

Lenox knocked. The door opened a few inches, and a fat round face, with a magnificent dark toothbrush mustache appended to its upper lip, appeared. " 'Lo?"

"How do you do? My name is Charles Lenox, and I—"

"Ticket office to the left," said the face, and then the door slammed.

Lenox knocked it again. The door opened. "I am in some difficulty, and—"

"You can't imagine how little I care, sir."

"I wish you would address a perfectly civil inquiry with a greater respect."

"If wishes was horses then beggars would ride," said the man immediately.

"I'm looking for the conductor of the 8:38 to Canterbury, Padden."

"Who, what, Padden? Should have said so straightaway, daft of you not to. Can't think why you weren't clear from the start. George Padden!"

"Not in!" called a voice.

"You've a visitor!"

The door then closed in Lenox's face again, but he heard footsteps, and soon enough it reopened, and a thinner, paler face appeared. Its bearer was extremely tall. His face was impassive. "Yes?"

"Let me begin—"

"Sir, we have ten minutes now and again for a cup of tea. Otherwise it's tramping up and down a train all day, soot in your clothes, and a vagrant sleeping off the back porch as thanks. Say your piece quick, please."

"I'm worried about the safety of one of your regular passengers, a young woman who takes the 8:38 to Canterbury once each month. She might well have taken it several days ago on a Wednesday."

The conductor frowned and then, after a beat, sighed. "You'd better come in," he said.

The room was cozy, with a great silver-plated urn at one end, crowded around at its base with chipped blue and white cups and saucers. There was a bowl of sugar off to the side, and a whole jar full of spoons. Every surface in the room, tables and chairs and sofas, was covered in periodicals and newspapers. A few conductors and engineers lounged peaceably, drinking their tea—or, in the instance of the man who had first greeted Lenox, something that looked like a glass of beer—and reading, one of them drowsing underneath a crumpled paper. There was a bright fire in the grate, making the whole room sleepy and warm. An enormous clock stood at the center of each wall, no doubt to keep them to schedule.

More civilly now, Padden offered Lenox a cup of tea, which he took—it was rather a cold morning. He spooned a quick shower of sugar into it and stirred. "Lemon, milk?" Padden offered.

"Go on, then, if you have milk," said Lenox.

Padden pulled a pot of milk from its spot on the only windowsill in the room, where it must have kept reasonably cold. Lenox took a sip of the tea. It was excellent, very strong. Padden, glancing at his pocket watch, invited Lenox to sit down in the corner of the room. "Tell me more, then," he said.

As minimally as he could, Lenox explained

who he was, that he had acted on Dallington's behalf in meeting this young woman, and how she had been scared away. He also described her appearance, at least as accurately as he could recall it.

When he had finished speaking, he looked at Padden expectantly. "Well?"

The conductor leaned back in the chair, his long legs crossed. "I know the young woman you've described."

"Was she on the train recently?"

"Yes."

"Do you know her name?"

With a skeptical rise of his eyebrows, Padden said, "If I did know it, I'm not sure I'd give it straight to you. As it happens I don't know her surname. I heard her Christian name once."

Lenox's heart fell. "Can you tell me anything about her? Any detail at all? What station she leaves the train at, with whom she might travel, any distinguishing marks of apparel?"

"You said you were a Member of Parliament. Do you have a card?"

"Of course." Lenox took one from the thin silver case Jane had given him three Christmases before. "At your service."

Padden took the card and inspected it, then looked up. "If you don't mind, I'll look into your story for myself and call upon you in the next day or two, should I find that all's in order, like."

Lenox nodded at once. "I understand, though I would appreciate your haste. The matter may be pressing."

"Yes," said Padden. "She was more agitated than I'd seen her before."

At the other end of the room Lenox's first friend here—the man with the pink face and the toothbrush mustache—folded his paper. "Right, chaps," he said. "The 8:29 to Clapham Junction waits for no man, unless I should stumble and fall into the tracks and have my head stoved in by a train. Which it's very possible, clumsy as I am, and if it happens be generous when they pass the hat for the widow Parker. None of your ha'pennies, I want to hear a rattle of crowns, or I'll haunt you proper."

He tipped his cap, and there was a chorus of good-byes, Padden lifting a hand. "I'd better go myself, then," he said to Lenox, glancing up at the clock. "I don't like to leave it quite so late."

Lenox stood. "Thank you," he said. "Please call upon me as soon as you can. I shall be in Parliament after two, perhaps even earlier. I owe you a cup of tea. Or I'm happy to return here, if you send word round."

"I fancy seeing the inside of Parliament," said Padden, smiling slightly. He put his conductor's hat on. "This afternoon."

"I'll have one of the runners give you a tour after we speak. Only be quick about it, please."

As Lenox left Charing Cross he checked his own watch, before realizing that of course he knew what time it was—just far enough shy of 8:38, anyhow. He had, as ever, a great deal to do in Parliament, but he decided that he could put it off for another few hours. With any luck Audley and LeMaire would both be at work already; unlike Dallington (who had given him their addresses), they had proper offices, not far from each other in the West End.

As he walked out of Charing Cross Lenox pondered what the conductor had said about the young woman—that she was more agitated, on the train trip the previous week, than he had seen her before. For the dozenth time he pondered as well the motivations of the man calling himself Archie Godwin, and what he might have to do with her.

It was useless to speculate. Better to keep his mind clear of possibilities, and hope that he received more information soon.

As he walked toward the mall he saw flutters of spring everywhere. Flower sellers on the pavement, sweet little blossoms dotting some of the trees outside of Charing Cross, rather wind-shaken but sturdy enough to have survived to their bloom. Patrols of red squirrels were outside and vigilant again, after their sleepy winters.

He associated all of these things in his mind with the London season, which was to begin very soon now—always the Monday after Easter, just a week or so away. In every part of the country, young girls, accustomed to the drear of fox hunts and country balls, would be packing excitedly for the grander stages of the capital, trading letters with each other about how it would be, preparing to stay in town for the first time, and soon they would be crowding into the ballrooms of London to look for husbands, as gallant young fools nearby worked up the nerve to ask for dances and stodgy whiskered men looked on at them fondly from the dim corners, murmuring to each other over the punch in their cups. The London girls would feign boredom and superiority. In the first week there would be twenty engagements, a fifth of which would be tactfully canceled in the second, and in the third still more, the very plain girls and the very beautiful ones, settling and picking respectively. Though the season lasted until August, this first burst of activity was the brightest.

Lenox didn't know what would be on his own docket, aside from their supper for Disraeli, but it would be crowded, with several parties starting at each hour of the evening, mothers imploring Jane, a great arbiter in these matters, for her presence. They had gone to just as many last year as ever, despite Sophia. It was tiring to contemplate. Still, he enjoyed a glass of punch, and it was pleasant to be one of the older men in the corner. There was not all that much joy in aging—his back creaked quite often now—but he felt glad that at any rate he was beyond the age of wife picking. He thought of Jane as he walked and smiled to himself.

CHAPTER ELEVEN

He went to LeMaire's first. Halfway down Brook Street was a gray house, much like all of its neighbors save for a discreetly gleaming brass placard near the bell, which read J-C.LM, letters that stood for Jean-Claude LeMaire's name.

Lenox rang the bell. A handsome lad, very tall and with jet black hair, answered the door. "Have you an appointment?" he asked in a strong French accent.

Lenox sent in his card, perching himself patiently upon a small chair in the front hall to wait after the assistant disappeared. There were cards in the silver card stand of very grand personages, or at least one was intended to surmise as much—the names themselves were blacked out, in a flawed bid for confidentiality, leaving only the titles, *Monsieur Le Duc de*——, *Lord*——*of*——, *The Honourable*——, *Member for*——. Lenox wondered with some dismay if his own card would be superadded to this heap of distinction. Without even examining the stand's contents closely he had already spotted the card of that fool Lord Sharpley, whose crest was unconcealed. No doubt Sharpley had hired LeMaire to investigate the disappearance of his two prized hunting dogs, though everyone this side of Northumberland knew his own ne'er-do-well brother had stolen them from him and sold them to a Scottish baronet.

The fellow who had greeted Lenox at the door reappeared and with a bow requested that Lenox follow him. LeMaire's office was at the end of a small, dark corridor. The detective himself met Lenox at the door.

"Mr. Lenox! A remarkable pleasure, this!"

The old Vidocq touch, Dallington had called it, and he was precisely correct. LeMaire was a distinguished-looking fifty-year-old man, dark hair shagged down below his collar, a gallant small pointed beard descending from his chin, a twinkle in his eye. He was the Englishman's idea of a canny Frenchman—and no doubt he was very intelligent; one could gather as much from his face. Of course, one could be intelligent in different directions. No doubt there would be a small surcharge at the foot of each bill for that twinkle.

It would be gratefully paid, for it was Vidocq who still held the most powerful hold on the British imagination of any police officer, at least this side of Sir Robert Peel. Vidocq had been first head of the French Sûreté, work he had described at length in his bestselling memoirs. Lenox was skeptical of the humility of anyone who felt the need to discourse about himself for fully four volumes, but they were rattling reads, enlivened considerably by the fact that before joining with the forces of justice, Vidocq had been one of the leading forgers and jailbreakers in France.

After he had reformed, he had also been the country's first private detective—indeed, might have been the first in the world. His innovations had been legion: indelible ink, plaster molds for footprints, an index of the unalterable physical traits of known criminals, all the equipage that Lenox and Dallington and their kind now regularly employed. Lenox had narrowly missed meeting him many years before, when Vidocq was in his eighties and near death. It would have given him pleasure to look the shrewd old chap in the eye. Even after his celebrated reform Vidocq had not given up the old ways entirely, and in his seventies had briefly returned to prison, on a charge of fraud; when he died, not long after, eleven women came forward claiming to be the sole heir of his estate.

"How do you do, Monsieur LeMaire?" asked Lenox.

"I flourish badly, sir."

"In that case you do not flourish at all, I fear!"

LeMaire smiled. "My English is not up in snuff, I am sure. To use your parlance."

"It seems very fine to me."

"How may I help you?"

"You may have heard that I was once a detective—like yourself," Lenox added, thinking with an unbecoming note of pride that it was the other way around.

"Yes, of course. We are grateful you have cleared the field, though I read with very great ardor the account of the murders upon the *Lucy*."

At the last moment he transmogrified the last word into *Lucys*, willfully it seemed to Lenox. He suspected the Frenchman of shamming his awkward English, and had since the words "up in snuff" passed his lips. It was no doubt beneficial to be underestimated, and of course nobody disdained a funny accent like the British. "That was a hairy business," was all Lenox said.

"I thought you did capitally well."

Lenox inclined his head to acknowledge the compliment, then went on. "Once in a rare while, I do take on a case. I have one at the moment."

"I am impatient that I might help you," said LeMaire. "What is the case?"

Lenox had told the story of his encounter in Gilbert's not forty minutes before to Padden, and now he had the points of the matter set in his mind and told LeMaire with decisive efficiency about the entire sequence of events. The French detective listened with great interest, all the way forward over his forearms on his desk, at the very edge of his seat, occasionally looking down at his hands and twisting his little beard with two fingers when Lenox came to a puzzling detail.

He waited until Lenox had finished and then said that alas, no, no such woman had come to him, that his only cases at the present moment concerned a vanished husband and a stolen ruby necklace, that while he kept his "ear in the ground" and tended to hear from his spies of much of the private detective work in London, he had not heard of this woman, he was so sorry, he was a thousand apologies. He begged of Lenox his card and promised to call upon him the moment he learned anything relevant, anything at all.

Lenox thanked him warmly and accepted the offer of a cup of coffee before he left. It was a loss of fifteen minutes in his crowded day but gave him a further chance to study the Frenchman. They discussed old crimes, on both sides of the Channel. He was a sagacious fellow, this LeMaire. By the time Lenox departed he was still not entirely sure whether that sagacity was complemented by honesty.

If LeMaire's office had been very fine, ormolu and sterling, Robert Audley's was all oak and brass. It stood not far away on Mount Street, near the fine old pile called the Prince of Saxe-Coburg Hotel—named for the Queen's prematurely dead love, Prince Albert, for whom she still, by all accounts, mourned deeply. Indeed, Audley was the house detective at several of the grand hotels in London, including besides this one the Langham and Claridge's, responsible for any minor matters that their august guests brought to management. He had been on the police force until about six or seven years before; Lenox had known him then, a sturdy young man, impatient of nonsense.

He was also, according to Dallington, a committed alcoholic.

Audley greeted Lenox at the door himself, gruffly acknowledged the card he received, and said that he did remember their previous encounters, though from his tone you wouldn't have guessed the memories were altogether fond. In the plain, banker's-style office there was no whiff of spirits. Certainly he had no assistant.

There was another telltale sign, however, one that Lenox had observed in about a third of the alcoholics he knew. Audley kept a great deal of food on hand, none of which, Lenox would have guessed, he touched, beyond a biscuit every day or so. It was, as so often in these cases, too much food, betraying in its very ubiquity the illusion the drinker aimed to preserve.

Or perhaps not—Lenox reminded himself that Dallington had been wrong before. He tried to stem his judgment of the man.

"What brings you here?" Audley asked. "I don't have time to talk shop."

"No, certainly not," said Lenox.

"Well?"

Audley's bluntness, perhaps like LeMaire's bumbling Frenchness, was likely a reassurance to the customers who sought him out—though in this case it was an unaffected trait, accidentally useful to him in his profession. "I am worried about the safety of a young woman who came to me for help."

"In your capacity as a Member of Parliament?"

"No. Her information was out of date, apparently, because she believed me still to be a detective. It happens half a dozen times a year." This was true in general, if not in this particular case; Lenox simply didn't want to bring Dallington into the matter. "In the end she convinced me, against my better judgment, to help her."

"Why couldn't His Drunken Lordship do it?" asked Audley. "You usually pass your work on to him, from all I hear."

Lenox looked at Audley sharply. "I suggest you watch your words. In particular when you're with his friends, of whom I consider myself one. John Dallington is a very fine detective."

Audley hesitated for a moment, a bit of fight in his eyes, but then held up his hands in apology. "Withdrawn. It's a vice I can't abide, drinking,

87

and my temper sometimes overruns my mouth."

"I can assure you that he has no problem with drink now, if ever he did."

"I hope that's the truth. They're clever at hiding it."

Lenox was half-inclined to leave—but this was his best chance, short of Padden offering some revelatory information, of finding the young woman he had seen at Gilbert's. So he stayed and told his story. In the end he was glad he did.

"Light-haired, you say?" Audley asked.

"Yes. With a black-and-white striped umbrella, at least when I saw her."

"Her name is Laurel Wheeler."

CHAPTER TWELVE

Laurel Wheeler," Lenox repeated, his attention complete, his pulse quickening—but his voice cautious. "You seem very sure of that name."

He looked more closely at Audley. The man's face was difficult to read; behind him was a high bank of windows, showing the gray day along this quiet slice of Mount Street, and this faded light cast Audley in shadow.

He nodded. "Yes, I'm quite sure."

"Could you elaborate?"

Audley shrugged. "I've given you the name of the young woman in question. She left no address, so I cannot offer you that. And since she may yet need the services of our profession—"

"Your profession," said Lenox.

"Our profession. Since she may still need one of us, I don't see the advantage to me in telling you more."

"Yet the advantage to Miss Wheeler may be very great indeed."

"That remains to be seen," said Audley. There was a slight throb or shiver in his right hand, which he did his utmost to master. "For the moment that will have to be enough, Mr. Lenox."

"Tell me, at least, how you are so sure of her name."

"She left a card behind her."

"I don't quite understand you, Mr. Audley. She has come to see you, left her card behind, and yet you still wonder whether she might be your client? Surely it is beyond dispute now?"

"Evidently you were her first pick."

It was a fair point. "Then why give me her name?"

"The case she offered me was limited in scope. There may be other avenues you wish to explore, and if she is truly in danger I wish you luck with them. For my part I mean to consult her later this afternoon."

"Listen here, what if I tell you that I will take her case on myself, but you can keep her fee? In fact, I'm happy to match her fee—I can hire you."

This had been a misstep, Lenox saw immediately. Audley's face darkened with professional
disdain. "I have my own agency, Mr. Lenox. In
Whitehall word may no longer reach you about
your profession—your former profession, let me
grant your point—but my agency is rather a
successful one. Successful enough that I have no
need to subordinate myself to an out-of-practice
society gentleman who once dabbled in the art to
which I have dedicated my life."

A silence hung in the air for a moment. Then
Lenox said, "As you please. Thank you for the
name, at any rate, and if it can be of any benefit
to Miss Wheeler, she may reach me at the address
upon this card."

Audley took the card that Lenox proffered and
studied it for a moment. Perhaps he felt he had
been harsh, because he added, in an explanatory
tone, "On top of it all, a new client is always a
boon to me. She will have friends, she might
recommend me. It is how I earn my bread."

It was a just point, as far as it went. "Quite so.
Good day, Mr. Audley."

"Mr. Lenox."

As Lenox closed the door behind him and
ventured into the street, he could almost sense a
bottle opening in the room he had just vacated. A
strange man, Audley. Hopefully he had steered
Lenox closer to the truth.

It was drizzling outside now, the street dark

except for the jolly sparkle of light in the Queen's Arms public house on the corner. Lenox turned up his collar and ducked his head, looking up and down to see if he might hail a hansom cab—but without success. He had to get down to Parliament. It was just far enough from Mount Street to make the prospect of walking it in the rain an unpleasant one. He sighed and soldiered on.

Soon the rain intensified, however, and when he came to another pub, this one called the Bear and Pony, he couldn't resist it. He pushed open the door and went inside.

It was warm and dry. Crowded, too—evidently others had the same idea of escaping the rain. Still, there were a few empty seats at the bar, and he went and took one, asking for a hot whisky and water, just a small one. The brisk young ginger-haired man in his apron nodded and went off to prepare the drink.

"That you, Lenox?" asked a voice nearby.

Lenox turned to look, and when he saw the face to which the voice belonged he smiled. It was a man named Joseph Baltimore. "Hullo, Baltimore. Stand you a drink?"

"Brotherly of you, but I have a fresh one." The older man held up his tankard. "Is this your regular drinking house?"

"No, I just came in to get out of the rain. You?"

"I live two doors down. Liza sends me here

when I'm underfoot. Today she's seeing about the season. Boring as all hell."

"Are you very busy?"

"Only averagely, three dozen parties a night. I wish it were already over."

"Give it a skip."

"No, I shouldn't hear the end of it."

Baltimore was an American, raised in the northeastern part of that country, of an old family; his first ancestor in the country had been the bell ringer of Boston when there were fewer than eight hundred people there. Shipping had brought the family a fortune, and on his tour of Europe Baltimore, then less gray, his face less lined, had met Elizabeth Winston. He was handsome and rich, she plain and poor, though very wellborn, and yet it was said in the West End that there was not a couple more in love with each other. They had nine children. Four were in America, where their father had insisted they study. The remaining five were girls—and for all he cared they might study in Transylvania, he had once told Lenox.

Baltimore didn't work, precisely, and yet he was useful to many men, and it would have been surprising if he hadn't earned a great deal of money, through the years, by his intelligence. He was London's expert on America. He helped politicians, businessmen, and also parents, who felt both the risk and the allure of the American fortunes that courted their sons and daughters. ("There's a lot of *money* over there, you know," people had taken to saying in the past year or two at parties, with shrewd, naive eyes, as if they were discussing dragons' teeth; great rumblings of rail and oil fortunes had begun to reach the island.) Baltimore's discretion was supreme, nearly unexampled in the hurly-burly of London society, yet paradoxically he was known for putting in a soft word at the right moment, in time to avert mischance.

And in fact that was what he did now, for Lenox. "I'm happy to have run into you," he said.

"Oh?"

"Indeed, I thought of calling on you when I was in Parliament yesterday, seeing Amos Cross, but our meeting ran long."

Lenox's interest was piqued. "I hope nothing is the matter."

"It's about your secretary. Graham." He pronounced the name without acknowledging the *h* in the middle, "gram." Baltimore stuck stubbornly to his flat accent—closer than the English accent, he was fond of reminding people, to the tone in which Shakespeare himself would have spoken, because no German family had come marauding for America's crown, slowly modulating the fashionable accent all out of recognition from its previous sound, as the Teutonic tones of the royal family had in the last hundred years. "You may want to keep your eye on him."

"I would trust him with my life," said Lenox immediately.

"I don't doubt that. Your career might be another matter, however."

Baltimore was not a troublemaker. Lenox would have walked away from most men who said anything against Graham in his hearing, but now he stayed. "What have you heard?"

"Nothing substantial, only mutterings. Not about you, though—always about Mr. Graham."

"He drives a hard deal with the other side, to be sure."

"Not that," said Baltimore in a low voice. He took a sip of his porter. "The other thing. Money."

"Graham?" asked Lenox skeptically.

"Yes, him. That he can be bought. But I'm sure you know your man."

"What exactly have you heard?" asked Lenox.

"I won't name the person I had it from, for he himself had it secondhand. But he said that it was well-known among the other political secretaries with masters in the Commons that Graham had arranged some kind of fund to pay himself through, something cozy."

"There are no more specifics than that? Pah. It's a slur upon his class, nothing more."

"Perhaps," said Baltimore, taking a pensive sip from his pint pot.

Most political secretaries in Parliament were young men with political ambitions of their own, often from the great public schools and universities, cultivating the connections that would one day attain for them their own seat, even eventually their own ministry. Lenox had scoured their number for a suitable secretary when he was elected, but none of the candidates had seemed quite compatible; instead (to general derision) he had selected his butler for the post. He considered it the best decision he had made as a politician.

"Nonetheless I am grateful to you," said Lenox. "It's better to know of these things. I'll have a word with Graham this afternoon."

CHAPTER THIRTEEN

The next morning it was Saturday, and Lenox lingered in his bedroom until nearly ten, reading the weekend papers and sipping at a sweet cup of tea. Jane was away from the house early, out with Toto at a meeting for the Humane Society. (This was Toto's influence. Jane liked dogs and cats, but she had grown up among the rougher folkways of the country, and therefore perhaps didn't have her friend's total and consuming sympathy toward their plight. She also couldn't especially spare the hours it required once a month to pin her focus to them, when there was so much else to do, and she was reluctant to wear the gruesome large yellow ribbon that indicated her membership in the women's circle of the society. Still, friendship.) Finally he dressed and went downstairs to eat a small breakfast, a hot egg upon a piece of brown toast.

When he was finished, he set out to find Laurel Wheeler. The area in which he intended to search for her was small indeed: He planned to find her within his study, if she was there. A name, a city. This was as close to pure detective work as one could approach. As he ate he asked the new footman, a gawky Leicestershire lad by the name of Silas, to lay a fire in his study, and when Lenox had finished his egg he padded down the softly lit front hall to take a seat at his desk, the fire now crackling warmly at the far end of the room. He settled down into his chair with an exhale of pleasure, ready to lose himself in the hours of the day.

The first question, as he saw it, was where Laurel Wheeler might live. That she took the train once a month from Charing Cross suggested that she lived in London to him—though now that he thought of it, he would like to know from Padden, or one of his colleagues, whether she took a return in the evening. She could also have been connecting at Charing Cross; hence the wait at Gilbert's. It was often faster to go through

London even if it meant many miles more travel.

For some reason Lenox doubted it. The early hour of her departure suggested a day trip to him, to the country to see a parent or sister. As for Gilbert's, she might simply have been a nervous traveler, inclined to arrive at the station early. Lenox himself had that trait. So did his brother, Edmund—both men ascribed it to the bells of their boyhood school, Harrow, which had for years harried them from one moment of the day to the next.

Lenox turned in his chair toward the tall windows behind him, wet with rain, that looked out over the houses and small shops of Hampden Lane. Though it was Saturday men were out upon their city business, dressed darkly, umbrellas high, leaning forward into their stride.

"Kirk!" he called.

A moment later the house's butler appeared at the door, a large, good-natured soul, black hair thinned almost to the point of becoming theoretical. "Sir?"

Lenox pointed at a carved walnut bookstand by the fireplace, next to an overstuffed red armchair. "Where did the footmen take those books off to, Kirk? They were here yesterday."

"I believe they were taken down to the storage room in the cellar, sir." Kirk coughed discreetly. "Eight or nine months ago, sir."

Irritably, Lenox said, "Well, I need them."

"I was instructed at the time to clear the space for your blue books, sir."

Both men glanced toward the bookstand, which was full of the parliamentary reports. "Can this Silas fellow read?" asked Lenox.

"Yes, sir."

"Tell him I need Kelly's for London, Essex, and Kent."

"Yes, sir."

"And he might as well bring up the clerical directories for the same."

"Yes, sir. I will oversee him in the task myself, sir."

"Well, hurry about it, please. Don't wait until you have them all, bring them up piecemeal," said Lenox.

"Yes, sir."

When he had gone, Lenox muttered, "Damn your eyes," and went back to looking out of the window.

There was no truly great directory to the people of England. The Normans had made a good start with the Domesday Book, about eight hundred years before, but no census taker since had matched their enthusiasm or perseverance. In Lenox's youth there was Pigot's, a meretricious series of directories, all flash and little substance, in the form of classified advertisements. Pigot's still existed but had been superseded every-where except the north (Pigot was a Manchester engraver) by the directories of Mr. Frederic Kelly. Kelly was the chief inspector of all Britain's inland letter carriers, and after buying the rights to Crichett's directory of London, he had used his position—over some objection—to compile an excellent series of books.

There were also trade directories, but Lenox felt strongly that the young woman he had seen in Gilbert's was not the scion of a tradesman. Her appearance, her handwriting, the diction of her letter, all militated against that possibility. He would consult the trade directories only if he grew desperate.

Soon Kirk came with the first of the books Lenox had requested. It was a guide to Essex. Trains from Charing Cross went to Kent and Sussex, but Laurel Wheeler might have transferred along the line to go somewhere in Essex, north of Kent along the eastern coast of England. She wouldn't have been on the 8:38 if she wanted to go anywhere in Sussex, even by transfer. Lenox, who had grown up in that county, felt sure of that.

It would help if Padden could just tell him the stop at which she left the train—but he had waited the entire afternoon for some word of the conductor and hadn't heard from him.

Wheeler was a popular surname in Essex, apparently. Lenox took down his Bradshaw's and, through a little investigation, eliminated about half of the county, deciding that she wouldn't have practically chosen to take the 8:38 to reach those parts.

Still, this left him with about thirty-five Wheelers. None of them were named Laurel, but there was one tantalizing subentry for *L. Wheeler, daughter, 22,* in a town (he had never heard of it, and smiled at the name) called Mucking. He copied out the address, as well as three others that listed only the fathers' names but indicated the presence of adult children.

Soon after Kirk had brought up the guide to Essex, he followed with the ones for London and Kent, as well as the clerical guides for the same counties. These last were a waste, unfortunately, but in both the London and Kent directories Lenox found addresses to copy out upon his pad of paper. In Canterbury—destination of the 8:38, a train he was coming to loathe—there was even a *Miss Laurel Wheeler,* but she was *aged 61* and, distressingly, according to Mr. Kelly, *possibly dead.* Well.

Several of the London addresses were more promising and required investigation in person. He didn't have the time to do it himself, and so he began to write a letter with the appropriate information to a man named Skaggs, to whom he had once contracted out such work—a tradition Dallington now carried on—asking him to help.

Just as he was signing his name to the foot of the letter, there was a knock at the front door.

Lenox heard Kirk's footsteps in the hall but went out himself to see who was visiting. Someone hearty—the rain had gotten quite thick.

"It's Mr. Frabbs, sir," said Kirk, turning back into the house. "With another gentleman."

"Well, bring them in."

Frabbs required no such invitation, however. He was already charging ahead into the hall, pulling along his companion.

It was Padden. Lenox's heart leapt up. "Mr. Padden, you came by Parliament?"

Padden, in civilian clothes, shook some of the rain off. "I sent a note, and Mr. Frabbs was around my house what seemed six minutes later."

"I say, well done, Frabbs. Kirk, give him the run of the larder, make him something hot. Padden, will you take tea or coffee while we speak?"

"Tea, please, sir, strong as you like."

As Kirk handed each of the new guests a towel, Lenox led the train conductor into his study. "I'm very grateful to you for coming," he said, "though I reckon I've outrun your help on at least one small piece of information."

"Sir?" said Padden.

"The young woman's name—it's Laurel Wheeler, isn't it?"

To his surprise, Padden laughed. "Laurel Wheeler?"

"Is that not her name?"

They had come down to the end of the room with the fire, and Lenox gestured for his guest to sit. The tall conductor did, tolerably dry now, shed of his hat and overcoat. "No, it's not."

Lenox felt a wave of vexation. "Well, a reliable man informed me it was." Even as he said this, however, he realized that it was a falsehood. Audley was not a reliable man.

"You might not have heard it before," said Padden. "There are names we give—people like me, you see—to keep the police out of our business. Who knocked over the bobby? John Shawcross. What was the name of the child's mother? Laurel Wheeler. Someone was having a joke at your expense, unfortunately, Mr. Lenox."

CHAPTER FOURTEEN

There was a whole morning wasted. Lenox could happily have seen Audley hanged from London Bridge. He cursed.

Yet even as he heard Padden's laughter trailing off, Lenox understood that the truth made more sense than the lie, in the cold light of this new information. Why would the young woman have left a card at Audley's when her note to Dallington was anonymous? Why would Audley go as far as to give him a name but help him no further? In the initial keenness brought on by a new piece of the puzzle, Lenox had forgotten to properly query its reliability.

Still, here was Padden. "I appreciate you coming to see me," said Lenox. "Are you hungry?"

"A mite, perhaps."

The footman was already at the door with a tray of tea things—albeit without hot water, which he said was boiling downstairs—and Lenox asked him to fetch up a plate of sandwiches. He had the sense that Padden would be happier if he ate his fill, if he felt he had achieved some transactional parity with Lenox. It was an understandable impulse, for someone walking into a house in this rarefied part of London. As Silas was leaving the room, Lenox added, "And cakes and all of that."

"Thank you," said Padden.

"Not at all. Tell me, when we spoke you said that you knew this passenger's Christian name, if not her surname. It was not Laurel, I presume?"

"No, it was Grace."

"Grace. And who called her by that name?"

Padden frowned, as if he hadn't considered the relevance of this question. "Now that you pose the question, I cannot recall. Some fellow passenger."

"She has been traveling long enough, I may then assume, to have made some acquaintance upon the train?"

"About a third of my passengers on the 8:38 take it daily."

"I find that surprising—take the train out of London? Surely the opposite course would be more likely?"

"There are many small businesses in the countryside near London, within a short walk of the train station so they can take advantage of the labor force in the city. In my third-class carriage are the factory workers. Solicitors and investors in the second-class carriage."

"And Grace?"

"She took a second-class ticket."

"Not first?"

Padden smiled. "On her initial trips she took a first-class ticket—but the second-class carriage is roomy and half-empty, and first class rarely has more than one or two passengers in it. I suppose she felt she could economize."

Lenox was making notes as the hot water and sandwiches came in, and Padden took advantage of the silence to fall upon both the food and drink with ravenous appetite. Every conductor Lenox had met could have eaten for England—something about snatching a bite between stations, perhaps, and the continual ambulatory exertions that came with the position.

The question about which Lenox was most curious—where this young woman left the train—he wanted to approach delicately. For some reason he was still afraid that he might startle Padden away.

"Has she ever traveled in the company of another person?" Lenox asked.

"Once. A young man."

"Tall and fair-haired?"

Padden shook his head. "Tall, but dark-haired, with a dark beard."

Lenox's pen scratched over the pad of paper in long careless lines, recording as much as possible. "Age?"

"Near enough to hers."

"Which is?"

"Beyond twenty, anyhow. Twenty-five?"

Lenox looked up at the conductor, who was himself perhaps thirty or thirty-five. He knew from experience that it became more difficult to judge the age of young people as one departed their ranks. "What was their relationship?"

"I didn't inquire."

"But could you not say, based upon their demeanor?"

This seemed like another new idea for the young man, who was more methodical in his mind than the ideal witness—not much imagination. "They talked very friendly."

"Was her arm through his?" asked Lenox.

Padden, a new sandwich halfway to his mouth, paused, furrowing his brow, trying to recollect, and then gave it up for a bad job. "I can't recall," he said. "I should have paid more attention had I known it was significant."

"Of course."

"Could I take another half cup of tea?"

"Have another whole one, my dear fellow," said Lenox, leaning forward to pour it for him.

For the second time Padden spooned a shocking quantity of sugar into his cup, stirred it in, took a gulp of the concoction, and sat back with a satisfied sigh. "Don't feel human till I've had my ninth cup of the day," he said.

It was a very modest witticism, but Lenox laughed generously. At last, gently, he said, "Did you mention that she went all the way down your line, to Canterbury?"

"No, no, she's for Paddock Wood. Returns by the 6:14."

"Paddock Wood. How far is that from London?"

"Forty-seven minutes," said Padden and took another sip of the tea.

Lenox had a hasty taste of his own, eyes over the rim of the cup because he was still writing, and said, "So then from the 8:38 it arrives—"

"Twenty-five past the hour. Usually a minute or two before."

Lenox knew something of Paddock Wood. It was a small brewing community, where they grew most of the hops in Kent. He had a university friend who had grown up not far from there, outside of Maidstone. "Is the Canterbury line the only one that goes there?" he asked Padden.

"No, nor the most frequent. The line from London to Dover, via Redhill, also goes there."

It was possible, then, that young Grace went to Paddock Wood more often than once a month. He hoped so—he meant to have a word with the stationmaster at Paddock Wood as soon as possible. With this in mind, he asked Padden who that was.

"It's Eustace Wainwright. He's as blind as six bats, sorry to say, but a personable enough sort of fellow."

"May I tell him that I know you?"

"Oh, yes," said Padden. "As I say, we're stopped there a moment or two every morning. I give him the mailbag."

It was a common sight—the conductor of the train slowing it just enough to pass a light blue bag into the waiting arms of the stationmaster, then speeding off. Some took it slower than others. "This young woman," Lenox said, "has she any distinguishing article of clothing, or item of luggage, that you can recall?"

"She often carries a black-and-white striped umbrella."

"Anything else?"

"She dresses uncommonly well."

Lenox asked a half-dozen more questions in

this line, none of them very fruitful. Padden, satiated at last, sat back, hands circling the warm cup that contained the last of the teapot, and tried to recall anything else he could about his passenger. He added a few small details, which the older man dutifully transcribed—but nothing of particular notability.

When it was clear that the conductor had nothing more to offer about the case, Lenox thanked him effusively and then sat with him for fifteen long minutes, discussing the minor problems of the railway system that Padden felt a Member of Parliament ought to fix. Lenox promised (sincerely) to have a look at them and then, with a warm good-bye, walked Padden out to Hampden Lane.

Alone again, he raced back to his study and looked into the Kelly's for Kent, which was still sitting out on his desk. There were apparently just above four thousand adults resident in Paddock Wood, and he scrolled through their Christian names, looking for anyone named Grace, or initialed with a *G.* There were a few of the latter, none of the former.

Now he looked up at the clock in his study. It was not quite two o'clock. "Kirk!" he called.

The butler appeared in the doorway. "Sir?"

"Fetch my light cloak if you would, the gray one, and pack my valise with these things." He gestured at the blue books and Stirrington dispatches that sat piled near the edge of his desk. "Some kind of sandwich to eat, too, I suppose, if I get stuck in rural Kent. But tell Jane, if she returns, that I expect to be back before supper."

CHAPTER FIFTEEN

Leaving London by train always offered passengers a strange glimpse of the city's hinterlands, from rambling small railyards full of rusted cars to suburbs of varying gentility. Every mile or so just a little more green appeared between the buildings, until at last one reached the countryside; Kent was almost inexpressibly beautiful at this time of year. On its way to Canterbury the train passed whole fields of delicate pink and purple, thousands of small flowers fluttering with meek bravery toward the uncertain spring sun. To Lenox's London eyes, familiar with every shade of soot, or perhaps the garish colors that men made, it was restful indeed. He had grown up with more plants than buildings around him. Really they ought to get out to Sussex more, and see his brother; but when was there ever time.

The platform at Paddock Wood was so short that everyone wishing to leave the train there had to crowd onto the first two cars. As the train slowed, Lenox could see the stationmaster waiting for the mail. He was a trim, white-mustached man in a blue uniform, with thick glasses and a stoop. This must be Eustace Wainwright.

Eight or ten people left the train at Paddock Wood, and among them was a family with a very small horse. They had bullied it onto the train at the last stop—"It will only be seven minutes, don't kick up a fuss"—and the hapless conductor had stared at it despondently for the entire time since then. To the horse's credit it behaved with admirable decorum throughout its brief ride, standing near the door of the carriage and refusing eye contact with its fellow passengers.

Unfortunately the animal chose precisely the moments of its disembarkation to leave a memento of its gratitude for the conductor's tolerance. The family (evidently known to Eustace Wainwright, who called their names disapprovingly) hustled away from the platform, speaking loudly to one another to indicate that they hadn't witnessed their beast's trespass, leaving the dismayed conductor and station-master to confront the problem on their own. On the platform, two small boys in short pants and suspenders, unable to believe their good fortune, were doubled over in an almost impossible posture of mirth.

Lenox thought it best to absent himself from these proceedings and decided to walk into Paddock Wood.

It was a very small town. On one side of the tracks was a wide apple orchard, of the kind for which the county was justly famous—taste aside, tradition said that it had been a Kent apple that fell on Isaac Newton, giving him the idea for his theory of gravity—and on the other a small main street. Lenox strolled toward a small redbrick church, very recent, and as he looked around he realized that most of the buildings were similarly new. None of them looked to his inexpert judgment older than ten or twenty years. Very possibly Paddock Wood was a new town, grown out of not much at all by the flourishing hops industry. Indeed, up the hill that sloped gently above the town he could see field after field of hops, a becoming light green color. At the end of the summer, when the little clusters were ready for harvest, many London families of modest means would take a hop-picking vacation, father, mother, and children spending their days under the sun and making a bit of money for their trouble. It had always sounded idyllic as Lenox heard it described, especially because hop pickers were in such short supply that the wages were rather good. Because the families were paid by the bushel, rather than the hour, the children didn't have to break their backs.

When he had taken in the width and breadth of Paddock Wood, Lenox made his way back to the station.

The train was gone, the platform empty except for the two boys, who remained on a bench near the entrance, still grinning. Lenox peered down the platform and saw a brick hut with a low blue door, which he assumed to be the province of the stationmaster. It was also, a sign announced, the place to buy train tickets.

Lenox went past the two boys toward the hut and knocked on the door. "Round here!" a voice called.

The sound of a shutter going up on the other side of the edifice confirmed what the voice had said. Lenox went around; there was Eustace Wainwright, sitting on a stool, a book facedown on the brass countertop between them.

"How do you do?" Lenox asked.

"Where to?" asked the stationmaster.

"Ah—no, I have a return ticket." Lenox patted his pocket. "I was hoping to have a word with you. George Padden sends his regards."

"Padden? Saw him this morning. Don't know why he would send his regards again, unless he means to propose."

Lenox took out his card. "I had a few questions about one of his passengers, and he wished you to know that you could trust me."

"Well, he can have my regards back, if it pleases him."

"Would you be willing to give me a few moments of your time?"

"Nothing else to say. I expect I'll see him tomorrow. If I don't I won't lose sleep over it."

"I'm a detective."

"I've no doubt of it at all."

It was hard to say if Wainwright, peering obstinately forward through his glasses, was unintelligent or merely had that deep country unwillingness (Lenox knew it well) to hear anybody else's business, unless he was absolutely forced to do so. "I'm concerned that one of your passengers is in danger, Mr. Wainwright. A young woman who alights here at least once a month, quite possibly more often, on the 8:38 from London. Or I suppose you would consider it the 9:25 from London. She's fair and usually carries a black-and-white striped umbrella. Her first name is Grace."

Wainwright frowned. "You say you're a detective?"

"I am."

"Who's hired you?"

"The young woman herself, after a fashion."

"What do you mean?"

"Well, do you know her?"

It was clear from his face that he did. "Perhaps. How do you mean, she might have hired you?"

Lenox explained the encounter he'd had with his client in Gilbert's and then described his efforts to find the woman, beginning with

113

LeMaire and Audley and concluding more recently with Padden, who had directed him to Paddock Wood. "I would like to help her."

"I have one question."

"Yes?" said Lenox.

"How can I be sure that *you* aren't the man who came into the restaurant and frightened her?"

Lenox sighed. It was a fair question. "You have my card."

Wainwright looked down. "Yes. It says nothing about you being a detective."

"Yes, but you have my name and my address. I am at your mercy. And here." On Lenox's watch chain there was a small, heavy pen, made of gold and with his initials inscribed along its side. "Take this. It was given me by my wife, and I don't readily part with it, but I trust you to return it. You see that it has the same initials as the name upon the card. Keep it for a day or two as a token of my goodwill—indeed, take it to the police in London and ask them about me if you wish—and then return it by the post when you can. Here's three shillings to send it."

Wainwright looked down at this rather poor bit of proof. Lenox reckoned that if the man was venal he could keep it—a small loss—and that if he was honest it might persuade him of Lenox's own honesty.

Which perhaps it did. "Her name is Grace

114

Ammons," said the stationmaster. "Once in a while she picks up mail left for her here."

Only now did Lenox notice the small wall of pigeonholes behind Wainwright in the hut. He evidently ran a postal clearinghouse of sorts, in addition to his railway tasks. It wasn't uncommon in the smaller country stations.

"Thank you very, very much," said Lenox. He pulled out his pad of paper and then reached down to his watch chain for his pen—only to find it wasn't there. With a smile he took the pen back up and wrote down the name, asking Wainwright to spell it. Then he returned the pen to the counter. "Do you know why she comes to Paddock Wood, or how often?"

"Once a month, as you said. I imagine she has some acquaintance here."

"And do you know where she's from?"

"All of her letters come from the West End of London."

Lenox noticed that the next London-bound train was approaching on the other side of the station. If he moved quickly he could make it, and spare himself another hour in Paddock Wood. "Do you remember an address?"

"No. Although her outgoing mail I do remember—if she's really in trouble, this young woman."

This felt like an intrusion, but it might prove useful. "Where did she write?" asked Lenox.

"It was only twice, but I remember because she addressed the letters to herself, and then of course because it was such an uncommon address. She mailed them to Buckingham Palace."

CHAPTER SIXTEEN

It was twilight when Lenox arrived back in London. Despite the misdirection of Audley, he had a name, and perhaps even a location. He felt energized.

From Charing Cross he took a cab to Half Moon Street. Mrs. Lucas answered the door. "How do you do, Mr. Lenox?"

"Is the patient receiving visitors?"

"At their own peril. Please, come along inside. Would you like a cup of tea?"

"Badly. If you could run a spoonful of sugar in it I would be in your everlasting debt."

She smiled. "You know the way up, then. I'll bring it along shortly."

"Thank you, Mrs. Lucas."

Dallington greeted Lenox, ushering him into the room and onto the sofa near the hearth, taking for himself the armchair opposite. Unfortunately it seemed that he had taken a step back in his recovery; he looked pale and clammy, his eyes overbright from the lingering effects of fever.

"Have you managed to leave your rooms at all?" Lenox asked.

"Not yet. I still don't have the vitality for it, I'm afraid. Rotten bore."

"At least Mrs. Lucas is here."

Dallington smiled wryly, as if he were reflecting upon the mixed nature of that blessing, but said, "Yes, she's a brick."

"Is there anything Jane or I could bring you?"

"Only news. The dullness of being ill is beyond anything you ever experienced. For a few days one can adopt a posture of statesmanlike gravity, hushed tones, weak broth—but after that it's simply an inconvenience, unless you attain the dignity of a very serious disease. I don't recommend it."

"The good news is that I have found out her name—your client's, the young girl at Gilbert's."

"You haven't!"

"I have. She's called Grace Ammons, and she may or may not receive mail at Buckingham Palace." As he said this Lenox was attempting to break off a loose thread hanging from the pocket of his houndstooth jacket. When he looked up he saw a change in Dallington's face. "What?"

"Grace Ammons?" the younger detective asked, concerned and alert. "You're quite sure that was the name?"

"I'm sure. You look as if you know it."

"Indeed I do. She is one of the Queen's social secretaries."

Lenox stared at him for a moment. "You're joking."

"I'm not. I've seen her once or twice, a very pretty young woman. I know for a fact that Jasper Hartle from the Beargarden was in love with her, until his aunt forced him to marry that aluminum heiress from the States."

"What is her history?"

"Her grandfather was a butcher in Chicago, as far as I understand it, and—"

"No, Dallington, not Jasper Hartle's poor wife, you fool, Grace Ammons."

"Oh, her. She's nobody much either—by the lights of the palace, I mean, not my own. She came from up north, some small landholding family there. Good stock. She must be very discreet, since she works directly for Mrs. Engel."

This was the Queen's forbidding principal social secretary, an iron-willed German woman, thin as a coatrack, of more than seventy years, who traveled with Victoria and kept the grand ledger of her appointments. "This makes the letter to you look rather more significant," said Lenox.

"Perhaps."

"Is she well-known?"

"In court circles," said Dallington. "I haven't seen her out upon the circuit much, but simply by virtue of her position she is a part of London society. Jane will know her name. Doubtless you've been in the same room with her."

"If she's not out much, how did Jasper Hartle meet her, or come to fall in love with her?"

"When I discover the private habits and yearnings of Jasper Hartle you will be the first to know them."

Lenox smiled. "Perish the thought."

There was a knock at the door. Mrs. Lucas came in, bearing a tea tray. "Here you are, sir," she said.

"Thank you," said Lenox gratefully, taking a cup from her. She smiled and withdrew. "This looks like a proper tonic. It's been a long day. I've yet to tell you about my adventures among your peers."

"My peers?"

Lenox described his visits with LeMaire and Audley. "It was irritating. In the end it caused me only a brief delay, at least. Thanks to Padden."

"That was foul of Audley."

"The usual brinksmanship."

"No, not when he knew that a person's life might be in danger. I call that more than run-of-the-mill competition."

Lenox looked down into his steaming tea, which he was stirring with the miniature spoon that Mrs. Lucas had left cradled between the cup and the saucer. "Grace Ammons, then. Can we call upon her?"

"We can leave our calling cards. There's no mystery about where to find her."

"At the palace."

"Yes." Dallington had stood and gone toward his mantelpiece, where he was shuffling through a thin stack of papers. "I went to a garden party there six or eight months ago and thought I had kept the invitation. I suppose I mislaid it. I think it might have borne her signature upon it, however."

"She has been there for some time, then."

"At least three years."

Lenox had been to the palace several times, in both official and unofficial capacities, though he knew for a certainty that Queen Victoria couldn't have distinguished him from her chimney sweep. He tried to recall the invitations—he felt sure that Lady Jane, though usually imperturbable in the face of any manner of social honor, would in this instance have been excited enough to show him—but couldn't.

"The real question," he said to Dallington, "is whether her troubles are connected to the palace, or the royal family."

"It would be easier if they were to do with Paddock Wood and the 8:38. I don't remember hearing of any member of the royal family taking up residence there."

Lenox remembered the little horse on the train. "No," he said.

"Shall we meet in the morning and call upon her?" asked Dallington.

"We cannot simply walk up to the front door."

"You're a Member of Parliament. Have Graham arrange for you to see Mrs. Engel if you like."

"Not a bad idea." Graham's name returned to Lenox's mind a faint sense of unease, left behind after his conversation with Baltimore. He would have to attend to that business as quickly as possible—cut it off at the head. "In that case I'll fetch you here in my carriage at, what, nine o'clock? Are you quite well enough?"

"I can shrug myself into a suit of clothes, yes. You'll have to do most of the talking. If I faint you can tell her that I'm pining for Jasper Hartle, see if it gets a reaction."

As it happened, however, this plan was never meant to come to fruition. Just as Lenox was taking his final sip of tea, there was a ring at the front door of the house. On the stairwell they could hear the footsteps of Mrs. Lucas, descending to answer it.

Dallington, curious, went to his window, leaning out over the sill to see who was calling. "A bobby," he announced. "Could be for me."

A moment later the housekeeper knocked on the door. "There's a visitor," she announced.

"Thank you," said the bobby. He was clutching a piece of paper. "I come with a note from Inspector Jenkins for Mr. Dallington."

121

Lenox could see plainly upon the young bobby's face, which was shining with excitement, that he could tell them what had happened as easily as the note could. "What is the news?"

"There's been a murder, sir," said the bobby, "in Knightsbridge. A single pistol shot to the temple, it was."

"Who died?" asked Dallington, still holding the unopened note.

"That was why Inspector Jenkins thought you might be interested, you see. It was a gentleman named Archie Godwin, sir."

CHAPTER SEVENTEEN

For the first time since he had fallen ill a week before, Dallington dressed to leave Half Moon Street, and the moment Mrs. Lucas understood this fact she raced into his rooms with pans of sulfur, blocking the keyhole with cloth as they left and opening all the windows. It was the usual manner of cleansing a sickroom. The smell was dreadful even from the street three flights of stairs below, where Lenox and Dallington waited for a cab to fetch them.

They passed the ride to Knightsbridge largely in silence, Lenox gazing out at the busy evening, angry with himself, Dallington, on the other hand, taking even breaths, trying to conserve his energy.

Soon they came to the address that Inspector Jenkins had given in his note. The bobby, having delivered word to Dallington, was now returning to Scotland Yard with a report, so the two men traveled alone.

It appeared that Archie Godwin had died in a hotel; the cab stopped in front of a modest, cheerfully bright hostelry, white with black beams in the old style of the Tudor coaching inns. It stood on a dignified side street, usually sedate no doubt, but at the moment flooded with activity. There were police carriages out front, which held extra lamps aloft and lit the pavement bright. Several bobbies were congregated around the hotel's doorway, barring anyone from entrance.

"This is the Graves Hotel," murmured Dallington. "You know it?"

"Passably well. My mother's uncle used to stay here, my great-uncle. Very quiet place. He thought it too noisy in our house. Anything above a whisper shattered his nerves, however. He was a general in Crimea."

Lenox and Dallington alighted from the carriage and approached the door. There they saw, in among the bobbies, Thomas Jenkins. He had a bit of gray at his temple now and was certainly into the thin end of his thirties, though Lenox still tended to think of him as a young man. He was issuing instructions when he spotted them and strode over.

"Lenox, Dallington," he said briskly. "I'm glad you're here. Lord John, in your last note to me you mentioned the incident with Godwin. I thought of you when we took in this case, naturally. Or perhaps you're the one who can help, Lenox?"

"Little enough, unfortunately," said Lenox. He described their encounter at Gilbert's Restaurant and his subsequent investigation at White's. "I'm curious about the body you found. Is it a tall, slender man with light hair, or a short—"

"No, no, quite the latter," said Jenkins impatiently, eyes roving the scene. Lenox remembered Dallington mentioning that the inspector was all haste for a promotion, now that his name was commonly found in the papers. He had recently been promoted and was now one of three chief inspectors at Scotland Yard. The job he wanted—which had rotated among several men, none of them satisfactory, since the death of Inspector Exeter—was superintendent. The other CIs wanted it, too. "Bald, short, stocky. The true Archibald Godwin, I fear."

"Then at any rate I can provide you with a description of the man who ought to be your primary suspect. He is a shade above six foot, a handsome fellow, dressed like a gentleman, with a silver watch chain, light hair, rather an upturned nose, and a blond mustache."

The inspector pulled a pad of paper from his breast pocket and transcribed this capsule biography, the eager young bobby just behind him, one Lenox had never seen, doing the same. Jenkins turned toward the lad after he was finished writing and said, "Get that description around, if you would."

"Immediately, sir," said the apprentice and vanished.

Lenox went on. "I think you'll find him in the West End, if you want to inform the peelers there in particular. He bore every mark of a gentleman."

"Shall we place someone inside Gilbert's?"

Lenox shrugged. "You might. If he is indeed a criminal, he has likely investigated my name by now and knows that I am—that I was once a detective. If so I sincerely doubt that he shall return to Gilbert's. He will likely be wary regardless. Plainly he is armed, if we assume he is the murderer."

Dallington, hands in his pockets, leaning against the building for support, asked, "Where is the body? How long ago was it done?"

"Not above seventy-five minutes ago," said Jenkins. "He is lying upstairs, in the corridor outside of his room. His cloak and pockets were stripped of all their contents. His hat and watch and watch chain—presuming he wore a watch— are gone also. So is an overnight bag, which the bootboy carried up to his room yesterday morning."

"His hat!" cried Dallington. "How very odd."

"Could they have been stolen by someone who came across the body in the hallway? Perhaps even one of the people working in the hotel? How long was he lying there?" asked Lenox.

Jenkins shook his head. "The sound of the pistol firing roused half a dozen people immediately. It's a miracle that none of them saw the face of the man who did it, though they gave chase to a figure that fled down toward Gloucester Road."

Gloucester Road was the main thoroughfare of this area; a man might have lost himself very easily in the public houses and restaurants there, even late in the evening. Still, Lenox said, "Have you sent bobbies down to—"

"Yes, they're conducting a thorough canvass."

"Do we imagine that the murderer took Godwin's effects in the hope of concealing his identity?" asked Dallington.

"No," said Lenox. "He was staying at the hotel. More likely the person wanted it to look like a robbery."

"Or it was a robbery," said Dallington. "At any rate, if his effects are gone, how can you be sure that it was Godwin at all? I suppose it was his room?"

"Yes," said Jenkins, "and the fellow at the counter took a look and confirmed that it was the same man."

"May we see the body?"

"Follow me."

They entered the Graves—a discreet front desk to the right, a wide stairwell straight ahead of them, and to their left a quiet restaurant, with two or three customers sitting at the bar. "You haven't let anyone leave the hotel, obviously?" Lenox asked.

Jenkins smiled. "Can you imagine that I would?"

"Forgive me. I've been away too long. One grows fretful—and witless, I don't doubt."

"No, no. We read about your case in Plumbley even here in London."

"Well."

Up the crimson-carpeted steps, lit with flickering gas lamps, was the hotel's first floor of rooms. Jenkins turned left, nodding the three of them past a constable at his post. "The fourth door on the right was his."

They could already see the shape of the body, under its white sheet, lying across the threshold, protruding slightly from the open door of the room.

Jenkins went to the body and lifted the sheet. The corpse answered exactly to the description the porter at White's had given Lenox, a short, round, and bald gentleman, with a thin nose and a fringe of dark hair. The bullet hole was a very tidy red circle at his temple. There was no exiting wound. The poor chap.

"A small pistol," said Jenkins, before adding grimly, "though it has done its work well enough."

"Have you looked at his room?" asked Dallington, peering over the threshold.

"It is more or less empty, but I invite you both to inspect it."

"Before we do that, John," said Lenox, "do you recall his address in Hampshire? I believe it was Raburn Lodge."

Dallington nodded. "That was it."

"We ought to send a telegram to them inquiring about Godwin's movements, what brought him to the city. Return paid, with the lad who delivers it to wait upon reply."

"An excellent idea," said Jenkins. "Here, write the name and the message on this scrap of paper and I'll have one of the boys run it to the Yard's office. They receive priority on the wires."

"Should we inform them that he is dead?" asked Dallington doubtfully.

"Perhaps not at the moment," said Jenkins. "Yet what will they think, receiving a message from Scotland Yard? It might be more humane simply to tell them."

"I cannot see the harm in it," said Lenox. "He is unmarried—thankfully, one might say."

He and Dallington spent some minutes conspiring over the precise language of the message then, careless about length because the Yard would pay for it, and giving both of their names, too, that whoever responded might reply to all three. When they were finished they passed it to a constable to send.

When at last this was done they turned into the room, hoping that it might offer some suggestion about the crime—about the vicious person who had rendered lifeless this body, across which they had to step to enter.

CHAPTER EIGHTEEN

The room was capacious but plain, with windows overlooking the street. It held a large four-poster bed with a white canopy at the top, a desk whose surface was empty save for a copper ewer and a stack of writing paper, a wardrobe, and a plaid horsehair chair by the fireplace. There were no ashes in the fireplace, nothing in the rubbish bin. In truth, no sign of Godwin's habitation here.

Lenox went to the desk and shuffled through the writing paper to make sure that it was all blank. He peered into the ewer and shook it: empty. "I suspect this was his first day in London."

"Yes, the hotel confirmed as much. But why do you say that?" said Jenkins.

"The state of the room." Lenox went to the wardrobe. In it was hanging a single suit of clothes. It was disheveled and gave off something of an odor. "Too tidy. More than a day in London and things begin to accumulate in one's pockets."

Dallington, looking ill, set himself gingerly down on the armchair. Still, he mustered enough energy to ask if the hotel had given Jenkins any other information.

"Nothing of very great utility. He arrived this morning with one bag, and—"

"What time?" asked Lenox.

"Before midday at any rate, since the two women at the desk just now were not yet on duty."

"He must have signed the book," said Lenox.

"They don't have one here. Discretion, they say."

"That's a fine way to be robbed."

"If anyone is thieving it's the hotel, if the rates they list are accurate."

Dallington shook his head. "You two don't understand. My uncle stayed here, as I was telling Lenox. It's full of country gentlemen who dislike the city. They're happy to pay for the quiet of the place, and its plainness, too. They bring you breakfast in your room at the crack of dawn, no doubt a single egg boiled hard and shoved in a newly killed rabbit, or some similar countrified nonsense. They're strict about guests. The bar is quiet. They won't object to muddy boots. It's Pall

Mall for people who can afford Pall Mall but don't like to stay in the din of the city. No questions from the staff, or even greetings really. The patrons know what they like. My uncle Gerald shot about forty men at the Sea of Azov and found he didn't care for much company after that. This was where he stayed in London. I don't think he ever tipped me once, the old sod. May he rest in peace."

"That sounds like Godwin," said Lenox. He had been surveying the room and now took a lamp, went down to his hands and knees, and peered into the stygian recesses beneath the bed. "Certainly he wasn't a Londoner."

"How do you mean?" asked Jenkins, then added, rather irritably, "I did look under there already. I looked all over the room. At the notepaper too."

"A new pair of eyes can never hurt," said Lenox mildly.

"Mine hurt terribly at the moment," said Dallington, pale, pinching his brow with a thumb and forefinger.

"John, tell Jenkins what we read of Godwin in *Who's Who.*"

In the end there was nothing under the bed, or in any of the drawers of the desk, which Lenox removed altogether and turned around, inspecting— an excess of caution that had once or twice borne fruit. He saved for last the suit of clothes hanging in the wardrobe. It was a heather gray suit, made of heavy wool.

"It is in shockingly bad condition," Jenkins called out preemptively when Lenox began to examine it.

Indeed it was. The cuffs of the suit's arms were unraveling, and there were large holes dotted along the hem of the jacket. Its distinctly unpleasant scent grew stronger in the room every time the door of the wardrobe was opened. "A gentleman's country suit, I suppose," murmured Lenox. "I have seen worse garments upon the shoulders of earls who were looking after their pigs. Not much worse, mind you."

"Certainly it could not respectably be worn in the city."

Lenox frowned and turned toward the doorway of the room. "What was he wearing when he died?"

Jenkins began to speak but then stopped, nonplussed. "A suit" was all he said in the end.

Lenox went to the body and uncovered it, despite the attendant bobby's initial objections. "A much finer suit of clothes," he announced to Jenkins and Dallington. "Very nearly new."

"We checked the pockets," said Jenkins quickly.

Nevertheless Lenox carefully went over the body himself, dutifully rolling its unpleasant limp weight side to side, removing the shoes, feeling the lining of the suit for padding. (In such a fashion he had once come across a large ruby on a costermonger's corpse, its origin and the history of its acquisition still, to this day, unexplained.)

Here Lenox did find something. The pockets of the suit were empty, but in the rolled cuff of the pants was a small ticket, evidently left there by the tailor, for delivery. It was dated to that day.

He showed Dallington and Jenkins. "It's not much, but at least we know he had a delivery this morning."

"I'm surprised he didn't simply bring up a nicer suit of clothes."

"I'm betting he wanted to travel lightly and knew that the suit in the closet had seen its best days. He knew he could wear the replacement back to Hampshire tomorrow."

"Now what?" asked Jenkins.

"The hallway," said Dallington and Lenox at the same time.

"We have scanned it closely—in increasingly large concentric loops," said Jenkins.

Lenox felt a surge of pride: It was his method, one that he had urged the Yard to adopt. Now he employed it again, for the first time in a while.

Unfortunately the killer had left no telling detail behind this time.

"I take it there is a second stairwell?" asked Lenox. "The murderer could scarcely have strolled down this primary one, through the entrance of the hotel."

"Particularly if the gunshots attracted people right away," added Dallington.

"Yes—it is to the right, rather than the left. The staff use it, but it is much less trafficked than the main staircase."

"The killer must have been familiar with the building," said Lenox.

"Or done a little bit of preliminary investigation. After all, what do we make of this murder? Was it planned with forethought?"

Lenox thought for a moment. "Obviously it is significant that Godwin was nearly never in London—yet here we find him, appearing in the city only a few days after an impostor gave me his name."

"Likely they will have information about his coming to the city at Raburn Lodge," said Dallington. "I suppose we must be patient."

"For my part, I wonder whether this was a long- or short-term impersonation. In the meanwhile we can hope to ascertain what he did in London. I think we might ask at White's, John."

Dallington nodded. "We can go there when we are finished here."

"I'll accompany the body back to the medical examiner's," said Jenkins, "if you two don't mind handling that end of it. There are a great many cases on my ledger at the moment. Though this one, in such a quiet and respectable neighborhood, may attract more notice, I suppose, in the papers."

"Happy to help," said Dallington.

"Before we leave—were there any witnesses in the hotel?"

"We have interviewed everyone once now, I believe. Let me check." Jenkins called over a young constable and conferred with him for a moment, then returned to Lenox and Dallington. "Yes, we have spoken to everyone. The results have been disappointing. Nobody saw the murderer—they only heard the gunshot."

"Nobody was upon the back stair, I suppose?" asked Lenox.

"No."

"We should look at it."

"Be my guest. But there is one witness who saw Godwin earlier this morning. Perhaps you would like to speak to him first? He is staying in the room next door. Sooner or later we must permit him to leave the hotel."

"Let's see him now, then," said Lenox.

CHAPTER NINETEEN

As Jenkins led them downstairs, a different constable approached him with a report: Nobody along the Gloucester Road, or indeed anywhere in these environs, had anything useful to offer the police. It didn't help that there was a fog that evening, thickening now to a degree of murkiness that meant cab drivers would soon start charging steeper fares, if they hadn't already.

There were clusters of onlookers around the door of the hotel, waiting for the body to emerge. Lenox scanned their faces. It was almost axiomatic among his peers that murderers returned to the scenes of their crimes, but there was too great an element of calculation in this death, of murder by design, to think that it was somebody who killed for the excitement of it. Worse luck. Still, he advised Jenkins to have the bobbies take the names of everyone stopped on the pavement.

The witness who had seen Archie Godwin earlier in the day was a young man named Arthur Whitstable, in town from Liverpool upon business; he was a broker of stocks in that city. He looked the perfect exemplar of quiet English rectitude, a tall, square-jawed, deferential gentleman, sitting on a hard chair and reading the newspaper in the hotel manager's office. He stood and shook hands with Lenox and Dallington—Jenkins had shown them into the room and left—without any evident impatience.

"I apologize for the inconvenience of another interview," said Lenox.

"Not at all. This is a dreadful business," Whitstable said. "I've been staying at the Graves for years, and count upon it absolutely as my home from home in London."

"Had you ever met Godwin before, or seen him?"

"No."

"But you saw him this morning?"

"Indeed, twice."

"Can you tell us what happened?"

"I can tell you all I told Inspector Jenkins, at least. At around eleven o'clock, Mr. Godwin knocked on my door, apologizing for the intrusion, and asked if I had a pen sharpener he could borrow. They didn't have one at the front desk. He was just on his way out but needed to finish a letter before he went."

"He was alone?"

"No, he had a companion, a tall gentleman with blond mustaches."

Lenox and Dallington exchanged looks. "Did he speak?" asked Dallington. "This other fellow?"

"No, and Mr. Godwin did not introduce him. I gathered that he had come to fetch his friend for some errand—he looked impatient to be gone."

"The second time you saw Mr. Godwin was when he returned the pen sharpener?" asked Lenox.

"No. I had to go out upon a matter of business—in fact, just as he knocked on my door I was readying myself to leave—and told him he could leave the penknife with the front desk, under my name."

"Did he?" asked Dallington.

"Yes, I have it right here." Whitstable patted his breast pocket. "I usually carry it upon my person, because in my business one signs a great many contracts. As it happens I didn't need it this morning."

"What was Mr. Godwin's demeanor when you first saw him?" asked Lenox.

"He was a very friendly chap, apologetic for the intrusion, and quite solicitous that I had no immediate need of the penknife. He said he would go borrow one elsewhere if I did."

"And the second time you saw him?"

"Ah, yes. As I say, I went out upon business shortly after he knocked on my door. When I returned at noon I met him on the street, on Gloucester Road. He was in a great rush, not at all eager to speak with me—even rather avoiding me, until it was clear that I had seen him, when he thanked me hurriedly. He was with two men this time, one of them the same as earlier."

"Did you get the sense that he was in danger?"

"Not at the time. Now, knowing that he is dead—perhaps. He wished to avoid meeting me."

"Who was the third gentleman with them?"

"I didn't speak to him, or look at him—just a normal sort of person."

"You cannot think of anything physically distinctive in him?"

Whitstable narrowed his eyes, thinking. "He might have been rather shorter than average."

"Fat, thin?"

"Neither, I don't think."

"You are sure he was with Godwin?" said Dallington.

"Yes, quite sure."

"Did you have any sense of where they were going?"

"No. Probably I haven't conveyed how brief the encounter was—no more than five or ten seconds. I should have forgotten it forever, if the gentleman hadn't been murdered. Now I've wondered all evening whether it was those two companions of Mr. Godwin's who did it."

Lenox wondered the same thing. They asked Whitstable a few more questions, some in a futile effort to acquire a more detailed description of this unidentified third man. At last, Lenox thanked him and said, "We may find you here, if we have further questions?"

"Upon my word, no," said Whitstable. "I couldn't stay in that room, after all that has passed. I've already had the porter remove my things to the Chequers, two streets down by Onslow Square."

"How long will you be in London?"

"Another eight nights. It is my semiannual trip to London, always two weeks."

"Then we will see you out at the Chequers, if

we have further questions. Thank you very much indeed for your patience."

Whitstable shrugged, his face philosophical. "I wish there were more I could do."

Lenox and Dallington made their way back upstairs and down the hall, headed for the hotel's second staircase—the one by which, presumably, Archibald Godwin's murderer had left the building.

It proved a disappointment. Dallington sat on a rickety chair at the top, out of breath and ill, as Lenox spent twenty careful minutes examining the area both inside and outside, hoping the murderer had dropped some small totem or left behind some smudged footprint.

There was nothing, however.

"It has the look of a careful crime," said Dallington.

"Perhaps, but I cannot think why Godwin and his companion were together for so many hours before it was done."

"Murder must have been a last resort. Bargaining first, then threats. Finally violence. So often one sees that pattern."

"I suppose," said Lenox, unpersuaded.

They traced their steps back down the hall— Godwin's door shut now, a bobby standing by it, the blankness of his face hiding either boredom or stupidity, or who knew, great internal self-sustaining brilliance—and went back downstairs.

As they came to the front hallway they saw that four bobbies were leaving the hotel, together bearing the stretcher that supported Archibald Godwin's corpse.

They followed the body out of the door. On the pavement the crowd parted and grew reverently quiet, granting Godwin the prestige that belongs to the newly dead. Two or three men took off their hats. The local pub's potman, roller of big cigars, with a wooden tray of beers hanging from a leather strap around his neck, had stopped here, attracted by the crowd no doubt, but now, perhaps out of respect, melted away, returning to his regular deliveries. This was death. Soon the body was out of sight, and the crowd, after the dissipation of tension that follows a long exhale, began to murmur again and then depart.

Lenox and Dallington had seen this kind of scene, each of them many times. It was always strange, jarring, raggedly human. After watching for a moment they decided to leave. There was nothing more for them here; they would be more useful calling in at White's on behalf of Jenkins.

"Although you might go home if you like," said Lenox as they got into his carriage. "If you're ill."

"I shall manage," said Dallington.

He looked awful. "As you please."

They rode in silence. Lenox must have seemed preoccupied, for as they were nearing White's his younger friend said, "Are you quite all right, Charles?"

"I am," said Lenox, shaking his head sharply to return it to attention, and smiling wanly. "It is only guilt that keeps me silent."

"Guilt? Over what?"

"I sincerely hope that the young woman I saw at Gilbert's—this Grace Ammons—is not in danger."

CHAPTER TWENTY

The windows of White's were, at this hour in the heart of the evening, very bright, crowded with lively figures, all of them holding drinks. Dallington, a member of the club, tipped his hat to the porter—a different fellow than the one Lenox had met before—and led the way inside.

"Shouldn't we ask that porter about Godwin?" asked Lenox in the front hall.

From upstairs came the merry noise of glassware breaking. "It will be Minting who knows," said Dallington. "Let's go to his office."

As they passed an open door someone cried "Dallington!" The young lord, face still pale, soldiered onward, and a moment later Lenox heard the same voice say idly, "Could have sworn it was Johnny Dallington."

He led Lenox up two flights of stairs and down a narrow passageway, lined with caricatures of the club's members that had appeared in *Punch* and, lower to the ground, glass-topped cases full of old rifles belonging to past members.

At the end of this passageway they came to a door marked HEAD WAITER. Dallington knocked at the door, and it was drawn open at once, revealing a jowly man, nearly as large as the tiny room he inhabited, with white hair and thick glasses. He sat at a desk covered with papers.

"This is Minting," said Dallington. "Minting, Charles Lenox."

"M'lud," said Minting, just rising an inch or two from his seat and then, this tremendous exertion concluded, emitting one or two very heavy breaths as he sat again.

"You are the head waiter here?" asked Lenox.

"I doubt Minting has lifted a tray in fifteen years," said Dallington. "He keeps the club bets."

Hence the paperwork on the desk. "With all due respect, how would Mr. Minting, in this office, know better than the porter who had entered and exited the club?"

"He knows," said Dallington simply. "Minting, we want to learn whether Archibald Godwin was here in the past day or two."

"Arrived at 12:40 this postmeridian, departed 1:50, on his own, placed no bets." The velocity with which Minting delivered these facts seemed like a rebuke to Lenox for his doubts. "Sat alone for lunch. Spoke with several young men in the card room but played no hands."

"When was the last time he was here prior to this afternoon?" asked Lenox.

Without hesitation Minting answered. "November 1873."

"Minting's got an excellent memory, you see," said Dallington to Lenox. "Everyone in the club rats to him, too, it's a disgrace."

"False, m'lud," said Minting complacently.

"Did Godwin stay here?" asked Lenox.

"No, sir. In '73 it was the Graves Hotel in Pall Mall, not half a mile away. Quieter, he said. He's a country gentleman. The lads can get a bit noisy in the lower rooms here. Carries into the quarters."

"Did he drink?" asked Dallington.

"Half-bott of the Ducru-Beaucaillou with lunch. Deplorable vintage, if I'm being honest."

"Did he tell anyone of his plans, of what brought him to London?" asked Lenox.

"Business, he said."

"Did you see him?" asked Dallington.

"No, m'lud."

The two men standing exchanged looks, to confirm that neither had another question. "Thank you, Minting," said Dallington and passed a coin to the man.

It disappeared into one of the folds of his voluminous waistcoat. "Sir," he said and then, as they were closing the door, added, "Congratulations on the Dwellings Act, Mr. Lenox."

Dallington smiled as they walked down the corridor again. "He's a genius, Minting. Laziest chap you ever saw, though. Otherwise he might have been a very great man—perhaps in your line of work. Perhaps in business, for I know him to have a remarkable knack for figures. As it is I think he's grown richer than half the club's members over the years. He made a packet when Siderolite won the Goodwood, though he gave some of it back on Doncaster last year."

"Strange fellow."

The consultation over, and therefore his duty discharged, Dallington had gone from looking poorly to looking positively deathlike. "Would you mind if we sat down for a moment in the back bar? It will be quieter there."

"You poor soul. Come, let's skip the bar. If you can make it into the carriage we'll take you home."

"That might be for the best."

As they drove, Dallington slumped into the corner of the carriage, eyes closed and breathing reedy. He could barely make it up the stairs at Half Moon Street; Lenox hadn't entirely realized the effort it had required for him simply to leave the house this evening. When he did reach his rooms he collapsed, gratefully, onto the divan in his sitting room. Lenox would have stayed to look after him, but Mrs. Lucas was already attending to it. A smell of sulfur lingered in the air.

"I'll be around in the morning," said Lenox. "We'll hope for some response from Godwin's people in Hampshire before then."

Dallington lifted a hand in response, and as Mrs. Lucas hustled a bowl of soft broth up the stairs, the older man took his leave.

At home Lenox said hello to Lady Jane—it had been a long day since he had seen her that morning, and he spent ten minutes acquainting her with its events, and another ten hearing of her own activities—and then scribbled a note to Jenkins, telling him what they had found at White's.

Now, both rather exhausted, Lenox and Lady Jane ate supper together, a comfortingly warm soup, to begin, and then a roasted pheasant with peas and potatoes. The best part of the meal, though neither was a nightly drinker, was the bottle of red wine they shared, quieting their brains, making the candlelight look soft and sleepy, dividing the buzz of the day from the peace of home. Slowly their voices relaxed, and their thoughts seemed to linger in the air. The conversation had nothing sharp in it. When the plates were cleared away they went to the sitting room, each with a small cup of coffee, and sat and read for a little while, hands occasionally touching—a reassurance. After a drowsy half hour upon the sofa they retired, both ready for sleep.

When Lenox woke in the morning there was a telegram for him, handed in at Raburn Lodge, Hampshire. Both Jenkins and Dallington were copied. It read:

Dear Sirs STOP I hope you have somehow mistaken your man and that my brother is alive, but fear that the worst is indeed true STOP Despite my distress I know that Archie would wish you to be in full possession of the facts of his trip to London STOP As such I will be in London by our 3:18 train and staying at the Graves Hotel STOP You may call upon me there at your convenience STOP Henrietta Godwin

Lenox took down his copy of Bradshaw's and looked up the timetables. The 3:18 would put Henrietta Godwin in central London at half past four, and from the station she might take another twenty minutes to arrive at her hotel. To permit her some time to settle he decided that he would call in on her at a little bit past five o'clock in the afternoon, teatime, and wired to both Jenkins and Dallington that such was his plan. This wasn't quite his case; then again, he was involved and felt a measure of responsibility, and unless he was positively making a nuisance of himself he was determined to stay on and see it through to the end. He wanted a word with that light-haired man from Gilbert's. Pride, he supposed. By that sin fell the angels.

Graham was up, too, and having taken breakfast in his own rooms now called upon Lenox. Seeing his secretary sent a shadow of unease across the Member's thoughts. He ignored it. There would be time to speak with him later, and the day was busy. "You are meeting with Lord Heath at nine o'clock," Graham said, "and with Phillip Marsden at ten, both to discuss the naval treaty."

"Could you push them?" asked Lenox.

"Marsden perhaps," said Graham, frowning. He looked tired, and Lenox realized that when he slackened the pace of his work Graham was the one who took up the extra line. "Lord Heath is insistent that he must see you."

"There was a murder in Knightsbridge last night."

"So Kirk told me, sir," said Graham, smiling faintly. "I recall a time when such affairs were your chief interest."

A very distant time, his tone seemed to imply. "Dallington needs my help."

"Very well, sir, I will change Mr. Marsden's place upon the schedule. Lord Heath you will see at nine?"

"Yes, fine," said Lenox. "But in exchange I need a favor—I need you or Frabbs to find me a moment in the schedule at Buckingham Palace, to visit with a woman named Grace Ammons. She is one of the Queen's social secretaries. She is in Mrs. Engel's office."

Graham raised his eyebrows slightly but merely nodded.

Throughout Lenox's meeting with Lord Heath, which lasted three-quarters of an hour, his mind dwelled not, sadly, on the proliferating French navy, nor on the quantities of armaments that Heath was positive Parliament must vote to order, but upon Miss Grace Ammons and the corpse of Archibald Godwin. Halfway through the meeting Frabbs entered the room.

"What is it, boy?" Heath asked with tremendous vexation, a huge lump of a man.

"Pardoning myself, sirs, Mr. Graham wished you to know, Mr. Lenox, that you will be welcome upon your errand any time after ten o'clock."

"Yes, all right, thank you," said Lenox, trying to match the peer's tetchiness, though in fact he could have stood Frabbs a pint of ale, he was so pleased that they would finally find Grace Ammons that day. The rest of the meeting seemed a long blur of impossibly slow exchanges. When Heath was at last satisfied, Lenox shot from the room and went directly to Half Moon Street.

CHAPTER TWENTY-ONE

His haste was not misplaced; when he arrived, Dallington was up and pacing his rooms. He looked ill, even febrile perhaps, but his jaw was set with determination.

"Do we have an appointment?"

"I'm not sure they'll want you to introduce the plague to Buckingham Palace," said Lenox.

Dallington managed a smile. "I'm fit enough. Mrs. Lucas had me swallow some beef broth this morning."

It was the kind of moment when Jane would have said she wished that Dallington had married by now, and had someone to care for him. Of course, Jane was very close with Dallington's mother, whose own interests also lay in that direction. Personally Lenox felt grateful that Mrs. Lucas was present. That was enough. "If you're sure you can do it, let's be on our way," he said.

They drove toward the palace by way of the Mall, green on either side of them, until they came to the roundabout that lay before the eastern front of the building. The carriage turned and they could see Nash's grand facade, brick and painted stone, with the sovereign's guards standing motionless at short intervals in the white gravel. Off to one side was a very small door that had a bit of bustle about it. Lenox took it for the visitors' entrance.

He and Dallington applied here for entrance to the palace and were told they must go around the corner. This they did, and after a very cross-grained porter looked up their names in several different ledgers, he locked the door of his post and beckoned them inward. The fate of any visitors who might arrive in his absence was apparently of negligible interest to him.

"They could sell one of these paintings and hire another chap," muttered Dallington, gesturing at the brightly adorned walls.

Indeed, the entire building, even in these back channels, bore a kind of heroic concupiscence, like a child adding twenty spoonfuls of sugar to his tea. They were walking on a red and gold carpet of intricate design, and it was so thick that one's footsteps wobbled into it. (Lenox thought of Sophia, who would have enjoyed it for crawling.) A less charitable Englishman might have believed that he discerned a certain German richness of taste—or absence of taste, supplemented with richness—but it was doubtful that the Queen had ever thought of these halls, much less designed them herself. As they walked, Dallington steadied himself upon a succession of priceless French side tables.

"Here you are, sirs," said their guide, rapping snappishly against a heavy door. "Mrs. Engel."

The door opened immediately, a sinewy woman with thick glasses and white hair standing behind it. "Yes?" she said.

"My name is Charles Lenox. My colleague and I made an appointment to call upon Miss Grace Ammons."

"I am Grete Engel," she said. "Come in."

The room the Queen's social secretary had for her use was tiny, but there was a small Rubens upon one wall, a Winterhalter portrait of Prince Albert upon another, and best yet a lovely view of the palace's large interior courtyard, crisscrossed with a complex geometry of paths. On a cloak stand in the corner was a smart jacket, which Lenox guessed that Mrs. Engel might wear over her rather plain smock when she went to see the Queen.

The largest object in the room was the secretary's desk, an oak and mahogany object the size of a small seafaring vessel. There were dozens of tiny cubbyholes in it, each brimming with paper. Only a madman or a genius could find organization in such profusion. Then again, Mrs. Engel took credit, one heard from those in the Queen's circle, for being a genius. Victoria's own version of Mr. Minting, as it were—likely with a slighter attentiveness toward horseracing results, however.

The actual surface of the desk was clear, except for an inkstand and a single sheet of paper. Lenox sneaked a look: It was a menu. Mrs. Engel, standing by her chair, must have seen his eyes, because, with a faint smile, she said, "Pigeons in jelly, hare soup, galantines de veau, and saddle of mutton. And plum tart, Her Majesty must have plum tart."

"Do you plan the food at the palace, too?" he asked. "Surely your responsibilities are heavy enough."

"I check the menus against the guest list." Her English was excellent, albeit with a slight German crispness around the vowels. "The Prime Minister cannot abide onions in any hot dish."

That was actually a useful bit of information to Lenox, and he filed it away in his mind to tell Jane later. "This is Lord John—"

"I know both of your names, Mr. Lenox," she said. "Why do you hope to see Miss Ammons?"

Lenox's face became serious, and his voice confidential. "You may once have heard my name connected with criminal investigations," he said, "though perhaps not. Lord John is still involved in the field. Together we have reason to believe that Miss Ammons may be in danger."

Mrs. Engel looked at them both with an appraising eye. Then she nodded. "Give my regards to your mother," she said to Dallington. "Miss Ammons is waiting in the East Gallery now. The door into it is at the end of the hallway.

There are guards at all the other doors. I tell you this simply as a matter of course, not because I expect you to leave the room."

They thanked her, and she set one foot into the hallway to watch them go down the corridor. At the end of the hallway Lenox tried the door; it was open, and together they stepped into one of the most beautiful rooms, he thought, that man had ever produced.

It was a long, thin gallery, with a curved glass ceiling. Because the Queen and her guests processed down it before official state banquets, it was empty in the middle other than a rich, slender carpet, but along the walls were long couches, upholstered in white with a very thin gold stripe. Then there was the art: High on the vaulted walls were massive paintings by Van Eyck, Rembrandt, Lawrence, and Constable. In the center of the gallery were two doorways, and all along it were ranged a series of marble fireplaces, carved with cherubim.

The two nearest were lit, and sitting on a sofa between them, looking very small in these surroundings, was a beautiful young woman: Grace Ammons.

She stood; there was already something defiant in her posture, and Lenox said, a propitiatory hand held in the air, "Miss Ammons, I'm afraid I owe you—"

"You cannot harm me here," she said. "There

are guards at every door, who will be here in an instant should I call for them."

"You have my solemn word that we would never harm you," said Lenox.

"It's my fault," said Dallington, coming forward. "I wish you would let me explain. Here, sit."

Each fireplace was flanked by chairs, and Lenox pulled two forward, so that they could all sit, though he left them at an angle to the sofa, not wanting this young woman, whose nerve he already admired, to feel surrounded.

Slowly, and interrupting each other, Lenox and Dallington laid out the facts of the case in their entirety: Dallington's illness, the missed signal in Gilbert's, the roundabout way that Lenox had found out her identity, and finally, though it might frighten her, the death of Archibald Godwin at the Graves Hotel.

"What do you mean, that Archibald Godwin is dead?" she asked, leaning forward eagerly. "The man who came into Gilbert's?"

"No," said Dallington. "A different gentleman, whom perhaps your foe was impersonating."

She slumped back into the sofa. Her face, though still wary, had relaxed slightly, and Lenox sensed that she believed their account, or wished to believe it. "Will you tell us your story?" he asked.

She shook her head. "It is too great a coincidence that Mr. Godwin—the man I know as

155

Mr. Godwin—appeared in Gilbert's at the same moment as you."

Gently, Lenox said, "Is it not possible that he tracked you there, or knew your habits? Had you been dodging him?"

From her face he could see that this was a plausible suggestion, but she shook her head again. "It's no matter. I've hired a different adviser."

"Who?" asked Dallington.

"Miss Strickland. Her agency has been excellent so far."

Lenox suppressed a sigh. "Miss Strickland."

"Yes."

"We don't need payment," said Dallington, "and as we're helping Inspector Jenkins at Scotland Yard with his murder investigation, you needn't even hire us on. We're simply investigating a case related to your own. Here is Jenkins's card, if you wish to contact him."

She took the card from Dallington and looked up at him, hesitating. At last, she said, "My friend—you may as well know it was Emily Merrick—said you were very reliable."

"You can trust us, Miss Ammons, I promise."

"Very well," she said, then began to tell her story.

CHAPTER TWENTY-TWO

I was born twenty-six years ago in a small town in Yorkshire, where I lived until I was seventeen. I have no family members still alive, save a few distant cousins who live in that part of the world, my mother having died just before my thirteenth birthday, and my father three years later. I stayed in the village long enough to speak to the executor of my father's will, to reassure myself that I had enough money upon which to survive until such time as I found either a husband or employment, and then I took the next train to London, and from there to Paris."

"Paris!" said Dallington.

"My mother and father were sophisticated people for their part of the world, and my mother traveled to London to buy her dresses, from a Frenchwoman. She had been to Paris twice in her youth. It was the place she loved best."

"You had no connections there, no family?"

"My father knew that his own death was coming, and wrote me a letter of introduction to his business partner, and to a very dear friend, in London. I saw them, and they arranged for me to stay upon my arrival with Madame de Vincennes, a young relation of the Duc d'Espaille, whose mother is English. She began to introduce me into the world of Paris society."

These names were unknown to Lenox (though he had taken his honeymoon partly in Paris, and dined out a great deal). "Go on," he said.

"I stayed in Paris for six years. I knew nothing of English society in that time, and traveled back to Yorkshire only once. Eventually, however, the money my father had left me began to dwindle, and I knew that I'd better either get married or return to London to find work. I had a good education and now spoke French fluently. So I began to plan my return. Then, in the last few weeks I was in Paris, I met a young man named George Ivory."

She blushed as she said the name, and Dallington, ever gallant, broke into a fit of coughs, whether by design or happy accident allowing her a moment to regain her composure. "Excuse me," said the young lord. "Still a mile or so under the weather."

"George and I are to be married—for the past three years we have both been saving money to be married. He doesn't have any family either, except for his mother, who lives—"

"In Paddock Wood," said Lenox.

She looked at him. "Yes. In Paddock Wood."

"You go down to visit her each month?"

"George lives there, rather than in London, to save money. It is really very close. My work is taxing, but I have one weekday off a month, and I take it to visit him. On weekends George comes

158

into London, and on Sundays he brings his mother, and we go to St. Paul's for the nine o'clock service."

"Why do you write to yourself from Paddock Wood?" asked Lenox.

"Oh, that. Occasionally I work as I ride down on the train. It's easier to mail the work back to myself than to worry about losing it, especially if it's not urgent. I'm forgetful about papers. It was at Mrs. Engel's suggestion, in fact."

"What work does George do?" asked Dallington.

"He's a solicitor."

"Please, go on."

"I came back from Paris and, with the help of a friend there, became secretary to the wife of the Earl of Axford." This particular Earl Lenox knew—the greatest womanizer London had ever seen. "From there I went to her friend Lady Mannering's, in the same position, and she was so pleased with my work that when Mrs. Engel needed a new secretary, she recommended me. These women like to be in Mrs. Engel's favor, as perhaps you can understand.

"It all happened so smoothly and easily—until two months ago. That was the day that Archibald Godwin called upon me."

"Here at the palace, or at your home?"

"At my home. I wish he had tried to see me here—he shouldn't have been allowed through the door."

"What did he want?" asked Lenox.

"To be placed upon a guest list."

"It is your job to make up the guest lists?" he asked.

"One of my jobs—in consultation with Mrs. Engel."

Lenox was writing now, in a small notepad. "How did he discover your home address?"

"I don't know, and it frightened me. He was horribly bullying. Very polite, all the while, but somehow at the same time threatening."

"You have the power to place people on and take people off of guest lists?"

"For larger events, yes. Mrs. Engel checks them, but she trusts me."

"Why did he believe you would do it?"

Her steady gaze faltered now, and Lenox felt they were close to the truth. "He said that he would have George fired."

"But how could he have the power to do that?"

"He was a director of a company—"

"The Chepstow and Ely," murmured Lenox.

"Yes. How did you know?"

"Only a suspicion."

"They are a large client of George's firm— possibly the largest client, I think, though George himself is extremely discreet. This man said he could have George fired at any time."

"So you placed him upon the guest list."

"Yes—once. It was a reception here for the

ambassador from Spain, nearly eight hundred people. I could not see the harm in it."

"Did you see him there?"

"No—but he came. His name was checked on the list."

"What then?"

"Nothing. I had a horrible fear that he would steal some priceless sculpture, or insult the honor of—well, you can imagine my fears. The party ended, and I thought that the worst had gone with it."

"Until?"

"He came to see me again. He was in a terrible knock, for some reason, and said that he needed to go to another party. I said that I couldn't allow it, and I thought he would thrash me then and there. He told me that if he didn't receive the invitation in the next three days, George would be fired."

"And you sent it to him."

"I told him it must be the very last time, and that I would go to the police. He sneered and said I didn't dare, and that if I did George would be fired. The next day I moved rooms, though I had lived in Caxton Street for three years and considered it a second home. That was also the day when I wrote you, Lord John."

"I sincerely doubt that his injunction was made to the exclusion only of public criminal investigators, and not private ones," said Dallington.

"I hoped for your discretion. That was why I was so alarmed when I saw him at Gilbert's, just after having taken the drastic step of moving house," she said.

"He must have heard that you moved and known his best chance of finding you again was on your regular morning at Charing Cross," said Dallington. "How frightening it must have been."

She looked down at the floor. "Yes. That is nothing to the fear I feel now, though, having heard of this murder."

"Just to clarify," said Lenox, looking at his notes, "when you refer to Godwin you mean the man at Gilbert's—tall, fair-haired, with a blond mustache and a gentlemanly appearance?"

"Appearance—oh, yes, that is he. But he has the soul of a devil, Mr. Lenox."

"What has Miss Strickland advised?" asked Dallington.

"She is going to find him for me—"

"That will be a neat trick."

"And discover his motives."

"What will you do then?"

"I don't know."

"At some stage you will need to consult Scotland Yard," said Lenox.

"He was so clear—that if I went to the police, it would all be over."

"Did he come to the palace again?" asked Dallington.

She nodded. "Yes. A little more than a week ago. There were six hundred guests this time. He came to me at the party and said that he needed to return one more time, to a smaller party the Queen was having the next week. I said he couldn't."

Dallington and Lenox looked at each other, and then Lenox said, "Did he insist?"

"Yes. It was a terrible scene—and George was to be at the palace. My heart was beating terribly. I told him he would be too noticeably out of place at a party for a hundred people. He seemed to understand that, at last, and stalked off."

"He didn't insist?"

The secretary's large brown eyes, full of apprehension, were wet with tears nearly ready to fall. "No."

"Were there any differences between the first party and the second?" Lenox asked.

She pursed her lips in thought. "The second was a garden party. It was finally warm enough, though we opened the residence, too, in case it started to rain or anyone took cold."

"And the third party that he proposed to attend?"

"That was altogether different—in a different quarter of the house, with many fewer people."

Lenox thought for a moment and then said, "This man has proven himself dangerous. I can only suggest that you take precautions for your safety."

"Miss Strickland has had two gentleman walking me to and from work. They make sure that we aren't followed. We change carriages, also."

Lenox frowned at this; his estimation of Miss Strickland (or more likely Mr. Jones, or whatever his name might be) ticked upward with that bit of information. It was the course he would have suggested.

They promised the young woman that they would give her troubles their full attention, and then, after asking a few more questions, they rose and left by the same hallway through which they had entered. Mrs. Engel was at her desk, door opened, and saw them out, with a few parting words.

"She is the third-best girl I ever had doing this particular job," the small German woman said. "Treat her well."

"We will, certainly," said Dallington.

Out on the gravel again, Lenox looked at his pocket watch. It was far later than he expected. "Damn it all to hell," he said. "I have to go meet Marsden now—twenty minutes ago, in fact. John, take my carriage, you're ill. I'll get into one of these cabs; it will be quicker."

Lenox was already walking away. Dallington called after him, "Wait—what did you think?"

Lenox was stepping into the cab, Dallington running up to come within earshot. "I liked her. I don't know why she lied."

"Lied?"

"To Parliament, sir," he said to the driver, who flicked the horses. "John, let's speak about it this afternoon—I really must go, I must."

CHAPTER TWENTY-THREE

There was so much upon Lenox's mind now: at the forefront Archie Godwin and Grace Ammons, in the wide middle band his work in the Commons, his meetings, his evening sessions, and at the back, occasionally pushing forward for his attention, his concern over two friends, McConnell and Graham.

He took for his luncheon a quick bite of bread and cheese between meetings, and survived a meeting with the treasury minister only by gulping down a cup of hot sweet tea beforehand.

As he left the meeting he glanced at his pocket watch and, with a sigh, quickened his step. It was five minutes past five o'clock, which meant that already he was late to meet Henrietta Godwin at the Graves Hotel, and that evening he had to return to the House by seven for an important debate concerning naval matters. He felt a twinge in his back, which heralded a day or two of discomfort. Funny, how as one's age advanced, fewer and fewer people seemed ridiculous. The hunched-over white-haired man approaching him on the street now seemed a figure of sympathy and caution. The portliness of the middle-aged, the mania of the mad—only the young, as callous in their health and beauty as beasts of the field, harts at the drinking pool, could find such complaints comic. Live to the age of back pain and one began to understand them all, Lenox thought.

But there was still youth stirring within him; he was on the trail of a murderer now, not simply an impostor, and he welcomed the fight.

As chance would have it, despite his late start Lenox beat Inspector Jenkins to the hotel by half a step. He checked his watch; 5:20. He was glad he hadn't missed anything. Dallington wouldn't have started without either of them there.

A bellman showed the two to a small tearoom, flooded with pink evening light, where a woman was sitting with a cup of tea, the remains of a light supper at her elbow. The plate had been pushed aside to make room for a notebook, in which she was writing intently, though when the door opened she put her pen down and looked up at them.

"Miss Godwin?" said Jenkins, removing his hat. Lenox did the same. "I am Chief Inspector Thomas Jenkins of Scotland Yard."

She offered him her hand. "And you are?" she asked Lenox.

"Charles Lenox, ma'am."

"Ah, Mr. Lenox," she said, "yes. Yes, how do

you do. I am Hetty Godwin. Thank you for coming to see me, gentlemen. I dearly hope that between the three of us we may find the man who murdered my brother."

Both men apologized for their tardiness. She waved away their explanations and invited them to sit.

She was very clearly the older sister of the deceased man, was Henrietta Godwin; if he had been thirty, she must have lived ten or fifteen years longer than he had, and if someone had told Lenox she was fifty he wouldn't have been surprised. She still had dark hair, however. She was a very thin, plain woman, with a sharp nose—in fact, sharp features in general, elbows and shoulders at angles to the world—but there was something indomitable in both her aspect and her speech. Her brother had died the day before and here she sat, far from home and in a great metropolis she might not have visited above once a year, calmly in command of this meeting already. Lenox admired her composure.

"Tell me of my brother's death, if you please," she said to Jenkins.

The inspector described, with appropriate restraint, Scotland Yard's discovery and identification of the body. "We have men attempting to ascertain Mr. Godwin's movements before his death yesterday. We know that he was in the company of a tall, fair-haired gentleman at ten o'clock, and a little while later they were with a third fellow, walking in a group down Gloucester Road."

She frowned. "A group? Who was the third man?"

"We do not know the identity of either man—unless you know the second."

"Not on such scant description. Is there a fuller account of this third man?"

Lenox shook his head. "Only that he was average-looking, dark-haired."

A fretful look passed across her face. "I told him to stay at the Parchment, in Willoughby Lane. The Graves has grown too noisy. I myself shall move this evening; they are fetching my bags now."

The Graves, whose tearoom at the moment was about as lively as a cemetery at midnight, seemed to sigh into even greater quietude, by way of solemn riposte. Here was another indication that Godwin had been a particularly retiring person, and Lenox asked his sister to confirm as much.

"Yes," she said. "He was a member at White's because our father was, and because he liked to spend half an hour there every year or two, but there was nothing my brother cared for less than visiting this city. We grew up quietly. Our father lived upon the land of his ancestors, which now, I suppose, must pass to my cousin Oswald."

Lenox wondered whether this would mean she was turned out. "Archibald was unmarried?"

"Oh, yes, dear me. When he was at Oxford there was a brief affair, but the match was unfortunate, and my father stepped in. A girl from a stage show playing at the corn market. Fully half a foot taller than Archibald was, too."

"When we came in you were making notes," said Inspector Jenkins. "Have you formed a theory about your brother's death?"

"Yes. I think his impostor killed him."

A thrill went through Lenox. "His impostor?"

"For the past month, somebody here in London has been impersonating my brother."

"Do you know what he looked like? Or his name?" asked Lenox, barely daring to hope.

"Neither of those things, no. But it was this man's activities that fetched my brother here, and I should be very astonished indeed if they weren't the reason that he died."

For the first time she evinced some emotion now, a small sob into her handkerchief. Jenkins and Lenox said words as comforting as they could muster, which she acknowledged. When she had composed herself again, Lenox said, "Do you have some relation, here or in Hampshire, from whom you might seek comfort, Miss Godwin?"

"My brother was my closest friend. We spent nearly every evening together, playing cards or reading aloud to one another. I have cousins and nieces and nephews nearby, but they cannot make up for the loss. Obviously. Our father would have been distraught—I only thank the Lord that he is underground."

It was damnable. Lenox glanced over at Jenkins and saw that he, too, felt a fresh anger at the murderer. The inspector said, "Perhaps you could tell us in more detail about this impostor. How did he come to your brother's attention?"

Hetty took a sip of her tea, to settle her nerves perhaps. Then she spoke in a steady voice. "My brother's tailors are Ede and Ravenscroft, and have been since he was a very small child and our father had his first suit of clothes made up. Generally he corresponds with them by letter, after a local tailor near us takes his measurements. They send us a complete catalog.

"Last month, Archie received a bill from them, though he had ordered no clothes; he generally only places his order just before Christmas, at the end of November. The bill Ede's sent in was for half a dozen shirts, two suits, three pairs of trousers, and a few odds and ends, handkerchiefs, spats. The letter said they had sent the same accounting to his London address but copied it to Hampshire for Archie's convenience."

"Do you have a London address?" asked Lenox. "Or rather, did he?"

"No."

"I thought not."

"Needless to say, Archie wrote by first post to query the bill. The cost was substantial, but that was not the issue. My brother and I are comfortably provided for. The issue, of course, was the clear attempt at fraud that had been perpetrated in his name. The impostor hadn't counted on Ede's sending a duplicate of the bill, but then they're very thorough, very professional."

"Of course," said Jenkins.

"My brother, too, was a very thorough man," said Hetty. "Along with his letter to Ede's, he wrote to half a dozen of the other merchants in London that he uses."

"Who are they?" asked Lenox and Jenkins almost simultaneously, pens poised.

"That is precisely the list I was making when you entered. There is Berry Brothers, his wine merchant. His hatmaker is Shipp's. His saddler is Hunt's. His gunmaker is Mr. Parson, near St. James's. I am forgetting one or two. At any rate, to consolidate several weeks of anxious correspondence into a brief tale, he wrote to each of them to tell them about the fraud at Ede's, and to ask them what the last charge upon his account had been."

"And they replied?" asked Jenkins.

"At four of the six places there had been no activity. At Berry Brothers and Mr. Parson's, however, there were recent and, of course, improper transactions. The bill at Berry's was particularly stiff."

"Parson's is a gunmaker," Jenkins murmured, looking at Lenox.

"They do not make small arms, however," said Lenox, "and a hunting rifle did not kill Mr.—did not murder your brother, ma'am."

The door of the tearoom opened, and though the light, in the last fifteen minutes, had gone from brilliant to shadowy, Lenox saw that it was Dallington. The young aristocrat, making his apologies to Henrietta Godwin, sat down, after asking for a cup of hot water with lemon, and bade them continue; Lenox would provide him with the earlier aspects of the narrative after they were finished here.

CHAPTER TWENTY-FOUR

How did your brother proceed, Miss Godwin, when he heard from Parson's and the other merchants?"

"He wrote to the police immediately, and of course to Berry's and Parson's, telling them that the items for which they had billed him were not ones that he had ordered. They were apologetic. Since my brother conducted most of his business through the post, it was apparently easy to deceive the clerks at these shops as to his appearance."

"What strikes me," said Lenox, "is that this person must have somehow known your brother—his habits, where he shopped—in order to impersonate him. Who were Archibald's acquaintances?"

Hetty, with a frustrated shake of her head, said, "That was precisely what so vexed us. My brother had few friendships outside of the valley. The one time that brought him into contact with the broader world—the London world—was his time at Wadham, I suppose, at Oxford. It is the only period of his life when he did not live in Hampshire."

"Could any of the shops provide a description of the man? Or the address he left?"

"The address he used was a false one in South London. Rather than have them delivered he sent a man, by his description his valet, to pick up the goods he had purchased upon my brother's name."

"I am amazed it was so easy," said Jenkins, perhaps thinking of the stingy lines of credit extended to members of the lower classes in England, who might find it difficult to buy ten shillings of groceries without ready money.

"A genteel manner goes a very long way in this country," said Lenox. "Did the clerks describe this man physically?"

"Yes. They all agreed that he was a tall man, well turned out, with a trim mustache and light hair."

So. It was the man from Gilbert's, or somebody of such a similar physical aspect that it was a very great coincidence. What relation could he bear to Grace Ammons?

Lenox still had one important question. "If your brother handled these matters of business by mail, Miss Godwin, may I ask why he ventured to London?"

"Three days ago my brother received a letter from his school friend Michael Almerston, who lives in Grosvenor Square. In his letter, Mr. Almerston mentioned that he had thought to write because nearly every night he saw a man dining alone at Cyril's Restaurant, whom the waiters all called Mr. Godwin. Mr. Almerston takes most of his meals there, too, from all I gather. Hearing the name had reminded him of Archie, living down in the country, and he wondered whether Archie might get up this season for a visit. Well, Archie, whose suspicions were already high, of course, wrote back by the next post to ask what the man looked like."

"Yes?" said Jenkins.

"Almerston's description fit the man who had been shopping at Berry's, Ede's, and Mr. Parson's," said Hetty. "My brother came up to confront the man at Cyril's, to see this charlatan with his own eyes. He thought it would be a simple matter for the police, once he could be sure."

"Would he have consulted a police officer when he arrived in London?" asked Jenkins.

"I do not know—but I wouldn't think so. Now as a result, as of course you know, he is dead."

Upon saying this Miss Godwin, who had been strong indeed to tell her story so clearly and carefully, broke down again into tears. It was some time before the gentle words of the three men could tame her agitation, and in the end Jenkins, an experienced hand in such matters, was forced to resort to the expedient of a tall glass of sherry.

Henrietta Godwin, her tale delivered, said that she thought she would now go to the Parchment and rest: She and her brother kept country hours.

Jenkins, his whole manner beautifully tactful, asked if she might have the strength, it would only take the briefest moment or two, to view the victim's body, and confirm that it belonged to her brother. The sister hesitated, plainly pained, but at last agreed to make the trip.

"You will remain in London?" asked Lenox.

"For a day or two, more if I am needed. It was always very hard upon our nerves, both of us, coming to London. Archie is spared that, anyhow. I wish he had never come to this beastly place."

Dallington, unoffended by this slur upon the city that had nursed him from childhood, said, "Did you ever hear the name Grace Ammons?"

"Who is she?"

"The same fellow who practiced upon your brother may have had other victims."

"I'm sorry to say that I do not know the name. How did you find her? I pray she did not meet the same end that Archie did?"

"She is still alive, and when we catch this blackguard will feel safe again," said Dallington.

There was vehemence in Dallington's voice—and Lenox perceived for the first time that for his young protégé, the fact of George Ivory's existence might not seem the unalloyed delight it did for Grace Ammons.

"You have business with Inspector Jenkins," Lenox said to Miss Godwin. "Thank you so much for your patience, and your admirable equanimity. Were it my brother I doubt I could have done half as well."

"Hear, hear," said Dallington.

As soon as Jenkins led Henrietta out of the room, Dallington plummeted into his chair and took a gulp of cold water. "Damn," he said.

"Are you still so very ill?"

"Yes."

"You should consult with McConnell again."

"There is a doctor at my door every morning at nine, there to interrupt the first peaceable half hour of sleep I've had all night, thanks to my mother. Anyhow McConnell is busy, from everything I hear."

Lenox ignored that. "You should go home, then."

"Are you not curious why I was late?"

"Because you are ill, I assumed. As it happened all three of us were late—no great credit to Jenkins or ourselves."

"You said that Grace Ammons lied to us."

Lenox hailed a passing waiter. "Bring my friend another glass of water, please," he said. "I'll take a whisky and soda."

The waiter left. "A whisky? Aren't you in the Commons this evening?"

"You think I should have made it a double?"

Dallington grinned, a little more color in his face now that he was seated, and not making any special effort to keep his spine straight. "Back to Grace Ammons. I wondered all through lunch what you meant, and I decided to start with George Ivory. You were correct. She lied to us."

"Oh?"

"First tell me what you meant—the suspense has been long enough."

Lenox was disappointed that Dallington had found out Grace Ammons on his own; he had a secret weakness for showmanship, though he deplored it as a trait in others. "There were two things," Lenox said. "The first was that she would not go to the police. In her account there was no compelling reason whatsoever that she would simply submit to such blackmail. Her future husband's firm of solicitors certainly wouldn't stand for the harassment of a woman. The story didn't make sense."

"And the second?"

"She said that the man who threatened her was 'in a knock.' There is a very narrow section of the country in which that is a common phrase, and it's several hundred miles south of Yorkshire—near my own part of the world, unluckily for her."

"Shall I tell you what I have done?"

"Please."

"I spoke to George Ivory's firm, Joseph and Joseph. You'll recall that he often spoke to her about his clients—the Chepstow and Ely?"

"Yes."

"Then you may be surprised to learn that they are not, and have never been, a client of the firm."

Lenox was silent for a moment, staring with a furrowed brow at two unconsolable pieces of bacon, left over from Henrietta Godwin's tea. "What do we know of this George Ivory?" he asked.

"For that matter, what do we know of this Grace Ammons?" Dallington responded.

CHAPTER TWENTY-FIVE

Lenox spoke several times at the Commons that evening, Graham close at hand, ready to dart down the aisle with relevant statistics, scrawled quickly on a scrap of paper. He left just after eleven, tired but pleased—one of those evenings when he felt his own party, and its principles, had inched forward across the battlefield slightly. There was nothing urgent to wake him in the morning, either. He would sleep late, and perhaps give over some of his day to his daughter.

In Hampden Lane, late that evening, he found Lady Jane sitting in the drawing room with Toto, both of them talking in low voices. Jane rose and gave him a kiss on the cheek.

"I come bearing very important news," said Lenox. "Benjamin Disraeli does not like— cannot abide—cooked onions, in any hot dish whatsoever."

"Where did you hear that?" asked Toto. "I call it nonsense. They add such a savor."

"It's good to know, if it's true," said Lady Jane.

"The Queen's social secretary provided me with that information, Mrs. McConnell," said Lenox with dignified superiority, then, coming out of this pose, smiled lightly at her. "And how are you?"

"Miserable—but who cares, why were you with Mrs. Engel?"

"Yes, Charles, what took you to the palace?" asked Jane.

He had gone to the sideboard and now was fixing a weak whisky and soda—in truth he did not think he could remain upright for very long if he had a strong one. When he was finished, he carried it to the armchair near them. "The case that John Dallington and I are working on."

He told them about his day in broad outlines: the paintings at Buckingham Palace, the East Gallery, Mrs. Engel's desk. Toto looked as if she welcomed the distraction, but Lady Jane seemed unhappy. "Hadn't you better leave it all to Inspector Jenkins? A murder!"

"That used to be my profession."

"Then you married, and had a child."

"If there's any danger I will dodge behind Dallington. He's nearly in a coffin already, poor fellow, he's so ill."

"You won't, and you oughtn't to make such jokes."

"It's been another very long day. What were you speaking about when I came in?"

Toto sighed and waved a hand. "Thomas."

Nothing had changed, apparently. McConnell was puzzled by his wife's coldness but did not inquire, and in the meanwhile he seemed, otherwise, still unusually happy, absent from the house every day, looking in on George in the evenings but not, as he once had, in each hour of the day.

Gently, Lenox said, "And has he been in Hyde Park?"

"No. Evidently he and Polly Buchanan have tired of making a spectacle of themselves. Perhaps they found somewhere more private."

"Toto," said Lady Jane reproachfully.

"I'm sorry—you're right," said the younger woman and leaned on the sofa toward Jane, taking her hand. "But it is cruel upon me, I swear it is."

As Lenox was readying himself for bed he saw a telegram from Jenkins, which had been left upon his bedside table.

> The body is Archibald Godwin's STOP confirmed by sister STOP sending constables to shops in the morning to confirm story STOP ab TJ.

So. Confirmation.

Usually when he had a case like this one, Lenox's thoughts as he lay in bed were occupied with its specifics—but now, exhausted, he fell immediately into the black null of near-consciousness and then, after only a few moments, into a profound sleep, which carried him through to morning.

Miss Emanuel was away the next day—she had a day off each week of her choice, and the first half of each of Saturday and Sunday as well—which meant that it was Charles and Jane's turn to look after Sophia.

They took the child into the dining room, where she crawled around the floor, inspecting the robed legs of the furniture, while they flipped through the newspapers and ate eggs with toast. Bright sun streamed through the windows. Once in a while Lenox would rise to refill his coffee cup at the sideboard, preferring as he did to take a quarter or a third of a cup at once, so that he could have it hot, and on these short voyages he would stop and greet his daughter. By the time the footmen had cleared the food, Sophia was involved in an intense examination of an old piece of tartan ribbon she had found under the sideboard. Lenox sighed: How much pleasanter it seemed just at the moment to sit here and let the lingering hours pass slowly by than to run back and forth across London, but he knew his brain would begin to itch after the solution before too long.

The papers were full of Archibald Godwin. The *Times* headline read FARMER MURDERED IN KENSINGTON, which seemed inaccurate, while the *Evening Star* of the night before—a paper that members of Lenox's class usually called, with derisive smiles, the *Heevening Star*—declared GRAVES HOTEL LIVES UP TO NAME. The most accurate story was in the *Telegraph*. It relayed the essentials, and Lenox, reading between the lines, suspected that Inspector Jenkins, solicitous of the good opinion of the press, might have fed the story to the reporter. Well—he did have to look out for his own advancement, and there was a place at the top to be had.

Lenox looked at the police report in each paper, searching specifically for the crimes that had occurred in Kensington. Aside from the murder, they all reported a grocer's robbed at knifepoint, a horse stolen when a hansom cab driver stopped for a cup of tea, a homeless man who had gone missing (he always thought such notices paradoxical, and yet they kept appearing), and an active pickpocket along the Gloucester Road. Nothing easily linked to their suspect, though it might be worth speaking to the driver of the hansom cab.

When all that remained on the long table was a single coffee cup, Lady Jane's, Lenox picked up Sophia and set her on his lap. "Are you tired?" he asked his wife. "You were up earlier than I was."

"A bit." She paused, looking out at the fine day. "I do worry about Toto."

"She is hale enough."

"Last night she mentioned divorce, for the first time."

Lenox raised his eyebrows. This was somber news indeed; there were only two hundred divorces a year in England, often fewer. All of them were among couples of Toto's own rank, the very rich, who could afford the moral disgrace— and, in extreme circumstances, tolerate its public nature. The same papers now jumbled in an untidy pile on a chair would report, with breathless excitement, every detail of the case.

Very often the woman suffered more than the man in the opinion of the public. Lady Violet Lesslock had moved to Baden after her divorce, because of the press's intrusions a broken woman—though it was known among her friends that her husband had used her violently, cruelly, and had been entirely in the wrong.

"She cannot be serious," said Lenox.

"You know her. She is impulsive and stubborn. A difficult blend."

"Her father would never permit it." This was a small, kindly man, who doted on his daughter but had never in his life become accustomed to any variety of contradiction. "He would sooner see them both move to India."

"I pray it doesn't come to that." She reached her hand across the table to his. "Could you speak to Thomas? More directly this time?"

"I could not—I'm sorry, Jane, but I could not. It would be a terrible affront to his self-respect. Certainly I should not forgive him if the situations were reversed and he came to speak to me."

She sighed. "I know."

It was half past nine now. Lenox went into his library. In the night Graham had neatened his desk and left for him a sheath of documents to sign. Lenox was a Junior Lord of the Treasury now—nothing to do with money at all, as it happened, but a position within the hierarchy of the party—and a great many papers passed under his hand. There was also a new blue book to read about the tax on breweries, a subject of particular interest to Lenox's constituency, up north in Durham. (It was unnecessary—some would even argue undesirable—for Members of Parliament to have a geographical link to the districts for which they stood. Lenox himself had never set foot in Stirrington before he traveled there as a candidate.) He signed the papers and then took the book to a comfortable armchair, recessed between two bookcases in the wall, its arms a comfortable height, with glasses and a decanter of water on the small hexagonal side table next to it. For some time he read.

Thomas McConnell had made a morganatic union for himself, one in which his rank and wealth could not match his wife's, and he had never since seemed entirely happy. The terrible moment had come early: when Toto's family had pushed him, with kindly intended pressure, to sell his practice, medicine skirting too close to physical labor for their liking.

Was it entirely surprising, then, that he had sought happiness elsewhere?

If he had, if he had, Lenox reminded himself internally, gazing out at the spring day. The bookseller across the street was doing a brisk trade.

Yes, of course it was surprising, because in recent years McConnell had been so delighted by his daughter, Georgianna. It had seemed enough.

Divorce: such a far-fetched notion that it was almost impossible for Lenox to grant the possibility of it in his own mind. Still, Toto dug her claws into ideas and wrestled them until they died or she forgot she held them; she was the daughter of wealth, and of almost limitless parental love. It was a dangerous combination— one that imperiled even Sophia, perhaps, though he and Jane tried not to indulge her.

He sighed and looked away from the window, back toward his book, unsettled in his mind.

CHAPTER TWENTY-SIX

As Lenox ate his breakfast, constables from Scotland Yard were spreading out across London in every direction, armed with a description of the man they suspected of the murder of Archibald Godwin: tall, light-haired, dressed well, platinum watch chain, trimmed whiskers and mustaches, an "arrogant" bearing and gentlemanly accent, possibly though not probably in the company of a nondescript dark-haired gentleman of average size. They conducted interviews at West End hotels, restaurants, and clubs and revisited the places they positively knew that he had been—the tailor's, Parson's, Gilbert's.

Lenox knew that this was a unique moment in

the case. If the Yard didn't meet with immediate success, its overseers were unlikely to commit similar manpower to the investigation in the next days, even if this murder, by virtue of its affluent geography and affluent victim, had more press attention than the average gin-mill killing in the East End.

Between eleven and two o'clock, Lenox had meetings, but between two and the session that evening, he was free, and he decided to conduct his own small search.

The Oxford and Cambridge Club stood on Pall Mall, a wide building coated in the same cream-colored paint as all the rest in its row. Lenox climbed the wide steps up to the front doors, one of which was swung open.

"Good afternoon," said the porter.

Lenox didn't come here often—he more often visited the Athenaeum, down the road—but always felt welcome. He handed over his hat and his light coat and made his way upstairs to the library.

He had felt sure that the O&C, as members called it, would stock the college directories— each student at Oxford or Cambridge belonging to one of these constituent colleges, and thus to the university. (Lenox himself had been at Balliol, a quick stroll down Broad Street from Archie Godwin's college, Wadham.) He was not wrong. There was a whole wall of the leather volumes, the Oxford set bound in dark blue, the Cambridge in light blue, all of the most recent vintage.

Here he found the directory for Wadham, *1875,* it said on the spine, which meant it couldn't be more than a month or two old. (He still wasn't used to living in such a modern-sounding year: 1875! It gave one pause. Three-quarters of Victoria's century had passed now. As vaguely, as indefinitely, and as certainly as a lighthouse flashing across a fogged channel, the year 1900— so madly advanced, so futuristic—stood on the horizon.) He pulled the book down and took a seat at one of the desks in the center of the room.

There was an inkwell close to hand, and a stand full of paper embossed with the club's sigil. *Wadham,* he wrote as a header upon one sheet, and then settled back with the book.

It was no difficult task to find Archibald Godwin's name. Lenox began looking in the class of 1862 and finally alighted on his quarry in the class of 1865. Underneath each name was a terse biographical sketch. Godwin's repeated the details of his entry in *Who's Who*, down to the Chepstow and Ely.

Slightly chilling to think that in the next issue of this book Godwin's name would appear in the necrology.

Each class at Wadham had roughly fifty members; Lenox was willing to wager that if the fair-haired friend was from Oxford, he was from Wadham, a famously insular college.

It was easy to rule people out. Many were propping up, in small backwaters, England's imperial edifice, local wallahs with twenty native servants, who even upon retirement would never be quite fit to live in England again—the heat got into their blood, or so it was said. Another half dozen were professors at the two universities, and outnumbering them two to one were the religious men, scattered across the parishes of the isles. Before he had started trying, Lenox had rid himself of thirty names.

Now came a greater challenge. Could Arthur Waller, of Swallowtail Lane, be the man? Or Anthony Brinde, who lived not three blocks from Lenox himself? Still, there were names to cross off the list. The head of a large tin concern in Manchester was not likely to moon about London for weeks on end, buying guns in another man's name.

Lenox finished with eleven candidates he viewed as strong, most of them Londoners. Then, with a dutiful sigh, he pulled down the volumes for the matriculating classes on either side of Godwin's year and did the same task.

An hour later he stood up, having covered three sheets of club paper with names, addresses, and occupations. In all there must have been nearly fifty.

It was a job for someone with more time than he had.

Fortunately he knew the man. Lenox put the books away and nodded to the old gentleman who had been sleeping underneath his copy of the *Times* for the last hour, before waking up with a flustered start and feigning deep absorption in an advertisement for women's headache tonic. Then he went downstairs to the club's telegraph office and sent a wire.

Two hours later, as Lenox was sitting in his office at the Commons, this wire produced its recipient in person. "Fellow called Mr. Skaggs!" said Frabbs rapidly, poking his head around the door, then beckoning the visitor inward.

When Lenox had been a detective, he had often used Skaggs—a large, bruising man, once a fearsome boxer, now tamed into domesticity by a lovely wife and three children—as an auxiliary investigator. Though he was a physical specimen, his skills of detection were, in fact, primarily cerebral.

"How do you do, Mr. Lenox? Back in the game, based on your message?"

"It has been some time! I hope you're well?"

"Quite well, quite well, sir. Lord John Dallington hires me every so often, and then of course I get a number of lesser cases on my own."

There was a small ruby ring on Skaggs's left hand; Lenox suspected this self-accounting of modesty. "Does the Yard ever ask for your help?"

"They haven't yet, sir."

Lenox sighed. "I've told them they ought to. At any rate—are you free for a day or two? I've a job for you."

"Delighted for the work. Though my rates have gone up."

"I would be surprised if they hadn't, seeing that it has been, what, four years? But the job—let me tell you about it." Lenox offered a quick outline, omitting the role that Grace Ammons had played in the affair, and then described in close detail the man they were all seeking. Finally he handed over the list he had made. "I would like you to rule out as many of these men as possible."

"An achievable goal, sir."

"Ideally I would like you to find our man—or a candidate I could lay eyes upon myself."

"Of course, sir."

"In most cases a glance should be enough. How much time do you think you need?"

Skaggs read through the addresses on the pages Lenox had handed him, then said, "Why don't I check in tomorrow evening?"

"That will do splendidly."

"Here, or Hampden Lane?"

Lenox laughed. "Here, unfortunately. If I am in the Commons you can leave word with Graham, or write me a note—or wait, since there are frequent breaks, and possibly I could step out during a lull in the debate."

"Very good, sir."

"We might even scoop the Yard, Skaggs."

Skaggs smiled. "Touch wood."

It was still shy of suppertime, and Lenox decided he would call on Jenkins, to see what progress the police had made. First he went to see Dallington, however; the young lord was fitter today, after sleeping late into the morning, and came along willingly. Lenox told him about his researches into the graduates of Wadham College.

"I cannot imagine one Oxford man murdering another in cold blood."

"Then you are missing out on a whole class of villains you might study. Nobody goes bad faster than a gentleman, and we know that it was a gentleman who stole from Godwin, defrauded him. Murder is not a very long chalk further."

Dallington shook his head. "No, but the kinds of friends Godwin—someone as quiet as Godwin—would have made at Oxford . . . do you not imagine them all curates, or perhaps butterfly enthusiasts, dipping toast into weak tea? This daring adventurer you've described—I cannot credit Godwin with such an interesting companion."

Lenox laughed. "We shall see if I am wrong soon, anyhow. Skaggs has always worked quickly."

CHAPTER TWENTY-SEVEN

Dallington felt well enough, after his day of rest, that he asked the driver of Lenox's carriage to stop a few streets shy of Scotland Yard, that they might walk there in the evening air. It was the season for walking: warm enough to be pleasant even after the sun had gone down but not, as in the summer, so hot that the smell of London became hard to bear, women carrying nosegays to hold to their faces, and anybody who could fleeing for the country or the seaside.

A constable led the two men down a gaslit corridor. Jenkins had left their names at the desk.

"Has an arrest been made in this Graves Hotel business?" Dallington asked the bobby.

"I'm not sure, sir."

"No matter. We shall hear it all soon enough."

In the past twelvemonth Jenkins had achieved the dream of all of the Yard's inspectors, an office in the upper south corner of the building, with a distant view of the Thames. When they reached his office, however, Jenkins's back was turned to the river's evening splendor, and he was hunched over his desk, reading reports. He smiled with tired eyes when Lenox and Dallington entered.

"I have an account of every light-haired fellow who ever walked down the Strand since the reign of Aethelwulf. Too much hay, not enough needles, sadly."

"No progress at all, then?" asked Lenox sympathetically, sitting down across the desk from Jenkins. Dallington took the other chair.

"None that I can discern, though it is possible that we have interviewed the fellow eight different times. I had high hopes that they might know something of him at Cyril's, the restaurant where he ate every night—perhaps even that they would remember Godwin coming in to confront his impostor—but it is a large place. Nobody there recalled him particularly. I hope that you gentlemen have devised some alternative line of inquiry. Tomorrow I have an appointment to speak with Grace Ammons, but beyond that I am at a loss."

Lenox described his trawl through the Oxford annuals, and the results.

That brightened Jenkins's mood slightly. "Certainly we have a list of names to cross-reference against yours. I exaggerated their quantity—it wouldn't take one of these young fellows an hour to check the lists against each other. Let me know when you hear anything."

"Our best lead is still Miss Ammons," said Dallington. "Whether we believe her tale or not, she is the beginning and end of it all."

"What do you take to be her role?" asked Jenkins.

Dallington glanced at Lenox, then back at the inspector. "Allowing that it is purely hypothesis?"

"Of course."

"Then I take the situation thusly: A gentleman finds that he has fallen on hard times. Let us call him Smith. This Mr. Smith is not a person of many scruples. In some previous walk of life—perhaps at Oxford, perhaps in some manner of business, perhaps, who knows, with the beaglers of the Clinkard Meon Valley—he encountered Archibald Godwin, and learned that Godwin is at once extremely retiring and extremely rich. Also perhaps that he orders from shops in London. That is an enticing combination. He wonders, in his own mind, whether the vendors a man of Godwin's stock would frequent—Ede and Ravenscroft, for example—would even be able to identify this country gentleman by sight.

"Then, one day, perhaps Mr. Smith is desperate, perhaps merely venal—he decides to try it. He visits a small shop. Which shop did he visit first?"

Jenkins squinted down at a list on his desk. "Shipp's. The hatmaker."

"Mr. Smith walks into Shipp's. Looks at hats. Finally plucks up his nerve and orders one—and finds that they are more than happy to accept that he is Mr. Godwin. He can call round next Tuesday to pick up his order. So it's begun. Inspector Jenkins, I suppose you and your fellows compiled a list of everything he purchased?"

"We did."

"Were all of his acquisitions grouped close together?"

"Within a week of each other."

"Very well." Dallington was looking off into the distance, settling into his vision of the crime. "Mr. Smith begins to think very highly of himself. He is dressed finely, he is eating at wonderful places—and he is a handsome fellow; he gains access by chance to one party, and then another. Or perhaps he has picked up with old friends, whom he had dropped out of shame when he couldn't afford to keep up with them, and while he is Archibald Godwin in Jermyn Street, he becomes Mr. Smith among his friends again."

"He must have known that it was going to catch up with him quickly," said Jenkins.

"He would have hoped that Godwin received the first bill ten minutes after Smith picked up the last suit at the tailor's, of course. It is not hard to vanish back into London—easy as the waters closing over one's head. Anyhow, it did not work out that way, as we know. Godwin discovered the truth, came to London, and confronted Smith. Perhaps Smith pled with him, particularly if they had once been friends. He would return the goods, if Godwin spared him from the ignominy of the police courts."

"But Godwin refused," said Jenkins. "Listen

here, though, Dallington—what about Grace Ammons?"

Dallington shrugged. "He had bullied his way into one happy situation—why not another? Perhaps he had bragged to his friends that he would be at the palace. Perhaps he had overheard George Ivory's name and story at a club."

"Or perhaps Grace Ammons was selling entrance to the Queen's parties," said Jenkins, shooting them a canny look. "That was the suggestion of a bright young fellow we have, Finnering. What if she had taken Mr. Smith's money, been unable to place his name on the list, and then, when she saw him, feared exposure?"

Lenox had been silent throughout this long exchange, and now both men looked at him expectantly. He shook his head. "I cannot entirely imagine that scenario, Inspector Jenkins, simply because she went to the effort of writing Dallington to hire him."

"If she felt threatened, would that not be wise? Keep the police out of it, but get help?"

"Dallington isn't in the business of protecting criminals."

"She might have lied," said Dallington.

"I suppose. To what end, however—to gain your indefinite protection? To frame Smith? You couldn't have extricated her from such a situation."

"Dallington is from a well-known family.

197

Perhaps she hoped that he would offer the money."

Lenox waved a hand. "This is all speculation. John, I enjoyed your story, and in truth it is very similar to the one I had in mind—and no doubt you, too, Inspector Jenkins. Nevertheless, hearing it out loud, there are points within it that I cannot reconcile with the facts of the case."

"What are they?"

"Well, first, I do not understand why our Mr. Smith would have dined out at restaurants under Archibald Godwin's name. Surely Godwin would not have had a line of credit at restaurants, when he was so infrequently in the city, and dined either at White's or his hotel when he was?"

Jenkins frowned and made a note. "We will ask whether Godwin had an account at any of these restaurants."

"I imagine you'll find he did not—and no restaurant would have given Smith a meal simply on Godwin's name, as Shipp's or Ede's would have given him a hat or a suit."

"Mm," said Jenkins, still writing.

"By the same token," Lenox continued, "why give me his name as Archibald Godwin, that morning at Gilbert's? What could it have benefited him? Better he should have told me his name was Aethelwulf—or Mr. Smith, anything."

"Perhaps he had grown used to the lie."

"Very well," said Lenox, warming to his

subject, "even granting these points, temporarily, there is still no accounting for Smith's behavior toward Grace Ammons."

"Except that we do not know what his behavior was, precisely—her word having already proven unreliable."

"Still, we may assume that he somehow gained access to the palace. She is a bright girl—in truth I would even believe her a good one, based on our conversation, though I have been misled before—and I do not think she would claim that she had put his name on the list for these affairs of state if she knew we would not find it when we looked. Which, incidentally, you might do tomorrow, Jenkins, just as confirmation."

"What, look up Archibald Godwin's name?"

"Yes, on the attendance lists of the two gatherings to which he was apparently admitted."

Dallington brought the conversation back around. "Why is his behavior toward Grace Ammons unaccountable, Lenox? Do you think it far-fetched that he merely wanted admission to the palace, and found through the example of Godwin that he was now able to take what he wanted? Certainly you and I have seen that moment before—when a law-abiding fellow tips into crime and then realizes the full possibilities of his choice?"

Here Lenox paused. "Yes," he said at last.

"What is it?" asked Jenkins.

"No, nothing at all. Only, on that particular subject, I am in agreement with Dallington. I think this Mr. Smith had realized he might do more than order a suit and a hat."

"How, exactly?" asked Jenkins.

"I have a growing fear that he intends to steal from the palace—or, worse yet, has already."

CHAPTER TWENTY-EIGHT

B oth men looked at Lenox blankly for a moment and then simultaneously shook their heads and began to speak. It was Jenkins whose voice won out.

"My dear fellow," he said, "there are so many places in London, so many thousands, from which it would be easier to steal."

"Can you point them out to me?" asked Lenox. "There is great risk in entering a private residence, and no guarantee that it will hold much treasure, even at the finest address. The museums and societies keep everything of value under lock and key. By contrast, Dallington, consider the paintings we saw on the wall—or the medieval Bible stand in the East Gallery, with gold and rubies in it, with which we were allowed to remain alone for twenty minutes."

"With guards on every side of us."

"At a party of eight hundred, would they be such a problem? Heaven alone knows the value of the jewels in the Queen's vaults. Think of the boy Jones, gentlemen."

The example of the boy Jones silenced the other two men. Three decades before, Jones, a lad of not more than fourteen or fifteen, had gained entrance to Buckingham Palace, disguised as a chimney sweep. Guards caught him after only a short while, with an eccentric collection of the Queen's personal items, garments, letters, and knickknacks, none of it very valuable.

They expelled the boy and warned him not to return. Not much later, he scaled the walls of Buckingham Palace and wandered it for hours, sitting on the throne, lying in Victoria's bed, and stealing food from the larder. One of the wits of the age had dubbed the child "In I Go Jones."

At any rate, the palace was not unimpeachably secure.

Jenkins rose from his seat. The light was declining into shadow outside, and he lit a lamp recessed into the wall, making the room brighter. "But then we come to Grace Ammons," he said. "No intelligent thief would leave behind such a trail. If he merely wished access to the palace as a social matter, this light-haired gentleman could deny Miss Ammons's story. That would be very much harder if he stole something."

"Perhaps he counted upon her intimidation." Lenox saw that it was a fair point, and he fell into silence for a moment, as the other two men contemplated him. "I don't know," he said at last. "There are too many questions—why our Mr. Smith gave his name out as Godwin beyond the shops at which he used it, whether and why he killed the real Godwin, what he wanted to do at the palace."

"The behavior of Miss Ammons," added Dallington, eyes narrowed in contemplation. "Until we are sure of her story we are sure of nothing at all."

"Yes, indeed," said Lenox softly.

It was this problem—Miss Ammons's character, her honesty—that preoccupied Lenox all through the remainder of the evening. Soon he and Dallington left the Yard, agreeing to reconvene with Jenkins the next afternoon. (Hopefully Skaggs would have finished his canvass by then.) Lenox dined alone at the House that evening, and as he ate his chop and mashed turnips and read about the mining crisis, by the flickering candlelight at Bellamy's Restaurant, his mind kept circling back to her, to Miss Ammons. Even as he sat upon the benches of the House she entered into his thoughts—true, not when he was trying to catch the eye of the Speaker, or as he spoke, or for any of the insensible moments after he sat down, his heart still thumping even after these many years of speeches. In the slack moments, though—for instance, when someone with whom he agreed was entering upon the sixteenth minute of a speech, every word of which the bored scribes in the journalists' box could have written themselves—it would be Grace Ammons who returned to Lenox's mind.

There were several important votes that evening, and he didn't return to Hampden Lane until well after one o'clock. Even then, however, as his tired head fell to the pillow, its last conscious thought was of Grace Ammons.

In the morning it came to him.

In haste he dressed and ate, then hurried over to Scotland Yard, hoping to catch Jenkins before the inspector left for his visit to the palace. By great good fortune he managed it—the Yard's brougham was sitting outside its entrance, horses warmed, waiting for Jenkins, when Lenox arrived.

"Mr. Lenox!" said Jenkins, surprised, when he met the older detective in the hallway. "Are we not meant to see each other this afternoon?"

"With your permission I would like another word with Grace Ammons, before you speak to her. I think I know her motives."

"Do you, though? Perhaps you might explain them to me, if we ride to the palace together?"

It was not difficult to convince Jenkins, who agreed to wait in the carriage for half an hour. Soon Lenox found himself following Mrs. Engel once again down the small hallway toward the East Gallery, and once again Grace Ammons was waiting there. Her mood before had been fearful. Now she seemed puzzled.

"I am to see Inspector Thomas Jenkins of Scotland Yard shortly," she said, rising as Lenox approached her, "despite my sincere desire not to involve the police in this matter. Is it necessary that you and I should speak again?"

"I'm afraid it is," he said. "Please, sit. As for the police—once there is a death, their involvement is no longer a matter of personal discretion. I apologize, Miss Ammons."

They took their seats on one of the couches along the wall. "How may I help you, then, Mr. Lenox?"

"I have decided that I believe your story."

She looked lovely in the wan morning light, with her chestnut hair falling around her pale throat. "Certainly there is no reason you should not."

"Believe you, that is, despite the barefaced falsehoods with which your story was filled."

"I beg your pardon?"

"I think that for the most part your story is true—that this light-haired gentleman, this murderer, bullied and threatened you—and I think it has taken courage on your part to tell us of it. The trouble is that if you lie once, your whole story is thrown into doubt. Until we are sure of you, it is difficult to proceed."

"I really cannot imagine what you mean," she said.

So Lenox told her what they knew: that George Ivory had nothing to do with the Chepstow and Ely company, that he sincerely and apologetically was forced to doubt her tale of a Yorkshire youth, that, in short, it was impossible to parse what was true and what was false in her story.

She began to offer a faltering rebuttal of all this, but the truth told in her face. She seemed to sense that Lenox could read her, and changed tacks. "Whether or not you think I was lying, it is no matter. I have hired Miss Strickland to assist me in this matter, not Mr. Dallington, nor, certainly, you."

Lenox sighed. "I had a lengthy conversation with Inspector Jenkins this morning. He plans to place you under arrest."

"He would not."

"Your position here is no shield, ma'am. He believes you to be in league with this fair-haired gentleman—the murderer of Archie Godwin."

She gave out an involuntary and anguished cry. "In league with *him?*" she asked. "Of all people you must be the least likely to believe that. You saw how I reacted to him that morning."

Part of Lenox's belief in Miss Ammons's story, that morning, had been secondhand—he trusted Mrs. Engel's evident and sincere good opinion of the young woman—and now, looking into her eyes, he felt sure that at heart she was true. Still, he said, "It might have been a show, specially designed for me, or for Dallington."

"I had no idea whatsoever that you were present," said the young secretary.

"If you make a clean breast of it, I'm sure I can persuade Jenkins not to arrest you."

She hesitated—and then said, "No, he will have to do as he sees fit. Time will exculpate me."

Lenox admired her fortitude, and it was with a reluctant heart that he said, "He may have to arrest Mr. Ivory as well, in that case."

"George? Why?"

"As another accomplice."

It was here that her resolve broke. She stared at him for a moment, then said, quietly, "No, that will not do. I will tell you my story—my very shameful story—and then pray that you show me mercy, for I could not stand for any of that shame to cast a shadow over George."

CHAPTER TWENTY-NINE

Often in the course of his career as a detective, Lenox had done things that he would never have dreamed of doing outside the context of his vocation. He had picked locks, climbed fences, lied to witnesses—sacrificed many bone-deep integrities upon the altar of an inexact but higher good. These actions almost never cost him any unease.

This one did. When he heard Grace Ammons's story, the shame she had claimed for herself passed into his ownership. It had been necessary to extract the truth from her—but this was an ugly thing.

She had begun with a heavy sigh. "I was not born in Yorkshire, you are correct," she said.

"The western part of Sussex, if I had to hazard a guess."

She inclined her head, in no mood to offer admiration for his deductions. "Yes, in western Sussex, though I thought I had shed my accent. I never knew my parents. My father was a shopowner there, and my mother a woman of gentle birth, rather come down in the world. Both of them died in a fire when I was not three months old. They had scattered the old ashes from their fireplace on the kitchen countertop to scrub it clean, and there was a live cinder among them, which caught on one of the wooden boards there."

"Where were you?"

"At my grandmother's house. She took me when there was too much work in the shop. It was she, too, who took care of me after my parents were gone. She was a wonderful woman, my father's mother, though I just barely remember her. She died when I was seven, my second-to-last living relation. Would that she had lived longer.

"After her death I passed to my father's sister, my aunt Lily. She was a quiet woman, kind enough when she had the opportunity, but she lived in horror of her husband, my uncle Robert. He was a pious, sober man, with a prosperous farm, but he was a devil—still I believe him to have been the very devil, Mr. Lenox. I will pass over my time in that house, with your permission. I stayed there only until I was fifteen, and that history is not relevant to my current predicament."

"You may tell the story however you please," said Lenox. He was on guard, however; her face was so sympathetic, her story already so sad, that he was alert to the possibility that she was manipulating him. "Go on."

"Growing up in a house that is cruel, I think children either grow to be, as adults, cruel themselves or unusually kind, even soft, perhaps. At any rate, without too much self-regard I can say that I am of the latter sort—I have always been hopelessly soft toward people. It is not necessarily a virtue, I think. One must learn to fight back, and I never did. At fifteen, a very rich, arrogant gentleman, passing through town, took advantage of me."

"I am sorry to hear it."

"You asked me for the truth." She looked down at her hands, folded in her lap, and paused before speaking again. "The usual sequel of such an incident—that the gentleman vanishes, and the girl finds herself with child—did not happen, in this case. In fact, what did happen at the time seemed rather wonderful, to me, childish as I was. He took me out of my aunt and uncle's house—to Paris. That was the truth I told you, the last time we spoke. I went to Paris."

"Would I know this person's name?" asked Lenox.

She shook her head. "I thought him very grand when I was young, but he was not of much account. His father was a very minor squire, the son a spendthrift, shut out of much of the society to which he hoped to win admission. Paris offered him a better chance for that access than London, since the rules are looser there. He was a bad man, though generous to me. He is dead now—died two years ago, in a hunting accident. I read of it in the *Times*. I had not laid eyes on him for many years before that. We did have happy moments together, he and I."

"Please go on."

"My benefactor—as he chose to call himself—arranged for me to have a small suite of apartments in the rue de Verneuil, though he himself lived in the Crillon. He visited me every day and gave me a small amount of money and a maid. I was fifteen, fresh from Sussex. You cannot imagine the sophistication I saw around me. Really, of course, my maid was reporting everything to him, and laughing at me behind my back, and the trinkets I bought with my pocket money were hopelessly vulgar.

"My fortune changed—you may decide whether for the good or the bad—when, at a very threadbare sort of *salon* in the *huitième*, I met a woman named Madame de Faurier. She was as glamorous as you can conceive, and very warm to me initially, though ultimately as cold, in her way, as my uncle Robert."

Lenox felt a kind of sickness—it was so clear what was coming. "I am sorry to make you tell this," he said.

She ignored this apology. "One day not long after that *salon*, my gentleman did not appear. I assumed he was ill and sent word around to the Crillon. No reply. At last on the fourth day that he was absent I went to look for him, but he was gone. On the fifth day my maid ceased to come—her weekly wages not having been paid. I was frantic with anxiety, as you can imagine. I knew that my apartments were rented by the month, of which the end was coming soon, and I had scarcely enough money to buy bread. Somehow they knew at the corner that I was alone, because the butcher and costermonger immediately demanded ready money, when I had always bought my food on credit. I imagine the maid told them.

"I am more intelligent about the world now than I was then, Mr. Lenox. In retrospect perhaps I ought to have taken myself to the British Embassy. Certainly I might have fallen upon the mercy of the English church on the Auguste Vacquerie. I think of how young I looked, and imagine they would have taken sympathy on me.

"You will have guessed what happened next, perhaps. A visitor came. Madame de Faurier. I don't know if my gentleman was complicit with her, or if he had to scramble away from the city and she merely took advantage of the situation. I suspect the former. Anyhow, I came under her protection."

There were tears in the eyes of Grace Ammons now, and Lenox offered her his handkerchief. On some winter night Lady Jane had stitched his initials in the corner of it with green thread, and passing it across the sofa he thought of his wife, her own tender character. He felt a blackguard. "You needn't go on," he said. "Or you may pass over any details you wish."

She refused the offer. "Within two months I had become a prostitute. A very expensive prostitute—that is the blessing for which I remain thankful," she said. She looked at him with some bitterness in her wet eyes. "Have you met a prostitute before, Mr. Lenox?"

"They are common enough in my business."

"Parliament?"

He smiled gently at her joke. "What was my business, I should say. Detection, crime."

"My counterparts in London are not in the Seven Dials, or by the docks—but in Hyde Park.

211

I had a small pink carriage to myself, and a thirty-minute ride in the Bois de Boulogne with me cost several hundred francs, roughly twenty-five pounds. Of that I received six pounds for myself. The rest went to the carriage, the clothing, Madame de Faurier. You may be sure that I hoarded that six pounds, however—grew wise very quickly, cajoled the gentlemen who visited me for tokens of their esteem . . ."

Lenox looked up at the far end of the gallery, the invaluable paintings between here and there, the intricate carpet upon which the Queen of England, Empress of India, tread nearly every day, and then back at Grace Ammons. "You are very differently situated these days."

"I tried desperately never to entertain an Englishman. After a year or two, however, my reputation was such that certain Englishmen offered absurd sums—twice the going rate, three times—for my company, and when Madame du Faurier offered to halve these extra fees with me, I could not resist. One of those gentleman was the Earl of Axford."

"Ah."

"Yes. I told you that I returned to London from Paris in the position of secretary to the earl's wife. I saw your face when I said the name. He is fond of women, true, but whatever the circumstances in which he and I met, he will always have my gratitude. After six or seven evenings together, he finally extracted my whole tale from me—and insisted that I accompany him back to England at once. He made me his household's secretary, and I showed an aptitude for the work. The rest of my progress I related to you truthfully."

"What did de Faurier say to your departure?"

She shrugged. "I was not a prisoner. She was extremely upset, however."

"I ask because I wonder whether she might be involved in this business."

The young secretary—her face still, after her story, suffused with a preternatural innocence—considered this idea and then rejected it. "I knew her well, Mr. Lenox. She would be capable of murder, I believe, but not of crossing the Channel."

Lenox paused, thinking. At last, he said, "Then it was this fact from your history with which your blackmailer threatened you, and Mr. Ivory was the reason you wouldn't go to the police but sought out a detective."

Her face went lifeless at Ivory's name, dull and shamed. Her voice remained steady, however. "Yes. I have never deserved George Ivory, but I have been selfish enough to hold on to him. It would hurt him so deeply to know the truth."

"I am quite sure you deserve him, Miss Ammons," said Lenox, "and I am sorry to have forced this story from you. At least you may have

213

my word that no other human being shall hear it
from me."

"Not Jenkins?"

"He will trust me when I vouchsafe the honesty
of your story."

"Thank you," she said and then, lowering her
face out of Lenox's sight, began to cry.

CHAPTER THIRTY

Before he went out to speak with Jenkins,
Lenox asked Grace Ammons if she knew
how this man—the one from Gilbert's, the one
whom they suspected in the murder of Archie
Godwin—might have discovered her secret.

"I asked him, and he laughed."

"You did not recognize him from your years in
Paris?"

"If I did I would give you his name this
instant."

"Though it meant your own exposure?" asked
Lenox.

"Yes," she said swiftly. "It has been hell enough
to live with his presence on the edge of my vision
at every moment, and now I know that he is
capable of murder . . . I thought he was only
trying to advance his position in society."

It raised a question: Was Miss Ammons unlucky
enough to have had her secret fall into the wrong
hands, or had this fellow sought out someone at

Buckingham Palace who would be susceptible to blackmail? This was what Lenox asked Jenkins, after he left the palace and went to discuss the matter in the chief inspector's carriage.

"But what is the secret?" asked Jenkins.

Lenox implied that it was a child, given up many years before—damaging to a young woman's reputation, but not as irretrievably damaging as the story he had heard that morning.

Jenkins thought it over. "I think he found out by accident, however he found out. People talk."

Lenox nodded. "True."

"I liked Dallington's idea. This is a fellow of social ambition. His fraud against Godwin allowed him to acquire the outward appearance his ambitions necessitated, and his blackmail of Miss Ammons gave him a venue in which to show them."

"It is a plausible idea," said Lenox.

Jenkins, with a small smile, arched his eyebrows. "Yet?"

Lenox laughed. They were sitting in the carriage outside the palace, and he said, "You had better go in and speak to her. Please handle her delicately. I would stake my life that she is being honest. If she thinks you know her secret she will be a wreck."

"Has my discretion failed you yet, Lenox?" asked the inspector.

Funny to be sitting in this carriage. He could

easily conjure an image in his mind of Jenkins as an earnest twenty-five-year-old man, chasing a particularly incompetent safecracker across King's Cross Station. Now here he was, a man in full, headed to somewhere not far from the summit of their profession. "It never has, you're quite right," Lenox said. "Well, now I must go to the House—should have been there already."

"You and Dallington will continue on the case, however? There was a murder in Camden Town last night, and I've drawn it from the pool."

"Yes, of course. I'll let you know when Skaggs has news."

Soon after this Lenox arrived at his office and without a moment's delay pitched himself into the work of Parliament—for there was a great deal to do. At noon he had a meeting presided over by the Home Secretary, Richard Cross, at which a dozen men, including representatives of the larger trade unions, discussed how they might accumulate enough votes to make the Public Health Act a law. The union men declared their intention to begin a campaign of publicity in favor of the act, and Cross and Lenox promised to align their party's members behind the action.

After this meeting Lenox spent forty minutes with Graham, preparing for the evening's debates. Each night at the Commons several subjects came up, and Lenox liked to have thoughts prepared (albeit in rough outline) on each of them, because Gladstone occasionally looked down the front benches and nodded his head at someone—calling that person up to the crease, as it were. One could never be sure who was next in line, as Gladstone saw it.

Before Graham left, he said, "I have arranged for you to have lunch with John Coleridge later in the week, by the way."

"Coleridge? Never."

Graham smiled. "Yes. I hoped you would be pleased."

Coleridge was the Chief Justice of the Common Pleas, and widely known to be next in line for the most important judicial post in Britain, Lord Chief Justice of England, when its current occupant died. More importantly, he was extremely influential within Lenox's party. The positions he held were not political, but he was of that small, untitled council of men, along with Gladstone and James Hilary, who determined much of England's fate.

In this respect his power lay within his almost complete inaccessibility to all but a small handful of politicians, none of them less prominent than the Chancellor of the Exchequer. He kept his opinions quiet to all but a few men, who valued them highly indeed. Junior ministers, such as Lenox, hoped for Coleridge's notice; to receive it was seen as a mark of ascendancy, and it was in vain that both Lenox and Lady Jane had attempted to attract his attention in the past. It was nigh on a miracle that Graham had succeeded; very nearly the first step toward becoming Prime Minister, if such a thing was even conceivable.

"How did you do it?" asked Lenox.

"It is a long and uninteresting story. I will tell you it some other time, sir, but now you are late to meet again with Lord Heath. Mr. Frabbs will go with you to take notes, for Heath will certainly have a secretary there."

Later that afternoon Lenox sat in his office again, all alone now, reading a blue book on the subject of African mining. Frabbs and the other clerks had left for the day. When there was a knock on the door, therefore, he went to open it himself and found, standing outside, his brother.

"Edmund! Come in! I'm alone, or I would offer you tea."

Sir Edmund Lenox was cloaked in a light spring jacket, cheeks red from the outdoors. "No matter, it is a flying visit—I'm due home to Molly soon."

"You look as if you have been in the park."

"Indeed I have. I walked down from a call I had to make in Piccadilly. The forsythias are a beautiful yellow already, even at this time in March."

Edmund had the same hazel eyes and short beard that Charles did, but his face, especially in the mouth, was somehow soft, as if to show that his heart was still at home in the gentler pace of the country, just as his younger brother's aspect had been sharpened into shrewdness by years of city life. Because it was Friday, Edmund would be leaving for Lenox House that afternoon. He rarely missed a weekend there, unless urgent parliamentary business kept him in town.

Edmund's sons were both out of the house now, the elder at New College, Oxford, the younger at sea aboard HMS *Lucy*, a midshipman of advancing responsibilities, nearly primed for his lieutenant's examination; Molly came out of a naval family, full to the brim with every stripe of post captain and admiral, and her connections had clamored for Teddy to go to sea. (Many of them still looked down upon her husband, Member of Parliament though he might have been, as a rank landsman.) Still, Edmund and Molly had both spent their childhoods in and near Markethouse and had a lively acquaintance there, some solace for the deprivation of their boys' company. Lenox generally went for a week in each season to visit, longer at Christmas. They were some of his favorite times of the year.

"Pass along my best to Molly."

"I shall, but I have a favor to ask first."

"Unto half my kingdom, of course," said Lenox, smiling. "Is it something political?"

"Tangentially, perhaps. Charles, unfortunately it is time you had a quiet word with Graham."

Lenox started to speak and then stopped. At last, he said warily, "About what?"

"I've seen John Baltimore. He said he told you the rumors."

Lenox felt stung. "Have you been gossiping about Graham, Ed?"

"No, no, Charles, good gracious. It was in passing in the halls, here, but I must tell you, the same rumors have reached my ears. The other secretaries are at a high pitch of indignation."

"I have yet to hear a single substantive allegation against him," said Lenox, "even if I did I should not believe it."

Edmund smiled gently. "There is no need to look at me with such fury in your eyes, Charles. Graham once returned a pair of diamond cufflinks I had forgotten at Hampden Lane for a year. It is impossible to conceive of him thieving—I would no sooner believe it of him than I would of you."

Lenox leaned forward. "Then to what do you attribute these rumors?"

"I don't know. All I do know is that you had better speak with him, so that the two of you can handle it together. It is beginning to do material damage to your name, Charles. At least in Whitehall."

"Is it as serious as that?"

"I'm afraid it is." Edmund checked his watch. "I must go now and catch my train. I have defended

Graham wherever I hear him mentioned, but it has gone beyond my power to help him."

Lenox nodded. "Thank you for telling me."

"So has this business with Thomas McConnell and Polly Buchanan—they were seen lunching together today." Lenox's heart fell. "But he is your friend, not mine, for all that I like him, and I care much more about Graham. Now I must go, I really must. Good-bye. I'll look in on you Monday morning."

CHAPTER THIRTY-ONE

As the day went by, Lenox's mind returned again and again to his interview that morning with Grace Ammons, in the discreet beauty of the East Gallery. After she had told the long tale of her past, she had taken a few moments to compose herself and had then invited Lenox to ask any further questions he had.

The first he had asked was whether her blackmailer had ever offered her a way to reach him, an address, a club.

"Never," she had said.

"Did he say how he found you?" She shook her head. "Did you see him at either of the parties he attended?"

"I looked, but didn't see him."

After that Lenox had asked her, at least partially out of professional curiosity, to recount her experiences with Miss Strickland's agency. The young secretary had been forthright on the subject: She had hired Miss Strickland as soon as she believed Dallington to be untrustworthy, and since then her agency's protection and work had been sterling.

"Did you meet with Miss Strickland herself?"

"Of course."

It would be an actress, someone hired for the women clients and a few of the gentlemen. "What progress has she made?"

Grace Ammons had shrugged. "I'm not sure."

"She is not in touch?"

"On the contrary, she is available twenty-four hours a day, and her people are always nearby. She also lent me a small pistol with which to protect myself."

"What does she charge you?"

Grace Ammons had lifted her eyebrows at this—it was a forward question to hear from a gentleman. "A pound a day, and then expenses."

"It's a great deal."

"She could treble that amount and I would happily pay it." The young lady had paused and then gone on. "I was always very careful with my money in France, after that week when I was abandoned. I husbanded it. George does not know the extent of the fortune I mean to bring him."

Though their talk already seemed long ago after

the work of the day, it lingered in his mind. He was curious about Miss Strickland, and certainly very curious about the man who had tormented Grace Ammons and impersonated Archibald Godwin.

As the sun fell that evening, ten hours after the conversation, Lenox remained in his office in Parliament, and at half past eight he went down to the Members' Bar, leaving word with one of the porters at the gate that if any visitors should arrive—he was thinking of Skaggs—he should immediately be fetched back. Opening the door of the bar he sighed, wondering what Miss Strickland was making of the case, wherever and whoever she was. He was impatient for new information.

The bar was teeming with gentlemen, many of them taking a break from the evening session. (On Friday these were always sparsely attended, the benches not a quarter full.) Some of them hailed Lenox. He paused and shook hands but didn't stop for long. He had a specific target in mind: Willard Fremantle, the least discreet man in London.

Fremantle was the third son of a Northumberland marquess, most recent in a very ancient line. Willard's older brothers had both stayed close to home, but Willard, brighter and more restless, had strayed in the direction of the stock market, losing disastrous sums of money until his father, tired of underwriting these losses, found him a seat in Parliament to occupy his time.

There are gossips the world values and gossips the world despises. Willard, sadly for himself, fell into this latter category, and one felt that he could almost sense it; instead of driving him to reticence, it seemed to induce in him an even greater volubility, as if in desperate defiance of other men's opinion. Certainly it had been many years since anyone told him a secret. While his amiability assured that he had many friendly acquaintances in the House, one or two of whom could be counted upon to stop for a drink with him on any given night, he had no true friends. He was a plump, rapidly graying gentleman, unmarried.

Lenox found him near the end of the bar, drinking a shandy and perusing the court circular in the *Times*. "Anything interesting?" asked Lenox.

"Parties at the palace the next three nights, then a night for the Queen to rest, then the whole retinue makes for Balmoral."

"So early in the season?"

"Only for a week, however."

Lenox nodded. Unsurprisingly, the one way to quiet Fremantle was to make a direct inquiry of him. Then he would tap his nose, implying that he had a great deal of knowledge on that particular subject but couldn't possibly share it. Lenox started elsewhere, therefore. "Did you hear that Millwood's secretary resigned?" he asked. "Passed on if he might obtain Ursula Millwood's hand in marriage, no less!"

This was the stalest piece of tattle in London, and Fremantle treated it with appropriate disdain. "I hear she's said she'll run off if her papa doesn't consent."

Lenox smiled. "Count us lucky to have our chaps—Graham and Mollinger." Mollinger was an old Fremantle retainer, the gamekeeper's grandnephew. Like Graham, he was one of the very few parliamentary secretaries not to come from the ranks of the aristocracy. Rumor said that Willard had to draw his allowance from Mollinger. "Not above themselves."

Willard pursed his lips doubtfully. "Not Mollinger."

"Eh?" said Lenox.

"Well, your chap, Graham . . ." He trailed off as if no more needed to be said.

"What about him? Excellent fellow."

"The business with the trade unions."

"Oh, that," said Lenox scornfully. "What've you heard? I'll guarantee you I know more, and that it's wrong."

"Wrong!" said Fremantle and laughed heartily to himself, taking a sip of his shandy. "When he's been seen accepting cash from Whirral and Peligo? And others before them?"

"Who else?" asked Lenox.

Fremantle paused—perhaps he heard the urgency in his interlocutor's voice. "Well, if it's all false it can make no matter."

"Of course." Lenox took his watch from its pocket and looked at it, then said, sighing, "I suppose I'd better go into the chamber?"

"I wouldn't advise it, my dear chap. Twinkleton had just begun to expatiate on the state of the glue industry when I left five minutes ago. He won't rest until the whole country is covered in a thin layer of glue, you know."

Lenox smiled; in spite of it all he rather liked Fremantle. Perhaps he would ask Jane if they could have him to their supper—but then he remembered Disraeli and the onions (now famous in his mind) and thought that perhaps he had better reserve Fremantle for a less important evening. "I say, thank you. That was a near miss. Well, good evening, Fremantle."

Willard beckoned in Lenox close and said, "Before you go, a word. They do say that Cross has heard your secretary's name in a meeting— yes, Cross, and even Gladstone. I think you had better be shot of him, you know."

Lenox felt a faint dread, but he masked it, smiling knowingly at Fremantle as he made his farewells.

That was the slur, then: that in the negotiations over the Public Health Act, Graham had extorted the two great union leaders, Whirral and Peligo, for the support of his master, Lenox. It was a grave charge, and, Lenox knew, false.

So why hadn't Lenox himself been implicated in this corruption? Why was Graham's name the one on every tongue? Certainly Edmund would have told him, and perhaps even John Baltimore or Willard Fremantle—as well as a dozen other friends he could name, who would have come to speak to him the moment they heard any slander against him, and not his secretary.

Graham did have the power of scheduling. He could place a petitioner in a room with some of the most powerful men in the country, earning that ability in the last twelve months, when he had begun to arrange many of the meetings those in the upper hierarchy of the party took, coordinating his efforts with their secretaries. The charge was that Graham was selling access—and since Graham was not of the same class as most of the men in these hallways, it was easy to believe in his avarice.

Lenox knew he would have to take steps quickly to repudiate these whispered accusations. Already, he feared, it might be too late.

His heart heavy and mind preoccupied, he wandered almost inadvertently into the Commons—and there, indeed, was Twinkleton, upon his feet, a tranquilizing dullness in his voice.

Fortunately, a messenger came to fetch Lenox from the benches almost immediately. He had a visitor.

He walked to the small, comfortable room where visitors to the Members could wait. It was paneled in rosewood, with a green carpet, and always had a cozy fire running in every season, a tray of tea and sandwiches, and all the current papers and journals. The room was empty save for a lad in uniform waiting to deliver a telegram, and in the meanwhile eating his fill of biscuits, dunked in a cup of tea.

Skaggs must have gone upstairs; Lenox turned and then heard, behind him, "Just a moment of your time, Mr. Lenox." He turned back, and the delivery boy, shorn of his cap and kerchief, had become a middle-aged man—Skaggs himself. "Weren't you curious about my report?"

"Skaggs, you devil."

"Apologies, sir. Thought you might like to see the costume I wore when I approached most of the gents on your list."

"I had no conception of your dramatic talents," said Lenox, smiling. "Well done. Shall we go up to my office?"

CHAPTER THIRTY-TWO

Skaggs asked if it would be all the same to Lenox if they stayed there. "I've been in such a lather, rushing about London," he said, "that I've barely managed a meal, and there's such a lot of food here."

"We can offer you more substantial fortification than this." Lenox turned back into the hallways and hailed one of the many runners who waited at each gate. "Bring us a horseshoe gammon and a pint of porter from the Coach and Horses. As quickly as possible, up to my office. Will that do for you, Skaggs? It's the best thing they do at the pub."

"Perfectly, sir, thank you. I've run myself five-fifths empty."

Skaggs was large, and Lenox wondered what constituted starvation for such a creature—but there was no doubt that even if it would have composed a hearty day's meals for Lenox himself, Skaggs looked pale and ragged.

Parliament's runners were very pushing at the pub, because they provided so much business, and the gammon nearly beat them upstairs. Skaggs took a bite and then another, and within a minute much of the color had returned to his face. After he swallowed the meat he took a prodigious draft of porter, nearly three-quarters of the pint pot in one gulp, and then set it down, settling back into his chair with a look of bliss on his face.

"How did you get along, then?" asked Lenox.

"Not badly. Here is the list." Skaggs pulled a much-consulted piece of paper, battered into softness at every crease where it had been folded, from his breast pocket. "You gave me forty-seven names. Of these, forty I eliminated by a simple test of sight."

"Well done."

"I approached most of them in the disguise I was wearing when you saw me. About half at their homes, and for the other half it wasn't very difficult to find their offices. I would tell the maid that I had a telegraph for Mr. Harrison, or whatever the gentleman's name might be, that must only be delivered directly into his hands, and then when he finally came to the door of his house or office, I would feign where I had lost it, you see. There were a great number of exasperated men—some downright angry. I told them I would be back around with the telegram soon."

"And when you never appear?"

Skaggs shrugged. "Life is full of mysteries."

"Are you dead certain that none of these fellows could have been the man I'm looking for?"

"Of those forty, none had light hair as you described except one, and he was both very stunted and very unfortunate-faced, not at all the handsome type you described."

Lenox nodded. "The remaining seven, then."

"Those were harder, but I think I have eliminated three of them. I mean to try again tomorrow, but I am fairly sure I glimpsed all three—call it nine-tenths sure—one coming out of his club in Pall Mall, one at his residence in Belgravia, one in his office in the city."

"That leaves four men. Three of these are tall, fair-haired, relatively handsome gentlemen. One I cannot recommend as your suspect, Mark Troughton. He is a man with a family of six, extremely pious, and would not, in my opinion, sir, be especially compelling to a female eye."

Lenox nodded. "Good. Go on."

"The other three gentlemen are worth a visit. Of course, neither may be your man—your man may not have come from Wadham at all, as I understand it—but here are their names and addresses. Troughton's is there as well, if you want to have a look at him."

Lenox took the piece of paper and looked at it, wondering whether at this late hour Jenkins would still be at the office. Even if he had left for home, he was not the sort to consider his Saturday morning sacred. "What about the forty-seventh fellow?"

"He is an enigma. He would not answer his door. I staked it out for some time, and nobody emerged."

"What is his profession?"

"He listed none. His address, as you can see at the bottom of that sheet of paper, is a good one— the forwarding address he left at his last residence, which was where I visited first, a lodging house."

"He has perhaps had a rise in fortune, then?" asked Lenox.

"I thought that might intrigue you, sir. He has only taken his new rooms in the past two months. Mitchell, the fruit-and-vegetable man across the way, keeps close track of all the houses in his street and says this fellow is tall and fair-haired. But I fear Mitchell saw the prospect of a coin, and might have picked up on my suggestions to please me."

Three names, then, perhaps four. Lenox felt a quickening of excitement. It was just possible they were circling closer.

Skaggs finished his supper then, and the two men spoke, offering up conjectures back and forth as to the motive of Archibald Godwin's murder. When he was finished with his last potato, his last dab of gravy, Skaggs thanked Lenox and took his leave, reminding Lenox as he went that he was available for any further work.

When he was alone, Lenox sent a wire to Jenkins and Dallington. In it he suggested that, with a few constables for support, they all might call upon the four gentlemen whose names he listed at the foot of the telegram. For his part,

Lenox added, he could do it tomorrow morning.

Jane wouldn't like it, the chance of his coming face-to-face with a murderer. Lenox looked at his watch when he had finished and saw that it was now past nine o'clock. The season began on Monday; she would be among her dresses, finding nothing to wear, or sitting to plan out in her tidy script their schedule. It seemed ages since he had laid eyes upon Sophia. He looked at the mess upon his desk and decided, rather suddenly, to leave, standing up and taking his cloak and hat down from the stand at the door. Within half an hour he was sitting by the fire at Hampden Lane.

Lady Jane seemed particularly tired after the social exertions of her day, which she had spent moving between the houses of friends and commiserating with them about plans gone awry, servants who had given notice, daughters who refused to wear the proper dresses, all the gravely important trivia of the season.

"Are we at least finished planning our own party?" he asked her as they sat on the sofa, each reading a book.

She marked her spot with her thumb. "I find that word 'we' exceedingly droll, Charles."

"You'll recall that I had very definite opinions in the great debate about meringues or ices for dessert."

She smiled. "And that your side was routed in

the end. Even your own brother took against you."

"I consider that sort of loyal opposition essential to a successful party, however. In fact, to any communal endeavor whatsoever. When we first married, you might recall, I wished to paint this room blue. No, don't shudder. Anyhow it was a thought."

"To answer your question, the planning for the party is all but finished," said Lady Jane. "Kirk has been a saint. The silver will be polished on the morning of the party, and the tablecloths laundered, the food delivered, but everything else is ready—where people will sit, the menu, and of course all the invitations have gone out. Have I forgotten anything?"

"What will you wear?"

"My yellow dress, with the gray trim." She smiled. "Have you begun to take an interest in my wardrobe?"

"A very slight interest, perhaps."

"At any rate I won't be wearing any roasted onions. I warned everyone in the kitchen that if I saw so much as one upon the table I would turn them out into the streets. I hope they are suitably afraid. Kirk will look at each plate as it goes out, and of course the Prime Minister's own plate will be the most strictly examined."

"Thank you, my dear."

"I only wish Coleridge had accepted."

"Oh! I've forgotten to tell you! Graham has arranged for me to lunch with him!"

"He hasn't."

"Yes, it's true." Lenox thought for a moment about telling his wife of the defamations circulating against Graham but decided that he would rather not burden her with another anxiety, at least not yet, not until he could set it straight. She was already preoccupied. Toto had been around earlier in the day. "I don't know how he did it."

"What a coup!"

"Yes—I was very surprised. I don't know exactly how to thank him."

CHAPTER THIRTY-THREE

In the morning Jenkins replied to Lenox's telegram that he was occupied for much of the day but would be available in the late afternoon. (Alas, none of the names on Lenox's list matched the names Jenkins's men had gathered.) Lenox wrote back, promising to be at the Yard at four, and sent a telegram to Dallington to inform him of the new plan.

His morning suddenly free, Lenox dawdled around the nursery with Sophia for a while, chatting affably with Miss Emanuel as both of them observed the child's awkward and endearing feats of coordination.

At ten, however, Graham asked for a word in Lenox's study, and there suggested that since they were both free, they might take a round of the charities.

"We have been putting it off," said Graham.

"Yes, and there will never be a better opportunity," said Lenox forlornly.

"I will put the word around—if you would be ready to leave in half an hour?"

"Just as you wish."

Since he had become a Member of Parliament, and especially since he had risen into the higher echelons of his party, Lenox had found himself an object of deep interest among the charities of London (and indeed beyond). For one thing, the imprimatur his name lent to the list of a board of directors was a valuable tool in raising new funds; for another, his attention might one day mean, however glancingly, the attention of the House of Commons.

In the first flush of his electoral triumph, Lenox had accepted every such invitation. It had become apparent very quickly how calamitous a policy that was. There were a great many sham charities, badly run and, truth be told, meriting the investigation of criminal authorities, and only narrowly did Lenox avoid involvement with several of these. As his circumspection increased, he had reduced his commitments to a half-dozen or so charities.

There were always new requests, however, and Graham now insisted—wisely—that they visit each, preferably on very little notice, to make their selection.

The first visit they made was a mere formality, one with which Lenox would happily have dispensed. Graham was more cautious and had insisted they visit Mr. Soyer's establishment in person. Soyer had been a great man, but he was dead, after all, and one couldn't rely upon the integrity of his successors.

It was clear from the moment they arrived, however, that Soyer's food hall was still a model of efficiency. Lenox had now made several of these trips, and the signs of mismanagement had become instantly distinguishable to him: dirt, neglected duties, men lazing about on the job. None of those signs were here. The kitchen was housed in a long room, with a massive marble countertop at one end where eager young men offered a steadily flowing line of ragged-looking individuals and families both soup and bread. Some twelve hundred people ate here each day, according to the letter Lenox had received inviting him onto the board. On Christmas that number was closer to twenty-two thousand. Because it was cheap and made for a hearty meal, Soyer's kitchen mostly served soup; the men who frequented the place had started calling it the "soup kitchen," and that concept, of a hall serving

237

soup to the impoverished, had spread all across creation, to the Americas, northwest to Ireland, and southeast to the continent.

This was a testament to the genius and vision of Soyer himself, who had now been dead for nearly twenty years. A Frenchman, he had come to England as the chef of the Reform Club, which instantly became famous for the quality of its food. It was the famine in Ireland that drew his roving attention (for he was also an inventor and an artist) to charitable work, eventually leading to this establishment in Spitalfields. Lenox had already decided when they entered the room that he would join the kitchen's board of directors, and now, watching the men, women, and children take their food, he wondered at what life must have been like thirty years before, when there was no such resource. He gave credit to his age: Since William the Fourth had died and Victoria took the crown, somehow it had been decided, in the faint aggregate consciousness, that it was unacceptable to permit an English-man to die of simple starvation, that it was unacceptable not to extend a hand down in aid. The changes were individually imperceptible, and together enormous. Who could say how many tens of thousands of lives this kitchen alone had rescued?

Not all charities were so admirable, unfortunately. The next one they visited was the Osgood

Children's Home, not far away from Soyer's; it was a disaster.

The home was in Petticoat Market Lane, which might have been the most colorful street in London. All along it was a line of stalls selling clothes and cloth, in every possible color, quiet and garish alike; no doubt Lady Jane had bought dresses whose material originated in this street. Eel sellers and baked-potato men wandered among the crowds, offering their food, and little children, scampering between the stalls, stole what they could.

Near the end of the street was Osgood's. A nervous young woman greeted them at the door ("It would be ever so much better if you wrote to Mr. Osgood for an appointment," she kept saying) and only reluctantly escorted them to meet her master. Osgood was a type Lenox recognized at once, bluff, venal, arrogant, charmless, and full of the self-regard of a man who thinks he has made his place in the world on his own. Very possibly Osgood had—but by no savory means. The house was filthy, and the children that Lenox saw were all working, picking apart old rope. He only managed to see this much because he opened a door at random as Osgood hustled them along on a tour of the building.

When they returned to Osgood's office, Lenox was preparing to give the man a measure of his mind. "Sir, I—"

Here Graham stepped in. "Mr. Lenox is honored at your invitation," he said, "but wonders if it comes with any emolument, to ease the financial burden of his travel here, for instance, or the lost hours he would spend on behalf of the home's cause. Perhaps I could return tomorrow to discuss it with you alone? Mr. Lenox's time is, you understand, very valuable."

Relief flooded into Osgood's face. "Of course, of course," he said. "Any time . . . I shall be in any time . . . I shall—please, come along and we may speak. It is always a pleasure to speak with a gentleman who has a business head."

Graham, all graciousness, thanked their host and promised to return the next day. Lenox touched his cap and followed Osgood's secretary out of the door.

When they had returned to the carriage, Graham said, in a low voice, "I thought it would be intelligent not to forewarn Mr. Osgood of any potential investigation you saw fit to initiate. I sensed that you might be near to expressing your anger with him, sir."

"You were absolutely right."

Yet this method of their extrication—the unsubtle hint that a bribe would certify Lenox's good opinion of the home—hewed uncomfortably close to the slanders against Graham. Was it possible that just such a situation had led to the misunderstanding? Lenox nearly spoke the question out loud—but didn't, found he couldn't. His faith in Graham remained unshaken, and yet his disdain for the rumors about Graham had somewhat diminished.

The next two organizations they visited met with Lenox and Graham's approval, though the second, a library for the Jewish schools, would demand a great deal of time; if possible, Lenox intended to fob the job off upon some junior Member.

"Are we finished?" he asked Graham as they left.

"Two more, sir."

Lenox looked at his watch. It was nearly half past one. "I can do one of them."

Graham chose for them, directing the driver to Great Ormond Street. There was a hospital for children there, the first of its kind in Britain, and though it had started with only ten beds, in '52, it had been successful. One of its earliest supporters had been Charles Dickens.

"Stopping there has the virtue of bringing us back toward the west end of town," Graham said. He was looking down at a page of notes in his tidy handwriting. "Aside from that, it is the least disinterested of our stops, sir."

"Oh?"

"In fact, they did not inquire after your availability—rather the opposite; I inquired whether there might be a seat on their board for

241

you. It may mean financial outlay, even a personal donation from you."

"To what end?" asked Lenox, curious.

"If the rumors are to be believed, Queen Victoria intends to take an interest in the hospital. Better to be on the train before it stops for the multitudes, I think, sir."

It was the kind of minor, vital action that Graham had mastered. Lenox smiled. "Excellent."

The hospital, housed in a tall red building that curved around a corner, was a model of what such an establishment ought to be. The wards were clean and white, with the sharp disinfecting smell of soap strong on the air, and behind it occasionally a whiff of baked marmalade pie, which must have been the dessert the children received for lunch. Windows were open to circulate the air, but the beds looked warm. In tidy crates near the door were picture books and toys.

All of the patients here were between the ages of two and thirteen, with very occasionally someone who had been long in convalescence staying to the age of fourteen. Lenox's tour began with the infants; a nurse, after giving him a mask for his mouth, led him to each crib, where she described the child's illness and the steps that the hospital was taking. A remarkable variety of medical men, including dozens from the Royal Society of Medicine and the Society of

Apothecaries, gave freely of their time. There were six staff doctors who rotated in and out of the hospital daily.

"Here is our newest one now," said the nurse as they turned a corner. "Perhaps we can follow him for a few minutes in his rounds."

There, to Lenox's astonishment, stood Thomas McConnell.

CHAPTER THIRTY-FOUR

She is only suffering from thrush at the moment, the poor mite," said McConnell.

They were beside the bed of a small girl, who was in the throes of what looked like a terrible fever. Lenox and Graham stood a few respectful strides back from the bed. It was the fifth patient they had visited with McConnell.

"Are you sure?" asked the nurse.

"Quite sure. We must give her a bolus of laudanum." With great tenderness, McConnell tilted back the child's head, its face swollen and red, and tipped a liquid taken from his coat pocket between her chapped, cracked lips. She coughed it down without leaving her state of febrile semiconsciousness. The doctor patted her hand and, as they walked away, murmured to Lenox, "I very much fear that she will not live out the month."

"You said it was only thrush."

"Yes, but a growth in her belly is what has made her susceptible to infection. No surgeon will touch it, if I'm not wrong. Still, we may hope."

Thus far Lenox and McConnell had not exchanged any words beyond a polite greeting, but now, as the nurse pointed out the artworks along the wall to Graham, Lenox said in a quiet voice, "Thomas, why didn't you tell me you were working here?"

McConnell consulted his pocket watch. It had been a present from Toto and was beribboned with rubies and emeralds, a garish, rather beautiful thing. "I'm free in twenty minutes," he said, "and I'm ravenous. Will you sit with me to my luncheon?"

"We passed a chophouse on Rugby Street when we came here."

"Mr. Porter's house? I know it intimately. Yes, let's meet there. Call it half an hour."

They shook hands, and Lenox saw with his own eyes, for the first time, what Toto had been telling them: McConnell really did look happier than perhaps he ever had before, his eyes light and free of burdens. Was it work? Was it love?

Lenox spent the next half hour introducing himself to the staff at the hospital. With every corridor he traversed and every person he met he grew more impressed—with the people in particular, for all of them bore the same brisk, efficient, no-nonsense variety of good cheer, which in Lenox's experience approached much more nearly to sainthood than the breed of self-regarding softheartedness that one found in Mayfair. Better to clean one patient's bedding than to pour vague pity upon a thousand homeless urchins.

He made an appointment to return and meet the director of the hospital and then, telling Graham he had agreed to meet McConnell, made for Rugby Street.

Mr. Porter's was a rude chophouse, with sawdust on the floor and a matronly woman hustling tall pewter jugs of ale here and there. Lenox took a table near the door. Evidently many of the physicians from the Royal College nearby took their sustenance here; the walls were covered in scrawled prescriptions, some now decades old, some belonging to doctors who had become famous on Harley Street. "Advised: one night in the Rugby: four glasses sherry: four glasses ale: four glasses port: sleep till noon," read a sheet near Lenox's right arm, upon the prescription paper of a man who was now the royal family's own surgeon. Perhaps that was why it was the only prescription in a frame.

McConnell came into the room not long after Lenox had sat down. "There you are," he said. "I hope I am not late. Yes, I'll sit, there we are. Are you hungry? They do a capital game pie, with half-burnt mashed potatoes over it. That's what I mean to have."

Lenox had already ordered coffee, which arrived as McConnell was sitting. He peered into the pot. "There are white bits floating in it," he said unhappily.

"Eggshells—it takes the bitterness away. Old doctor's trick, you know. Could I have a cup of that?"

"You can have all of it."

"No, come, you must try it. There, half a cup each."

Lenox took a sip and was compelled to admit the efficacy of the eggshells. "Not bad."

They ordered, and for a while McConnell spoke about the patients Lenox had seen, giving him more detail on each one—a small boy with a teratoma, an older girl with the hundred-day cough, and a newborn, seemingly in perfect health, whose breathing was strained. "We shall pull him through, however," said the doctor. "I'm sure of that."

"Then I am, too."

McConnell paused now. "Tell me," he said, "did you come to the hospital because you knew I would be there?"

"No. Did you not observe the surprise in my face?"

"I thought I did," McConnell murmured. "I had kept it quiet. Still, it was a jolt seeing you there."

"You have a taken a job of work, then, Thomas?"

"You don't need to say it that way," said McConnell irritably, "as if you were Toto's father, the old bugger, and I had decided to shift vocations and become a chimney sweep late in life."

In that sentence was encapsulated the change in Lenox's friend—a new self-confidence, a new indifference to the opinion of others. "You seem happy."

"I have never been happier in all my life. I have been at the hospital for six weeks, and it has passed like six hours."

"But Toto doesn't know," said Lenox.

A defiant look came into McConnell's eyes. "I asked her if I should take the job—Dr. West was my professor, many years ago—and she pitched a fit, if you must know. Fortunately I am not tied to her apron strings."

"She thinks you're having an affair with Polly Buchanan," said Lenox. He had decided upon directness. "In fact, half of London thinks as much."

McConnell's eyes widened in surprise, and then he burst into a long and rolling laugh. After a few moments, catching sight of his friend's stern face, he laughed harder still. "Oh, dear," he said, wiping his eyes.

"I cannot see what is so funny," said Lenox, vexed.

"Only the idea—but I suppose that is why Toto has been so cold? What a relief!" McConnell emitted a final sigh of laughter and then, realizing perhaps that he had conveyed too much information about his marriage in that spontaneous exclamation, hurried along his next words. "No, no, Charles, I have no amorous affection for Miss Buchanan. I look forward to telling Toto as much this evening. I suppose I had better tell her about the hospital, too—yes, I will, and she can take it just as she pleases, for I don't mean to stop."

"You are friends, you and Polly Buchanan? She is a great rake."

"Just a minor friendship—no, I would not even call us friends, though I cannot dislike her. Still, I must keep my word, and not tell you why she and I have met in Hyde Park. For I assume our meetings there have given rise to these rumors."

"Yes."

"Trust me, Charles, in the fullness of time I shall explain it all to you. Polly Buchanan! You must admit that it's amusing."

Lenox, who conceived himself bound to admit no such thing, merely frowned. Their food arrived, and McConnell dropped into it ravenously, ordering a pint of ale to accompany it. For many years he had been too heavy a drinker, but even to Lenox, now, his thirst seemed healthy.

What happiness he saw in his friend's face! In

spite of his misgivings, Lenox felt a growing warmth of corresponding happiness, and blended into it an overpowering degree of relief. Toto would understand about the hospital. She was not a cruel-minded woman, not at all. The only shame was that it had taken so long for him to return to medicine.

Thomas had the same feeling, describing, as they ate, the sense of waste, of talent squandered, that the decade since his marriage seemed to represent.

"I don't blame Toto in the slightest. It was my own fault," he said, "and when her mind is at ease over Polly Buchanan, how much happier she shall be, knowing that I am happy. Do you not think so, Charles?"

It was an unusually intimate question, and an unusually intimate conversation, but something about the hominess of the food and the sawdust on the floor and the rising drunken voices toward the back of the room made it seem appropriate. They were friends of very long standing, after all. So Lenox replied that yes, he did imagine that Toto would be happier. "Perhaps your only error has been secrecy, Thomas," he said.

"One is bred to it."

"That is true." Lenox took a sip of coffee, sitting back from his half-eaten luncheon. He checked his watch. It was nearly three. "I must go soon. Tell me first, though, what I am to say to Jane?"

"You must tell her what you please," said McConnell lightly. "You speak as if it all must be such very heavy weather."

"I don't think you can understand how Toto has suffered, Thomas, and as a consequence how much Jane and I have suffered on her behalf. Your happiness has blinded you. If I still seem somber, that is the reason—not because I am not pleased that you have come to work at the hospital, which has already earned my full-hearted esteem. I give you joy of your new venture. Only you must recall the old ventures, too."

McConnell hesitated for a moment, thinking, and then nodded. "Yes."

"I hope you are not offended that I am candid."

"Never in life. I think you are right, Charles. I have been selfish—but it may be that I was overdue some selfishness, and now I can accord myself the proper prescription of it again. All those years I spent in a lab, such a wan imitation of life! You've no idea what it is to lose yourself for so long."

Lenox briefly alighted upon the feeling of avid anticipation he had of the meeting at four, then thought of the thousands of hours he had spent at his office in the Commons. "No," he said, "I don't."

"It is like coming back to the red-blooded rush of living, after being a ghost. I am certain that Toto will understand—Polly Buchanan, indeed."

CHAPTER THIRTY-FIVE

Lord John Dallington was unmistakably in better health. Lenox watched him stride down a wide central passage at Scotland Yard just after four o'clock. "Jenkins will be another moment," Lenox told his young associate.

"Is he bringing a constable with him, I hope?" asked Dallington.

"Two."

"Who are these four gentlemen we mean to visit, then? Old college mates of Godwin's?"

Lenox read out the names that Skaggs had given him. "Mark Troughton. Albert Walworth. Jeremiah Smith. St. John Walker."

"They sound a dreary lot."

"Let us hope they are dreary enough not to fire a pistol upon us, at any rate."

"True, I should hate to die just when I no longer feel like ten-day-old soup." Then, cheered by a thought, he said, "But perhaps they'll hit the constables!"

"Come now, Dallington."

"Only a joke."

They visited Mark Troughton first, and Skaggs had been correct; he was not the man for whom they were searching. They apologized to him and returned to the Yard's large, rather ratty carriage.

The remaining three gentlemen all, by coincidence, resided within a few streets of each other in Bloomsbury. The first they visited was St. John Walker—his forename pronounced Sinjun, one presumed. As they approached his door, Lenox felt a patter of anxiety in his chest. He braced himself.

The result of their inquiry here was disappointing, too. Walker was a tall, very thin person, with enormous red ears like bell pulls. When they explained their visit he replied that, instead of murdering and thieving, he occupied his time by buying antiquities and reselling them on the secondary market. "I've very sorry you've got the wrong man," he said.

"It's not your fault," Dallington told him glumly.

"I had never supposed it to be, but I can understand that it must be an exasperation to you nevertheless."

"Thank you, Mr. Walker," said Jenkins and motioned the two constables, hearty beef-fed lads with high hopes of making the arrest, to retreat down the steps of the house.

That left two men: Walworth and Smith. "Skaggs notes that Smith is the handsomest of the lot," said Lenox.

"Ah, Rupert Skaggs, noted judge of beauty," said Dallington.

Lenox smiled. "I suggest we leave him for last."

Walworth was out. He lived in a gloomy set of apartments, largely unadorned, with a single servant, a young and jumpy valet who introduced himself as Albert Wrightswood. "You're both called Albert?" Lenox asked.

"Yes, sir."

"He must sound mad when he speaks to you," Dallington said. "It's as if he's telling himself to fetch his pipe or lay out his clothes. 'Albert, you've done first-rate work today.' Eh?"

The junior Albert smiled weakly, the presence of five strange men from Scotland Yard evidently having dampened his appetite for witticisms at his own expense. "Perhaps, sir."

There was something Lenox didn't like in the young man's edginess, however. "Where is your employer?" he asked.

"Out upon a social call, sir."

"Do you know where?"

"At the Biblius Club, I believe, sir."

Lenox and Dallington glanced at each other. "I know it," said Lenox. "He is a member?"

"Yes."

"We shall seek him there."

When they left, however, Lenox, in a whisper, suggested that they watch the door for a moment. Sure enough, Albert Wrightswood appeared a few moments later, all in haste to be gone. Jenkins sent one of the constables along with cab money to follow him.

The party from Scotland Yard was down to four in number, therefore, when they knocked upon the door of Jeremiah Smith. It belonged to a lovely alabaster town house overlooking Bedford Square.

Jenkins wasn't pleased. "This hardly has the appearance of the residence of a gentleman who needs to commit fraud to buy a hat."

"Perhaps his frauds have run pretty large," said Dallington.

A white-haired housekeeper answered the door and led them into a drawing room, where they waited for three or four tense minutes. At last Jeremiah Smith entered the room, face serious— and confirmed all of Jenkins's fears. It was not the man from Gilbert's.

They made their hasty apologies and, without needing to consult each other about the decision, made for the Biblius Club, and Albert Walworth.

The club's steward acknowledged that he was in, and after a perfunctory objection to their intrusion upon a private clubhouse, which Jenkins immediately squashed, he led them upstairs to the club's back library, overlooking the garden.

"What is on the third floor now?" asked Lenox to the steward in a low voice, as they walked. "I know the society that was there has been disbanded."

"Yes, that was a terrible set-to. The Biblius Club

uses the space now—and got it very cheaply, because nobody wanted to rent the rooms of the September Society. Here we are, gentlemen. Mr. Walworth, you have visitors. Impertinent visitors."

Indeed, here Walworth stood, and the last of Lenox's hope dissolved. Jeremiah Smith had not been remarkably handsome, but in comparison with poor Albert Walworth, who had a bulbous nose and eyebrows the size and texture of two voles, he was like one of the ancient Greek gods, returned to modern times. For the fourth time they went through the same apology, which Walworth, befuddled, managed half to accept.

Out upon the street Lenox sighed and made his own apology. "I am sorry, gentlemen."

"It was worth the effort," said Dallington loyally.

"Perhaps the two of you would like a cup of tea?" asked Lenox.

Jenkins hesitated, plainly out of sorts, but then, manners winning out, assented. Soon they were all in a carriage bound for Hampden Lane.

As usual, Lenox was greeted by a raft of telegrams, many of them to do with Parliament. One of them, however, bore the return address of Skaggs. This he tore open as Dallington and Jenkins settled themselves into armchairs.

Misidentified forty-one, forty-three STOP addresses and names appended STOP Apologies Skaggs

Lenox handed this note to Dallington, who read it and passed it on to Jenkins.

"What sort of code is this?"

Lenox explained: Skaggs had dismissed forty of the names on his initial list, reserved judgment about the four they had just visited, and had all but certain confirmation on three: the forty-first, -second, and -third names on his list. Apparently his certainty had been misplaced, however, and when he had gone back to check those three he had discovered the fact.

"It's two new names," said Lenox. "If you have the energy to go out again."

"We've sent Constable Hardy home."

"I'll go," said Dallington. "Though I might swallow down a sip of that tea first."

Twenty minutes later the three men were in Lenox's carriage, bound for Belgravia. The first address was in Dalton Mews; the name of the man who lived there was Leonard Wintering. It did look rather a more promising location in which to find their impostor, a dingy building in an otherwise affluent street, no steward or porter or housekeeper at the door to greet them.

"The third floor," said Lenox, looking down at the telegram. "The door is marked with Wintering's last name."

"I look forward to apologizing to him for infringing upon his privacy," said Jenkins. "It will be our fifth apology of the day. Mrs. Jenkins will be delighted that I am so promiscuous with the things."

Lenox ignored this sarcasm and led them up the stairs. He was using no special caution, until, on the landing below the third story, Lenox suddenly felt a sense of unease. "Stop," he said.

"What is it?" asked Dallington in a low voice.

"Do you smell that?"

Both men turned their noses up into the air. "Someone has built a fire," said Jenkins. "It's cold out, after all."

"No—that is cordite you smell, not a wood or gas fire. A gun was fired here today."

Dallington and Jenkins looked at each other and nodded. "Carefully, then," said Jenkins and went ahead of them, leading the way up to the third floor and Wintering's door.

He knocked at it. "Delivery!" he announced in a confident voice.

There was no answer. "Try again," whispered Dallington.

Jenkins repeated the ruse. "Delivery!"

"See if the door is open," said Lenox.

It was. They crept inward, single file, down a shadowy front hall, closing the door behind them. Jenkins had his small revolver out. The smell of cordite was strong here; there was no noise inside, nobody moving toward or away from the door.

"He's killed again, and fled," said Jenkins.

Suddenly there was a hammering on the door that they had closed behind them, and all three men jumped, startled, at the same time. "Hellfire below," said Dallington. "What was that?"

"Delivery!" a voice called out.

Lenox's heart was racing. "We look inside before we go to the door," he said and, seeing that Jenkins wavered, strode with a purposeful step down the hall.

"Delivery!" shouted the voice again, and there was a fist on the door.

They came into a large living room, blue with evening light. Nobody was in it. In the corner of the room was a door, leading to a bedroom. "Follow me," said Lenox.

Here, where the smell of gunfire was so intense that it might have been only moments old, they saw it: the body of Leonard Wintering, long and lean, flung back on the unmade bed, one leg dangling off, a small bullet hole in its temple. Leonard Wintering—or, as he had called himself in Gilbert's, that day, Archie Godwin. He had not killed again; he had been killed, this time.

"My God," said Jenkins.

It was Dallington who had already looked away, back down the hallway. "Do we wait it out? Or do we go to the door?" he asked.

"We go to the door," said Lenox.

CHAPTER THIRTY-SIX

As they walked with quiet steps down the hall, Lenox's mind was racing: Their chief suspect was dead, shot in the temple, and their surmises about him would have to be adjusted. He thought of Whitstable's plain, honest face; thought of Grace Ammons; tried to move backward through his ideas about this whole business.

It was Jenkins who—bravely—threw open the door, all three of them pressed with their backs against the wall in case of a violent greeting, but none came. Instead an enormous, bristle-bearded fellow in a peacoat, hair black as night, barreled into the room. "Where is Wintering?" he demanded. "Tall, light-haired fellow."

"Who are you?" asked Jenkins.

"Who are you, for that matter?" said the man, eyes glinting dangerously.

"I am Inspector Thomas Jenkins of Scotland Yard, and I repeat my question: Who are you?"

"The Yard, eh? Is Wintering here? Let me see him."

"I am asking for the final time, before I place you under arrest. Who are you?"

The man looked at Jenkins, Lenox, and Dallington, perhaps reckoning his odds of outmuscling all three of them, and then said,

"Alfred Anixter. I'm here from Miss Strickland's Detective Agency. I want a word with Wintering."

The three men looked at each other.

"Wintering is dead," said Lenox. "How did you come to hear his name?"

"He was harassing one of our clients."

"Yes, Grace Ammons. My question stands."

Anixter looked as if he might remain silent, until Jenkins, irritated, said, "Unless you answer Mr. Lenox, we will have to consider you the chief suspect in this murder."

That drew him out. "I was following you," he said.

There was a pause, and then Dallington burst out laughing. "I rather like this new detective agency," he said.

"Which of us were you following?" Lenox asked.

He nodded toward Dallington. "Him."

"How did you know Wintering's name?"

"It was on the door."

"Then why not wait until we had gone to speak to him?"

"I wanted to see his face before you arrested him and hid him away. Miss Strickland has a portrait artist who can draw a wonderful charcoal likeness from a description. Takes him about six minutes. We could match it to Miss Ammons's description that way."

That was ingenious, Lenox thought, though he

didn't say anything. Jenkins, tone officious, pointed to a chair in the living room, "You may sit here until we decide whether we need to speak to you further."

"Why not let me help you?" asked Anixter.

"No, thank you. Don't think about leaving, either."

Dallington, Jenkins, and Lenox had a brief conversation. The first thing they had to do was to examine these rooms, then speak to the residents of the building. After that they had to learn as much as they could about Wintering—as they now knew him to be.

Jenkins went downstairs with his whistle between his lips, planning to blow for a constable, who could offer immediate assistance; in the meanwhile he could send Lenox's carriage to the Yard with word that help was required.

Dallington and Lenox went back into Wintering's bedroom. Lenox looked down at the body. It seemed infinitely long ago that he had spoken to this gentleman at Gilbert's. How much pain might have been avoided by detaining him then and there? If only there had been a reason to do so at the time.

"Quickly, John—you and I must search as rapidly and thoroughly as possible, for all I trust Jenkins."

Dallington looked at him and nodded, and they began.

Fortunately the flat was small, three rooms. There was the sitting room, with a gas stove and a crimson sofa, where Anixter was sitting and tapping his foot, restless; the bedroom, where the body lay; and the kitchen, which had a small breakfast table in the corner. Lenox took the bedroom, Dallington the kitchen.

The bedroom was small and unadorned. In it were a narrow bed and a bookshelf; Lenox turned his eye to the latter first. It was crowded with randomly shoved-in volumes of *The Gentleman's Magazine*, a digest for educated Englishmen (and the first publication to use the word "magazine," French for "storehouse," which was now becoming more and more common— although now, oddly, the word had migrated back to Paris from London and come to mean "journal" there, too). Lenox sifted through these as quickly as he could. There were no books on the shelves. Not a reading man. A few trinkets— a silver watch fob, a hinged pine box with *LW* carved into its top and tobacco spilling untidily out of it, a jar of loose coins. On top of the bookshelf were a number of bills and a book of checks—he banked at Barclay, Bevan, Barclay, and Tritton—and Lenox looked through both. All of the bills were invoiced to Leonard Wintering, none to Archibald Godwin. It made sense. He wouldn't have given out this address when he used a false name.

"Lenox!" called Dallington from the kitchen. "I'm not quite finished."

"You had better come in here anyhow."

Lenox went to the kitchen and saw Dallington sitting at the table there. "What is it? I've yet to even look at the body."

"Look." Dallington gestured at the small piles of paper and the other objects that covered the table in front of him, and Lenox looked more closely. There were newspaper clippings and a soft black cap. Dallington picked up a half sheet of paper. "Look at the dates that he circled."

It was the court circular from the *Times*, the very one Willard Fremantle had been reading when he informed Lenox that there were parties at Buckingham the next three nights, and then the party was off to Balmoral.

Wintering had circled two of the nights: tonight, tomorrow.

With dawning interest, Lenox began to sift through the other objects on the table. "What else have you found?"

"Look at this."

Dallington was holding a small square of red wax. Lenox took it and asked, puzzled, "What is its significance?"

"You have to open it in half."

He did this, and saw that in the soft wax there was a perfect impression of a key for a mortice lock. He whistled. "A proper housebreaker—and tomorrow was the third party he asked Grace Ammons to get him into."

"What better occasion to steal from the palace than during a crowded party, too? Ten to one it belongs to one of the doors at Buckingham Palace."

Lenox shook his head. "No—look at the size of the key. It belongs to a window. I would guess they left the keys in the windows during the party, in case it grew too warm. It's the season of unpredictable weather."

"And look at the rest of this." Dallington held up the newspaper clippings. "An account of the last party, the rooms that were used. The Queen's social calendar, and here is an odd little shorthand list of some kind or another—but it's placed with the things I think he meant to take, the wax, the cap, and this knife."

Dallington held up the knife. It was a short, ugly, efficient object. "This looks like the kit of a serious thief. It's hard to believe the fellow in the bedroom put it together," said Lenox.

"We must learn more about him. Perhaps he even has a criminal record."

"Yes, it could be."

There was a noise in the hallway and Jenkins came in, trailed by a constable. He found them in the kitchen—Anixter stood up at his arrival, and again offered to help, an offer the three men declined in unison—where Dallington reported on all they had found.

Jenkins blanched. "Thank God somebody got to him before he could steal from the palace."

"But who?" asked Dallington.

Almost at the same moment, Lenox said, "I'm not at all persuaded that the palace is safe even now."

"What do you mean?"

"Arthur Whitstable described three men walking up the Gloucester Road that morning. Now two of them are dead. Who was the third?"

CHAPTER THIRTY-SEVEN

Thirty-five minutes later they were in the Blue Drawing Room at Buckingham Palace. A grim-looking lieutenant stood watch over them. The Queen was on her way.

Jenkins paced the room nervously; they had left a passel of constables behind at Wintering's, to take care of the body and search the rooms, but he would have preferred to do the job himself. Meanwhile Dallington and Lenox sat on two uncomfortable chairs near the door. Despite its name, the color of the Blue Drawing Room was almost entirely gold—too sumptuous for Lenox's taste, though undeniably spectacular, with its long rows of high columns and its vast acreage of glossy royal portraiture.

"Have you met the Queen?" asked Lenox in a quiet voice.

"Several times as a child."

It was sometimes easy to forget that Dallington was the son of a duke. "Of course. You must have been a page."

"Yes, I still have the costume. Fearful bore."

"Come now, be respectful."

Dallington grinned, but when the door opened a moment later, he was just as quick to his feet as Lenox.

What was one supposed to feel, meeting one's monarch? She came in with a rollicking bustle of spaniels around her feet, four or five of them, tan, white, and black in coloring. (Lenox still remembered Dash, her first and favorite, who had been memorialized in the newspapers as if he were an officer in the Guards.) The most striking thing was her size, always—she stood just under five feet, a crumb of person. There was a reason the people called her "our little queen."

In public and social life Lenox had occasion to see Victoria relatively often, sometimes as many as six or seven times a year. He always felt the same complex blend of emotions. There was reverence, first, then incredulity that so much power and meaning resided in one rather inconsequential-looking person. There was even something comic, faintly disappointing, in her plain, rather portly personage, but this recognition was always succeeded by a great wave of affection and wish to protect her.

Perhaps this was because of Albert. On the day in her eighteenth year when she took the crown, she had once said, she watched two of the greatest men in the realm—her two ancient uncles—bow before her, and at that moment it had been borne in upon her that she would never again have a true equal. She had been wrong, however. In Prince Albert she had found both love and mutual respect. When he had died, fourteen years before, it was widely acknowledged that the world had grown dark for her—that even now she only went on out of a sense of duty, without any pleasure in life, even, somewhat shockingly, in her children.

Albert had been something of a laughingstock, in truth, a derision encouraged in part by Victoria's overfondness for him. When he had arrived she had been less kind: She had banished his childhood friends from his retinue, back to the Continent, permitting him to keep only his beloved dog, Eon, for whom she bought a silver collar, which in itself seemed a gesture of proprietorship.

Albert had handled his submission gallantly. He was exceedingly gentle and loving with the Queen from the start, until soon she came to depend on him utterly. She had made him a consort when the public took against him—they feared a war with the continent—and would have made him a king, if she could have.

After his death, nobody in London had seen her face for three years.

She emerged a statelier woman, her own sorrow close to death itself. She had strength, certainly. Often Lenox remembered the story, much whispered in his childhood, of her first days as Queen. During all of her adolescence she had shared a bed with her arrogant, domineering mother, but upon taking up residence here at Buckingham she had banished that woman, furious, to a distant suite of rooms. Yet she had kept through an adjoining door her childhood governess, who, until the day of her death, brushed Victoria's hair every night.

As she entered the room now, gray of hair and lined of face, that arrogant, vulnerable child-queen seemed both unreachably gone and at the same time visible in her lineaments, her expressions. Time had shaped her. It took no courage to be a nobleman, or even a prince, but to be a monarch for thirty-eight years, as she had been, took mettle. Privilege was no bulwark.

"Gentlemen," she said, as all four men in the room bowed, "I am told that someone may mean to make mischief here this evening."

"Yes, ma'am," said Jenkins, who was the official presence of their trio.

She had insisted upon seeing them herself,

apparently. "You are Charles Lenox," she said now, reaching down to scratch a dog's ear. "And you are James Dallington."

"Yes, ma'am," they both said, Dallington apparently willing to let her slip pass unremarked.

"Lady Jane Lenox is pregnant, Grete tells me," said the Queen. "It is the hazard of being a wife, unfortunately."

"She has had the child, Your Majesty," said Lenox and then, though the lieutenant had warned them to be as brief as possible, could not help himself from adding, "a girl named Sophia."

A flicker of a smile passed across the Queen's face. "I'll tell Grete she was wrong—she won't like it. Sophia, then. I don't dislike babies, though I think very young ones rather disgusting." There was virtually no appropriate response to this, but she didn't seem to mind the ensuing silence. She walked toward a window and pulled back the diaphanous curtain, looking out at the black of evening. "Our gathering begins in thirty minutes, gentlemen. Is that correct, Shackleton?"

The lieutenant—who had a thin martial mustache, a strong jawline, and hair slicked into a neat mold—consulted his watch. "Thirty-one minutes, Your Majesty."

"What a pointless correction."

"Yes, Your Majesty."

"I am surrounded by lawyers everywhere, making minor corrections. Such exactitude—

everyone wishes the Queen to know the exact facts. Shackleton, it is foolish."

"Certainly, Your Majesty."

"You have my permission to approximate the time by half a minute, if it will save me a further line of dialogue with you."

"Yes, Your Majesty."

"Mr. Jenkins," she said, "we are using four rooms this evening: this one, the State Dining Room, the Music Room, and the Ballroom. We will also walk down the East Gallery together, the King of Portugal and I. Will I be in any danger?"

"There are already dozens of constables from the yard around the perimeter of the palace, ma'am."

"You think this thief means to mingle with the crowds?"

"Yes, Your Majesty."

She was still looking out through the window. "What does he hope to steal?"

"We don't know, Your Majesty. There are no doubt a great many objects of value here."

She smiled again, as if acknowledging a certain dry wit to be found in such a trifling assessment of her possessions. "Yes, a few. Would he have gotten in, were all these constables not at their posts, Mr. Jenkins?"

"I cannot say, ma'am."

"Yet I insist."

"Then yes, ma'am, I believe he would have."

"Do you agree, Mr. Lenox?"

"I do, Your Majesty."

She looked back at them and inclined her head imperceptibly. "Then I thank you. Shackleton, let me know when he is caught, unless I am speaking to the King himself."

"Yes, ma'am."

"Good evening, gentlemen," she said, and, the dogs responding to some invisible tether they must have felt pulling them toward her—one that Lenox felt, too, and that he could see Dallington felt, Shackleton, Jenkins, every one of her subjects—she left.

There was a moment's silence. "She is very calm," said Jenkins at last.

"There is little enough that can surprise her after all this time," Shackleton responded. "At any rate you know her famous quotation. 'Great events make me quiet and calm—it is only trifles that irritate my nerves.'"

"One does feel—well, something," said Dallington.

Indeed there was electricity still hovering in the air of the room, or perhaps being communicated between the four men, including Shackleton, who must have seen her every day. "She was uncommonly obliging," said Lenox.

"Yes, I thought so," said Jenkins.

This was by her own standards, of course. In most people her behavior would have seemed inexcusably haughty, but such haughtiness, Lenox reflected, contained some measure of self-protection. He thought of the black crepe she still wore upon her shoulders, and then of the inexhaustible line of people who wished a word with her, a moment, beginning with the King of Portugal.

As in every occasion of life, Shakespeare had said it best. "I would not be a queen," he had written in *Henry the Eighth*, "for all the world."

CHAPTER THIRTY-EIGHT

The next night Lenox and Dallington sat in a carriage outside the bright palace, both full of nervous energy. The night before nothing had happened. It must be tonight, they agreed. It was ten, and the party—this one given for a retiring member of the Queen's retinue, an ancient woman called Lady Monmouth—was approaching its busiest moments. Now would be the time for the thief to strike. The men of Scotland Yard, as well as the Queen's own guards, had melted into the crowd, or attempted to, to give the thief the illusion that he was unwatched.

"Yet how could he obtain access to the palace?" Dallington asked moodily, lowering his head to peer through the window. "It is guarded on three sides, and on the fourth there is a high wall."

"That is his best chance," said Lenox.

"But it would be impossible to scale."

Lenox shrugged. "Whenever I have a moment of doubt I consider the key."

"The key?"

"How did you find the block of wax—opened or closed?"

"Opened in half. Why?"

"Whoever killed Wintering must have taken the key from the block. He had no time to do anything else, but he took the key."

The Yard had taken the wax impression and made a key from it, then tested it. As Lenox and Dallington had suspected, it belonged to a window on the lower level of the palace's east side—not far, in fact, from the East Gallery, and for that matter from the State Dining Room, where Lady Monmouth was at that moment being honored.

"Perhaps he has been scared off, because he killed Wintering, this person," said Dallington.

"I don't think so. We've kept Wintering's name out of the papers. All of the extra men on duty here are discreet, in plainclothes. Besides, the Queen is leaving for Balmoral—every item of value in the palace will go into a safe immediately."

"Bar the pictures."

"Which could not be resold with any ease," said Lenox. They had consulted with several members of the palace's staff, all of whom agreed that one of the decorations only put out while the Queen was resident—diamond-encrusted clocks, ancient royal artifacts, jeweled decanters—was the most likely target.

"I don't know why he would come," said Dallington dispiritedly.

"I think he will."

Two hours later, it was the younger detective's pessimism that looked more prophetic. Shackleton and Jenkins, who were both inside the palace, had promised to fetch Lenox and Dallington immediately should an intruder enter the palace, or any guest—for this third man might have obtained an invitation, for all they knew—be seen to snatch at one of the Queen's possessions.

They had occupied the time in reading about Wintering. Though none of his neighbors knew him—or had even heard the shot—the Yard had still managed to put together an impressively thorough dossier on the dead man.

Wintering was the scion of an impoverished but extremely ancient and distinguished family; there had been Winterings in Staffordshire at least since the Norman invasion, perhaps longer. His father, fifth son of a third son, was the curate of a small church just west of Stoke, where he lived with his wife. Leonard was their only child.

Lenox knew several curates. It was no life for a man without private means. The rector of a parish took for himself the greater tithes (traditionally

10 percent of his parishioners' income from the harvest of hay and wheat, or the sale of wood from trees) and the rector and the vicar split the lesser tithes, from the collection plate. The curate merely got a "cure," a small fee, and ended up doing most of the work of these two greater men. The curacy was where one found the true believers without a shred of social grace, and it inclined its holders toward either saintliness or bitterness. A curate bore the education and status of a gentleman, without the funds to live in a gentleman's style. There was many a stoop-backed sixty-year-old curate all across England, never able to marry on such a low income, eating only two or three hot meals a week, and then mostly of Mr. Campbell's tinned soup—and looking forward with tremendous excitement and hunger to the church supper on Sundays.

Of course, it was possible—the dossier offered no indication—that Wintering's mother had brought money into the family, but Lenox thought he discerned the beginning of Wintering's motive.

For at the age of seventeen, Wintering had gone up to Oxford, and if life in a northern curacy had seemed at all grand, Oxford, with its aristocratic disregard for money—such an easy pose to adopt when one *had* money—would have placed it in a different context. Wouldn't it have made Wintering yearn for suits from Ede's, for hats from Shipp's, for shotguns from Parson's?

After two years at Wadham, Wintering had left for London.

"Did you see this?" Lenox asked Dallington, as he came to this part of the report. "About his first job?"

Dallington looked across the carriage and smiled. "The Chepstow and Ely?"

"Yes. Sales representative to France and Ireland."

"Only for a short period," said Dallington. "Then the trail goes cold."

Lenox read on and saw that, indeed, the Board of Inland Revenue had lost track of Wintering entirely some six years before. "Hm."

"Godwin must have arranged for Wintering to get a job," said Dallington, "and then perhaps Wintering fouled his own nest. This has been his revenge."

"Why wait so long? Then, who killed Wintering?"

Dallington shrugged. "I don't know."

Wintering's residence in Dalton Mews dated back just three months. He had received no forwarded mail and offered no previous address. "I want to know what gave him the idea of robbing the palace," said Lenox.

For another hour the two men sat and traded desultory conjectures about Wintering, his motivations and history. Neither had his heart fully in the conversation; both, too often, peered out toward the palace, as if a flare might go up when the thief was caught.

At one o'clock, the final carriage having rolled away down Constitution Hill, Shackleton and Jenkins came outside. The party had concluded, they reported, without incident. Members both of Scotland Yard and of the Queen's guard would remain on duty throughout the night.

"They might as well go home," said Dallington dully. "To break into the palace without the noise and cover of a party would be tantamount to suicide. I was so sure of it, too."

Jenkins was more positive. "We scared him off, the scoundrel. I don't mind going back to good old detective work to find him, either."

"The Queen thanks you."

"Bother her thanks," said Dallington.

Shackleton, normally imperturbable, looked scandalized. "Will you withdraw that statement, sir?"

"Oh, bother you, too. We're sixty years past dueling, you know." Lenox had to conceal the look of amusement pushing its way onto his face, and then Dallington, with a change of heart, or perhaps just wishing to leave on good terms, said, "I only meant that we haven't deserved her thanks—that we ought to have done better."

Shackleton looked only slightly mollified but said, "Ah, I see. Yes."

"I apologize if it came out improperly."

The officer bowed slightly. "Not at all. Good evening, gentlemen."

It was very late, and the mood in the carriage, as they drove away from the palace, was disconsolate. Lenox had missed two important nights in Parliament. Dallington had said when the night began, only partly joking, that they were both sure of lordships. Now here they were, driving away empty-handed.

As they approached Half Moon Street, Lenox said, "Do you know who had the most to lose in this situation?"

"Who?"

"Grace Ammons."

Dallington shrugged. He knew that the Queen's secretary had lived in Paris for a while, and he had perhaps deduced that she had some unsavory past there, but he did not know the full extent of the story. "Her work?"

"And her fiancé, George Ivory. Everything in her life."

"Yes," said Dallington.

Lenox almost went on—but didn't, because the idea wasn't quite formulated in his head yet.

Still, he could not help but dwell on two facts, revolving them in his mind.

First, that as the representative in France for the Chepstow and Ely, Wintering had likely spent time in Paris when Grace Ammons was there, several years before.

Second, a single sentence: *She also lent me a small pistol to protect myself.*

CHAPTER THIRTY-NINE

When Lenox took his breakfast the next morning, it came with several letters tucked under his plate. One of them was from Hampshire.

He had forgotten writing to his old school friend Peter Hughes, who lived in his family's dilapidated castle not far from Farnborough. Once they had been very close friends indeed, and still, whenever Peter came to the capital, they had the same easy rapport they'd had when they were both fourteen, sneaking off to the shops near Harrow to buy sweets.

Leck Castle
March 26

My dear Lenox,

Are you sure you've come across Archie Godwin, and not mistaken someone else for him? He is not tall, nor fair-haired—quite the opposite, in fact. He is a member of White's, however.

The Godwins have an odd reputation in this part of the world—not so much

Archibald or Henrietta, for they keep very much to themselves, and decline nearly all social interaction—Archie barely even hunts, though he is, *ex officio*, as a Godwin, a member of the Beagles, which his great-grandfather founded. People in this part of Hampshire remember his father, Winthrop Godwin. I believe Winthrop was a cousin—who can say how distant—of William Godwin, the political philosopher, whose daughter married Shelley. Winthrop was a vicious old fellow, according to my own pater. He was always in and out of court, died some years ago. I believe very late in life he might have married again.

As for Archie—one would scarcely call him a farmer, but there is no other suitable description of him to offer. He is not an esquire in any proper sense of the word. He doesn't keep horses, other than for a handsome barouche Hetty uses now and again, doesn't take tenants (there is a great deal of money at Raburn Lodge, and the houses he might let sit empty and unused). His sister was near marriage once but it was called off, for some reason. Their mother died when they were very young. Frankly I cannot imagine him going to London at all—he cannot find the will to make it to Farnborough for a winter ball—but the whole countryside knows that he went to London a few days ago.

I fear this is unhelpful, but at least I can give you an accurate description of him, for I do see him now and then, perhaps every six months. He is very short, just above five foot I would say, and has a bald crown, with dark hair around the fringe. He has an unprepossessing face, with a bulbous nose and eyes set rather too close together, though last I saw him he was wearing spectacles. Certainly he has never been anything but gentlemanly with me in our interactions. I always sense in his manner a bit of atonement for his father's bad reputation—even apology, perhaps. It is no wonder he stays out of Farnborough, where they gossip like schoolgirls.

That is all the account I can offer for Archie Godwin. As for us, we are still struggling to keep the bones of Leck together, Frances and I, and there are many moments of worry—but as you know love and marriage are a tremendous solace, and we find great joy in each other's company still. It would make us happy indeed if you and Jane could visit. Name your date. Otherwise I will be up in September, as always, to see my lawyers and spend a week in London. I know that I will see you then—if not before—and regardless of when our next meeting may be, believe me to be,

Your very dear friend,
Peter Hughes

When he finished reading this letter Lenox felt a powerful wish to see his friend again. Leck was a beautiful place, with ancient magic in its gray walls, situated on a rise of hill just above a pristine, circular lake, and Peter, who had grown quite fat and red, was one of the funniest, gentlest people he knew. His wife, too, a gray-haired woman slightly older than he, was unusually caring and sweet.

He thought of how unpredictable life was. If Peter had decided to come live in London after he finished at Cambridge, the two men would have seen each other three or four times a week for the past twenty years. Instead their friendship consisted in this—letters, a week in September, and the abiding memories of a daily closeness that was now decades in the past.

Lenox wrote his reply, sipping his coffee and relaying his news, including reports on Sophia and particularly on Edmund, whom Peter had known more slightly when they were all at school.

He still felt disappointed that they had been

wrong about the robbery at the palace the past two nights, but it was absolutely essential that he devote the day to Parliament. As soon as he had finished his letter to Peter he stuck it in the silver toast rack where he kept his most pressing ingoing and outgoing correspondence, put on a light cloak, and left.

The next six hours were long and full of quick, significant meetings; Whirral and Peligo, the two men who rumor said were paying off Graham, appeared at his office, and though he tried to discern from their attitude whether *they* thought it was possible, somehow, that they had bought either his time or his favor, he could not see it. He was closeted afterward for several hours with the party leadership. There were significant speeches to be made that night. Gladstone parceled them out like favors at the end of a party.

None to Lenox, however.

When the meeting was concluded, and men began to stand up from the long oval table and break off into twos and threes, Gladstone came over to Lenox and asked, with a kindly smile, if the younger member would walk the halls with him.

"Certainly, Prime Minister," said Lenox. It was still customary to address Gladstone by this title among members of their party, though he was out of office now. They offered the honorific with the assumption that one day he would resume his proper place in government; namely, at its summit.

They walked into the halls together. When they were alone, Gladstone said, "I looked down the benches last night and could not find you."

"I was at Buckingham, sir."

In normal situations this would have excused one's absence from any social event short of a funeral or an invasion from the heavens, but Gladstone, like Disraeli, was unusually sharp. He raised his eyebrows. "A dear friend of Lady Monmouth's, are you? I understand the dinner was only for a hundred people. I had to decline."

Lenox smiled. "Not precisely."

"Ah. Precision. It is an interesting virtue, is it not? Too much of it can lead to fastidiousness— but on the other hand an insufficiency of precision, a perpetual inexactness, can lead, I think, to the more serious degradation of *moral* inexactness, though it begin as merely a trait of laziness."

"Sir?"

Gladstone stopped at a high arched window, recessed into the wall so that it offered a stone bench for passersby. He sat down and looked out over London through the glinting glass. Though it was a bright day the Thames was unusually turbid, churning up red clay along its two pebbly strands. At its depths toward the middle of the river, however, it flowed as sleek and gray as ever.

Gladstone looked back at Charles. "Sir Edmund assures me of your sincere belief in your secretary's honesty. Unhappily, it is no longer a mere matter of exoneration. The opinion of the world is set against Mr. Graham—set firmly against him."

"The opinion of the world is an ass."

Gladstone smiled mildly. He knew that fact better than most. For many years he had visited with prostitutes, with the aim of reforming them. He had even invited them to take tea at Downing Street. His wife was always present at these meetings, yet gossip ascribed his fascination to less noble motives than he claimed. Lenox happened to believe him, but of all men he ought to have understood the impudence of quick tongues in London. There were times when the opinion of the world, as he called it, was scurrilous indeed upon the subject of William Ewart Gladstone.

"Edmund tells me as well that you have a strong personal connection with this Mr. Graham. It troubles me all the more, therefore, to tell you that either he must go—or you must. Not from Parliament, for the seat is yours, but you will return to the back benches. Mr. Graham has attained some power in these halls, Lenox, and for our purposes, however baseless the rumors, that will not do. We cannot lose ground against Disraeli. He already has our backs against the wall.

"The stain has not yet spread to you, Charles. Yes, I see your grimace. This is politics, my dear fellow, nothing else." He stood and put a hand on Lenox's upper arm. "Let me know when it is done, and we will be delighted to have you speak again."

CHAPTER FORTY

It was impossible for Lenox to put his finger on what bothered him so much about the case— about Wintering's death, about this third man Whitstable had seen with Godwin and Wintering, about Grace Ammons, about the whole bloody mess.

He spent his evening thinking about it. Lady Jane was out upon the errands of the season, fluttering around the girls who were newly out, fixing their hair and dresses, consoling and congratulating their mothers. Lenox ought to have been with her, but he had begged off it. Something in his face must have told his wife it wasn't worth attempting to persuade him to come.

He gave the servants the night off and ordered supper in from the chophouse down Hampden Lane. He poured himself a strong whisky and soda and pictured the front benches that evening, without him; pictured the cold body of Wintering in the cellar of Scotland Yard; pictured the Queen's servants packing for Balmoral. It was a good evening, cool and remorseless, for self-pity.

After he ate he felt exhausted. He went over to the soft armchair by the fire where he liked to read and picked up the *Telegraph*, casting his eyes over the crime notices for London. There had been a stabbing in Bethnal Green, a fire in Bermondsey, a straightforward murder in Chelsea—the husband had already confessed to killing the wife. In Kensington that same paradoxical homeless man was still missing. Someone had cut loose all the horses in southwest Battersea. As he read these notices his eyes grew heavy, and soon he could feel, with some barely conscious part of his mind, his hands descending heavily into his lap, the newspaper softening down with them, and then he was unconscious.

He woke up with no particular sense of urgency, only a pleasant warmth, until he realized, with a start, that all of his deductions and suspicions had woven together in his mind.

He had it.

It was the newspaper that had finally given him this comprehension. He understood the whole thing now, he thought—or at least the who, the how, the when. The why was murkier.

He bolted out of his chair and to his desk, yelling for the only remaining servant in the house, Kirk, to come to his study.

"Sir?" said Kirk, looking alarmed.

"Telegram this around to Jenkins and call my carriage out."

"You have given all the stable—"

"Christ, call me a cab then."

The telegram he had written said:

> Must return tonight STOP Queen in danger STOP Dllngtn and I will be in same place as last two nights STOP URGENT

It would bring Jenkins. It had to. He sprinted down the steps of the house and into a cab, which he directed to Half Moon Street.

Dallington was in, fortunately. Lenox didn't even bother knocking on the door—he simply stood on the pavement and called up toward the open window. "Dallington, we have to go!"

Dallington's head popped out. "Righty-o. Down in thirty seconds."

Lenox, stepping from foot to foot, was too nervous to feel much amusement, but his friend's predictable gameness did put a brief smile on his face. When he heard footsteps on the stair, he got back into the cab and waited.

He had never felt entirely happy about the suit

they found in Godwin's wardrobe, he thought.

Dallington's tie was still only half looped around his collar as he stepped into the cab, and he was standing on the backs of his soft boots. Lenox rapped the cab's window, and they began to move. "Where are we going?" asked the young lord, bending down to fix his boots.

"Buckingham Palace."

"But there's no party tonight."

"I think we were mistaken," said Lenox, turning toward his friend. "What if Wintering's objective wasn't to rob the Queen?"

"Then what was it?"

"To harm her."

Dallington's face, never much inclined to seriousness, nevertheless now took on a look of severe concern, and the thought skimmed across Lenox's mind that his friend was a more serious royalist than he let on—more devoted to the Queen than he would have admitted. "What makes you think that?"

"The thought that has unsettled me is that the scene at Wintering's was too perfect—the dates circled in the newspaper, the wax impression carefully placed alongside it, the knife, the black cap, all of his kit so neatly laid out."

"That only means he was thorough."

"You saw his rooms—tobacco spilling, bed unmade, nothing put away. He didn't seem so orderly to me."

Dallington shrugged. "It hardly seems con-clusive."

"No. Only suggestive, but think—would he really need to have circled those dates in the newspaper? In his position I would have committed them to memory."

In this particular part of the West End nearly every house was busy and full, roused from the dormancy of winter by the season. The exception was Buckingham Palace, apparently. As they approached it along Constitution Hill, the flag was still high, indicating that the Queen was in residence, but all of the gas lamps lining the front gates were unlit and the interior was dark.

By some kind of magic Jenkins had reached the palace before Lenox and Dallington. He ran up to their cab when it arrived. "What the devil is this about, Lenox?" he demanded.

"I think they're coming back tonight."

"They?"

"He, I should say—the third man."

"And why do you think that?"

Now Shackleton was bearing down on their small group, his face irate. "Gentlemen, what is the meaning of this?"

Lenox explained again that he thought Wintering's rooms had been used by the murderer to misdirect them—but as he spoke, he saw three faces fill first with doubt, then with outright dismay.

"That is all?" asked Jenkins.

"No. That is far from all," said Lenox.

"Then tell us what you think."

Not wanting to look foolish—he had begun to doubt himself, very nearly—Lenox said only, "You'll see. Shackleton, if I'm not mistaken, this is the south end of the palace, and the Queen's rooms are on the north end?"

"Yes."

Dallington added, "The rooms of state—the East Gallery, for instance—are in between, along the west side of the palace."

"We have two men waiting by the window for the key of which you found the wax mold."

Lenox shook his head. "I think that mold was a blind, like the circled dates in the court circular in the *Times*. I think Wintering took a second mold while he was in the palace. That was why he had to come back for a second party—one in the garden, around the north end. The whole thing has been exquisitely planned from the start, Jenkins. Is the Queen guarded?"

"Of course. Always."

Lenox waved a hand. "No, I mean, are there still extra guards attending her?"

"Not from the Yard any longer."

Shackleton shook his head. "Two outside that window, just in case, and half her usual compliment in the palace. Many of us go ahead to Balmoral, to secure it."

Lenox looked at Jenkins. "He knew that."

"Who?" asked Jenkins, his voice full of frustration.

Lenox was about to explain—the suit, the newspaper, even the letter he had received that morning—when there was a crack of gunfire from the palace.

All of the blood drained from Shackleton's face. Without a word, he turned and began to sprint the hundred yards back to the palace.

Lenox, Dallington, and Jenkins hesitated for a moment and then ran after him.

The place was in chaos. A servant in a nightcap had woken and was stumbling down the hall with a candle; the porters had abandoned their stations to help the Queen; there were cries from distant rooms. Shackleton wended his way through the byzantine corridors with expert speed. They were just barely able to track him.

Leaping up the marble steps of the private residence three at a time, he called out, "Your Majesty!"

When they reached the top of the stairs—even in this hurry Lenox noticed how different it looked here than in the official rooms, more subdued, if no less richly outfitted—the Queen was standing there.

"He missed," she said and then added, "So did all of you, apparently."

Lenox felt sick with failure. "Where is he, ma'am?"

"My guards fell upon him. He will be bruised in the morning, I expect."

This was Victoria's famous calm, then. "You are sure you're not injured, Your Majesty?"

She gave them a small smile—but Lenox saw in her eyes fear, shock, something she was attempting to master, the old lessons of a youth dedicated to the exigencies of self-restraint. "I was at my desk. He entered the room and told me to raise my arms. I threw a crystal glass at him and yelled for my maid, and he fired his pistol wildly, the stupid fool. Shackleton, tell them to find Hannah and send her up to me. I will be in the Pink Study."

"Ma'am."

If only Albert were still alive, Lenox thought. Or if only the Queen's children didn't all live in Germany, sent out upon the transnational chores of royalty.

There was a hoarse shout two rooms away. Shackleton pulled a guard aside and told him to find Hannah. Then he gestured for the three men to follow him.

The assassin was being held in a small closet covered, rather absurdly in the circumstances, with murals of laughing angels, playing in a woodland. Fragonard, Lenox would have guessed. Another treasure—though too saccharine for his tastes.

It was dark in the room, and the three guards

turned with angry faces, until they saw that it was their superior officer.

"Is he secured?" said Shackleton.

"A sight beyond his liking," said one of the men, with grim satisfaction.

"Who is it?" said Dallington. "Ivory?"

"No," said Lenox and lit a lamp so that they all might see more clearly. "Gentlemen, unless I am much mistaken, this fellow is Mr. Archibald Godwin."

CHAPTER FORTY-ONE

The list of men who had tried to kill Her Majesty Victoria, by the Grace of God, of the United Kingdom of Great Britain and Ireland Queen, Defender of the Faith, Empress of India, was long, varied, and ignoble. The assassination attempts that had made the news occurred in 1840, 1849, 1850, and 1872—and most notably in 1842. During that year, when she was only twenty-three years old, a man shot at her carriage; the next day, the Queen insisted on riding the same route, in hopes that he would attempt it again. He did. He was a fellow named John Francis, and had been immediately arrested and charged with treason. In the end he had escaped the gallows and been transported to the colonies for life.

Later in the same year, 1842, a different madman had tried to kill Victoria, but his pistol was improperly loaded. He had received eighteen months in jail.

It took Lenox's breath away to think of that leniency, after what he had seen this evening.

On his person Godwin had a pistol, a sixpence, a key, and a shred of paper that said, in a firm, slanting hand, *We forgive; we cannot forget.* It was unsigned. He wore a beautifully tailored suit. Lenox would have bet sixpence that it came from Ede and Ravenscroft. It bore no resemblance to the tattered, odorous garment Godwin had left behind in the Graves Hotel—and that was where Lenox's train of thought had started.

He began his explanation instead with the nose.

"Do you remember seeing the body at the Graves?" Lenox asked Dallington. "Its features?"

Dallington nodded seriously. "Of course."

They were sitting in a jail cell at the Tower of London. In the normal course of events Jenkins would have taken Godwin to Scotland Yard, but the Tower, a castle dating from the twelfth century, was where the Queen's own prisoners went, a living relic of the Middle Ages. It was where the two little princes had died, where Henry the Sixth was murdered, where Anne Boleyn was imprisoned and executed. The whole history of England's monarchy could have been told by these yellowing walls, moated around with an empty gravel expanse, guarded by silent, dark-faced men. It was a solemn feeling that

Lenox had as he looked across the table at Godwin.

With Lenox were Jenkins and Shackleton; standing by the door was one of the Queen's guards. Godwin was, as had been reported, a short, fat person, with a face of dreamy innocence and a fringe of brown hair. The only evidence of his evening's activity was a rapidly swelling cut near his left eye and a matching one upon his upper lip.

His nose was fat.

"I had a letter from my friend Peter Hughes this morning," said Lenox, "in which he described Mr. Godwin. One of the details he provided was that Godwin had a bulbous nose. Yet the corpse at the Grave Hotel had a *thin* nose—I remember that specifically, and remarked upon it at the time, when we were looking at the body."

Dallington and Jenkins looked at the prisoner. "Mr. Godwin, who was it?" asked Jenkins.

The prisoner gave no indication that he heard the question, but Lenox thought he knew. "That suit of clothes you left behind in the wardrobe of your room at the Graves—I don't think it belonged to a farmer, as we originally speculated. I think it belonged to a homeless man. A vagrant. You found one who looked adequately similar to you, in shape and size, and somehow enticed him up to your room at the hotel. Was it with the offer of a new suit? A new suit and a hot meal?"

"A homeless man?" asked Shackleton curiously.

Lenox told them about the note in the crime column, during the last week, about the vagrant missing from the area near Gloucester Road—near the Graves.

"I don't know how they were sure he was missing," said Dallington. "Mightn't he have found another bench?"

"Yes, I wondered the same thing."

Jenkins shook his head. "These bobbies know their streets amazingly well—every brick, every face, every shop window. If an itinerant always slept upon a certain grate, or begged at a certain corner, his absence would be noticeable. Perhaps even alarming. Some of them are figures of quite popular local character."

Godwin still hadn't spoken, but a certain hardness in his eyes, or perhaps around his mouth, told Lenox that this conjecture was correct. "We wondered why the body at the Graves—your body, we thought—had been so thoroughly stripped. Hat, watch, everything in the pockets. It could not have been for the purpose of forestalling identification, since of course the body was lying across the threshold of your room, and looked like you. Those things were gone for a very simple reason, I suppose: because you needed them."

Godwin said nothing. Jenkins added, "The overnight bag the bellboy carried upstairs for you upon your arrival was gone, too, as I recall."

Lenox smiled faintly. "The suit the dead man wore—was it one of the suits that Wintering bought at Ede and Ravenscroft? We should have checked the sizes in which he ordered them. We would have found, I expect, that the tall fellow I met in Gilbert's was ordering clothes of a very different measurement than their customer Mr. Godwin usually did."

Dallington, frowning, said, "And Wintering? Where does Wintering enter into the picture? He was there that morning."

Shackleton banged the table with his palm. "Never mind this nonsense! Why were you trying to kill the Queen, you bastard?"

Godwin's interrogators let a moment pass, in case their subject chose to answer this angry query. When he didn't, Lenox said, "I'm guessing the two men with whom Whitstable saw you out upon Gloucester Road were Wintering and the homeless man."

"Whitstable," muttered Godwin.

It was the first word he had spoken. "You used him to place Wintering at the scene of your 'murder,' correct? Wintering thought he was still your accomplice at that stage. I don't know when he realized he was only your pawn."

Recognition dawned in Dallington's eyes. "Ah. I see it now. Somehow you convinced Wintering to impersonate you—then, when you died, the suspicion would fall upon him."

"What I don't understand," said Jenkins, "is why he needed an accomplice at all."

Lenox shrugged. "He needed someone to lay the groundwork—to meet with Grace Ammons, to buy suits and guns and hats, to go to Buckingham Palace. He couldn't do all that from Hampshire, and anyhow I'm sure he preferred to lurk in the background. It was intelligent. We spent days chasing a tall, fair-haired man around London, never suspecting that the real threat came from a different source entirely."

"But why kill anybody?" asked Shackleton. "Simply to frame Wintering?"

"Yes," said Lenox. "Why did you need so badly to be found dead, Godwin?"

The murderer—the would-be assassin—looked at them strangely and then said, with sudden decision, "What time is it?"

Lenox looked at his watch. "It's nearly midnight."

Godwin again stared at them and then, somehow, seemed to soften, relent. "Yes, I framed Wintering, the poor fool. He was always a piggy little fellow. His mother starved herself, gathered rope at that shambles of a curacy, so that he could play the tassel cap at Wadham. Back then I found him rather amusing. It was funny to order an expensive drink on his round and watch him pretend not to sweat out the arrival of the bill.

"Nobody wanted anything to do with either of us. I have my own ways, and Wintering . . . he was raised a gentleman, but he tried too hard to please other people. He was never comfortable in his own skin. One could always play upon his greed. I told him I had hatched a plan to rob Buckingham. He didn't believe me at first, because I've always had a great deal of money, but I persuaded him it was gone. And then of course my people have a grudge against the Queen."

Something blazed for an instant in Godwin's eyes. "What for?" asked Lenox.

Godwin was silent for a long time, perhaps a minute, staring into the damp upper corner of the stone room. Then he said, lightly, "Oh, no reason."

"Why did he use your name?" asked Jenkins.

"I told him to order himself suits, clothes, anything he liked—to use my name. I wanted him to for my own purposes, as you have guessed."

"It was an error to give it to me at Gilbert's," said Lenox.

Godwin shrugged. "I suppose he had become habituated to the alias, and no doubt he believed you to be a simple lovestruck fellow. Not a private detective. It was an error, to be sure—I wonder whether I would be here if he had told you that his name was Jones or Robinson. And yet here I am."

There was something sanguine, something troublingly calm, in Godwin's face as he delivered this statement, and suddenly Lenox wondered. Why was he being so forthright, so helpful? Why did he seem unperturbed by his predicament?

Then the answer came to him: It wasn't over. He felt a lurch of panic. "Shackleton, where is the Queen?" he asked.

"In her bedchamber, I hope, safe."

"Who is with her?"

"Her guards."

"You must go back—you must take her from the palace. There's going to be another attempt."

Shackleton frowned, half-standing. "By whom?"

"Hetty Godwin. Jenkins, someone must go and arrest her."

Suddenly there was a crack like the report of the pistol. It was Godwin's hand, slamming down on the table. "No!" he said. His face was transformed, hideous with fury.

"Jenkins, Shackleton, go—as quickly as you can, for the love of God, go."

CHAPTER FORTY-TWO

The two men flew from the room, as behind them Lenox, Dallington, and Shackleton's subordinate restrained Godwin—a small and fat man, but strengthened all out of proportion to his physique by emotion—from pursuing them. When at last Godwin was exhausted by his struggles they shoved him unceremoniously back into his chair. Lenox stood back, breathing heavily, as Dallington, still recovering, slumped into one of the other chairs. The palace guard kept his head better. He knocked at the door, and the keeper of the cells, a fellow named Matthew Almond, came to see him.

"Shackles," was all the palace guard said. He, too, was rather panting.

Almond nodded and left. Godwin was giving his captors a look of sheer malevolent hatred. "She'll get there in time," he said at last.

"What does that mean?" asked Lenox.

Then, as if remembering himself, Godwin modulated his voice and said, "She'll get there, back to Hampshire, in time that you'll miss her. They'll miss her. Then you'll look pretty foolish."

In his face Lenox saw that this was an effort not of weeks or months that Godwin had made, but of years, perhaps decades.

My people have a grudge against the Queen . . .

"What time was your sister supposed to follow in your footsteps?" Lenox asked. "Did Wintering take a third wax impression, at a different window?"

"We cannot leave the keys in the windows for garden parties any longer," muttered the palace guard, who seemed to take it all as a personal affront. "They'll have to roast or freeze by their own lights, the buggers."

"What made you suspect Hetty Godwin?" asked Dallington.

"Godwin's behavior in this past hour has been too strange for my liking—silence, followed by volubility. Then when he asked me the time . . . I didn't think anything of it at first, but it was followed by his change in attitude. It made me wonder if perhaps he was stalling."

"The only reason to stall would be to let someone else get on with the job," said Dallington.

Lenox nodded. "As soon as that occurred to me, I started thinking about the people involved. Then I remembered the body."

"What, Wintering's?"

"No. At the Graves Hotel."

"The homeless man."

Lenox shrugged. "That's only a theory, for Mr. Godwin here to affirm or reject—but that body, yes. You'll recall that the corpse had a single small bullet hole at the temple. It was not enough to interfere with the person's facial features."

Dallington snapped his fingers. "You clever fellow, Lenox. She identified the body."

The older man smiled, feeling a little surge of pride. It was quickly poisoned by the memory of the Queen telling them they had failed—and now the possibility that they had failed her again. "Yes, she went with Jenkins and positively said it was her brother on the slab. It strains credulity to think she could make an honest mistake in identifying her nearest relation, the person with whom she spent every day of her life at Raburn Lodge."

Dallington turned to Godwin. "What was the plan? If the news hadn't emerged by midnight that the Queen was dead, she was to follow you into the palace?"

Godwin didn't speak. "It was cunning," Lenox said. "At every step it was cunning."

Dallington was leaning back in his chair, arms crossed, studying the floor. At last he said, "She seemed cool, during that first meeting. Perhaps too cool."

"She knew her brother wasn't dead." There was a moment of silence, and then Lenox thought of something else. "Do you recall the one moment when she seemed surprised? When we said that Godwin had been seen in a group, out upon Gloucester Road. By Whitstable. She asked who the third man was. She seemed nonplussed, actually nonplussed. We weren't supposed to hear about anything other than Godwin and Wintering asking Whitstable for that penknife."

They asked Godwin a few more questions, receiving only blank stares. Almond came in and shackled the prisoner, using long medieval-style chains that extended from his ankles to a steel ring bolted into the wall. When the small drama of their binding was concluded, the whole room fell into a morose, tense silence. Three of the men were saying quiet prayers for the Queen; one, for his sister.

A few minutes later Dallington added another piece to the puzzle. "It's been troubling me that they didn't remember the name Godwin at Cyril's, too," he said abruptly.

"The restaurant?"

"Yes. If Wintering ate there every night, someone would have had some recollection of him. Now I remember that it was Hetty Godwin who gave us that information."

"But why?" said Lenox.

They both glanced at Godwin. Dallington shrugged. "She needed a compelling reason that Godwin would have come to London. He was corresponding with his tailors and his hatmakers and his gunmakers from Hampshire. Why would he have come to London?"

"True," said Lenox. "It also planted the idea in our heads that he was going to confront the tall, fair-haired gentleman, the impostor. We didn't look far when his body turned up."

"It's true. And then our whole sense of Godwin was confirmed by her, established in part by her—retiring, nervous, shy. She played that up, I suppose. For herself, too."

"Yes. She said she wished to retire at six, or whatever absurdly early time it was."

Lenox thought of Henrietta Godwin's determined, gaunt face. It was possible, he supposed, that it had been she who pulled the trigger at Wintering's apartment. They ought to have kept better track of her while she was in London.

But a woman! He ought to have known by now that women were capable of murder. Just think of Ludo Starling's wife. Still, somehow there was always a lag in his mind, a hesitation at the idea. It was a flaw of his detective's brain.

The next hour passed with excruciating slowness. Every so often one of the two men—and after a while the third, too—would throw out some question at the prisoner, perhaps taunting, perhaps conciliatory. There was never a response. Both sides had played out their strategy. All that remained to be seen was who would win—and when Lenox, intermittently, remembered the stakes, the life of the Queen, he would almost gasp, and then say a silent prayer.

"You will hang for this, you know," Lenox quietly told Godwin at one point.

"I hope not."

At length Almond the cell keeper came in with a pot of tea for them and water and a crust of bread for Godwin, who ignored the provisions. Almond took a message from Lenox for Lady Jane. The palace guard perked up considerably under the influence of the hot tea, and Dallington and Lenox, who had declined, changed their mind. Dallington looked as if he would rather have a glass of whisky, so etched was his face was with anxiety.

Just after a quarter past one, Almond came in. "DCI Jenkins has returned, gentlemen," he said.

Lenox turned automatically toward Godwin, who greeted this news with a look of wild hope. "What's happened?" asked the prisoner.

Almond smiled faintly. "The Queen sends her regards."

A powerful emotion—more than relief, closer to love—flooded through Lenox, corporeal. Thank God. He turned and saw that Dallington was experiencing the same thing.

Godwin looked stricken.

Jenkins and Shackleton were out in the small office Almond kept. A boy of fourteen or fifteen was there, too. "My son," said Almond.

"What happened?" asked Dallington.

"We took her as she was leaving her hotel. She had a bag with a pistol, a key, a rope . . . everything she needed. She kicked up every kind of wrath when we arrested her, and went for the pistol."

"And the Queen?"

"She has started early for Balmoral," said Shackleton. "We deemed it safer, until we can be sure nobody else will crawl out of the woodwork. The castle there is extremely isolated. Easier to defend."

Lenox shook his head. "Hetty was the last gambit, I think. Where is she, Jenkins?"

Almond answered. "In her own cell in a different part of the Tower."

"We will keep them separated," said Jenkins.

"Of course," murmured Dallington.

There was a pause. On the desk was a plate of biscuits, and Shackleton and Almond's son reached for the last chocolate one at the same time. Almond's son won the race—offered it to Shackleton—was politely rejected. There was a funny feeling in the little office: The Queen had been saved, just like the song said, and the capital was ignorant of her salvation. The brother and sister were secured. It felt a strange night in London.

Almond was a large, bright-eyed fellow, with a bushy black and gray mustache. He reached into his pocket. "I don't generally drink on the job, gentlemen, but in this flask there is a quantity of whisky, which I propose we take turns in. To the Queen," he said and took a sip.

"To the Queen," said Shackleton, who was next in the half-circle and took a solemn sip, too.

Dallington, his face shadowed in the shifting dim lamplight, took it next. "To the Queen."

Then Jenkins, then Almond's son. Then finally Lenox. "To the Queen."

CHAPTER FORTY-THREE

Neither of the Godwins would talk. Each of the detectives—Dallington, Lenox, Jenkins—shuttled back and forth between Henrietta and Archibald Godwin, trying to cajole them first into confession, then into conversation, and finally into any speech at all. Both were as silent and watchful as animals.

Henrietta seemed to Lenox the more likely to break down, because it was plain that she became upset when he mentioned the possibility that Archie might end at the gallows. Even after they learned this, making her offers and promises to the contrary, however, she remained stubbornly quiet. The two had made a plan, evidently, in the event that both were caught.

At last Jenkins had to let them see their solicitor. He could prevent them seeing each other—though there was no way of preventing them from communicating through this third party. He was an acute white-haired man with owl-like eyes, taciturn, no friendliness in his manner at all; immediately he called in a barrister from the Inner Temple to consult upon the case. Soon thereafter Jenkins told Lenox and Dallington, with regret, that they would no longer have access to the prisoners.

"If it's a consolation, they aren't talking anyway," said Jenkins.

Dallington shook his head. "We know the facts. I'd like to know the story."

"The story's in Hampshire, if we want badly enough to find it," said Lenox. "For my part I cannot go. There is too much to occupy me in Parliament, a fearful amount."

Dallington nodded. "I'll go, then."

Lenox had hoped Dallington would say that. "Good. You must consult with my friend Peter Hughes there before you begin your investigation. He lives not ten miles off of Raburn Lodge, and he knows that county as well as anyone."

"Excellent."

They were standing in Scotland Yard, a Friday morning; Jenkins was on his way now to see the Godwins again. It would be some time until the trial. The crown's best hope of a conviction in the murder of Wintering was a confession, obviously—there were numerous witnesses to his attempted assault upon the Queen—and though the hopes of one seemed faint, Jenkins was going to keep trying. The papers were obsessed with the affluent, wellborn pair; the reports they received (some, perhaps, from Jenkins himself) were muddled and contradictory, but that made no alteration in the ardor of their interest.

After they said good-bye to Jenkins, Lenox and

Dallington walked back toward Hampden Lane, discussing it all.

"By God, she was cool, wasn't she?" said Dallington. "I mean Victoria. Standing at the top of the stairs, making little jokes."

"Her reproof has stayed with me."

The young lord waved a hand. "There is almost always an element of luck in these things, or mischance. The only reason I have any success is that it's so damned difficult to commit a crime without leaving evidence of yourself, or without something going wrong. I could almost sympathize with Godwin. It must be maddening."

Lenox smiled. "Something maddened him long before this."

"Yes, true." They walked a few paces. It was a warm day, and London looked leafy, prosperous, peaceable. "Do you know what's been on my mind?"

"What?"

"Why was Wintering in Gilbert's that day at all? It couldn't have been a coincidence."

"I've been thinking about it, too," said Lenox. "I rather think it was more to do with Grace Ammons than Archibald Godwin."

"How do you mean?"

Lenox shrugged. "She is a beautiful woman. I wonder if he fell under her spell."

"And began to follow her?"

Lenox shook his head. "No. I would hazard that

311

he had an enormous amount of information about Grace Ammons, her habits, her residence, her circle of acquaintance. He would have known about her monthly visit to Ivory's mother."

"What makes you say so?"

"I am more convinced with every moment that passes that this attempt at assassination was years in the planning. The care that went into every step of it was remarkable."

"Or perhaps he simply followed her."

Lenox laughed. "Yes, I suppose so."

They arrived at Lenox's house. Waiting on the steps there was a guest: Alfred Anixter, Miss Strickland's operative.

"Mr. Lenox, Lord John," he said, standing up and taking off his cap.

"What are you doing here?" asked Lenox.

"I wanted a word. Miss Strickland is still acting on behalf of Grace Ammons, and will be until the case is resolved to her satisfaction."

"If she's still charging Miss Ammons a pound a day and expenses, she ought to be taken to court," said Dallington.

Anixter shook his head. "No. When the Godwins were arrested we stopped charging Miss Ammons, but Miss Strickland likes to do a thorough job."

"What does she wish to ask us?"

Anixter had a whole host of questions about the night that Archibald Godwin had attempted to kill the Queen, about Leonard Wintering, about the homeless man who had died in Godwin's stead at the Graves Hotel. (A constable from the homeless man's street had gone to the morgue to confirm that it was he, Joseph Thayer, a vagrant, at one period a blacksmith until an accident crippled his right hand, at which time he turned to drink, gradually losing his purchase in civilized society. The constable had described him as a gentle soul, well enough liked on the Gloucester Road. His had been a life like any other's, of course, his flesh as alive as the Duke of Omnium's—it was a sentimental view, but one the papers had adopted, and with which Lenox, though a relativist, tended to agree.) Anixter read these questions from a neatly written list he pulled out of his pocket.

When he had concluded, Lenox said, "I would be delighted to answer these questions for Miss Strickland in person."

Anixter shook his head. "I'm the point of contact on the Ammons case."

"Where are her offices? In High Holborn, I believe? I would be happy to call on her there."

"She doesn't work out of the office," said Anixter quickly. "We meet new clients there, and if their cases are of sufficient interest they meet Miss Strickland elsewhere."

Lenox smiled wryly. "Is that right?" he asked. "Well, if she would like to speak to us in person, please get in touch. Until then."

Anixter watched both men touch their hats and then, his face darkening, turned on his heel. "I would like to help Miss Ammons," said Dallington as Anixter stalked away.

"So would I. Quick, let's follow him."

"Who, Anixter?"

"Yes. Or Miss Strickland, as he chooses to be called."

"Lenox, you reprobate. I've never been fonder of you." Dallington pointed up the street. "He's getting into a hansom."

"Then we'll hail one, too."

They followed Anixter's cab through Mayfair, down Brook Street, then turning into Davies Street and passing Berkeley Square, before finally arriving, twelve minutes later by Lenox's watch, at a small, ugly brick house in Hay's Mews. It was a fashionable address.

Anixter left the cab—Lenox had directed the driver to keep going when the cab they were following stopped, so they passed him—and went into the house. At the end of the street Dallington and Lenox got out.

"What's our plan?" asked Dallington. He looked uncommonly happy to be engaged in this kind of subterfuge, the sprightly white carnation in his buttonhole matching his mood. "Do we climb in through a window? Jimmy open the cellar and sneak upstairs?"

"I think we should knock on the front door."

"Cunning."

The house was only two stories high, small though well maintained. Was it Anixter's own house? Lenox knocked on the door.

A housekeeper appeared. "May I help you, gentlemen?" she asked.

"We are here to see your mistress," said Dallington, in a voice he occasionally summoned— a domineering voice, to the manner born. He held out a card for her to take. "Please tell her Lord John Dallington and Mr. Charles Lenox have arrived. We will wait in her sitting room."

The housekeeper, face doubtful until she heard the word "Lord," said, "She's just here—she'll want to see you straightaway, I know, m'lud."

The house was bright and cheerful, with small French paintings lining the front hall. They came into a sun-filled sitting room. Anixter was upon a sofa there, speaking to Miss Strickland. She turned a sly, pale, beautiful face up to them in surprise—the face of the woman who was still being called Thomas McConnell's mistress all over London: Polly Buchanan.

CHAPTER FORTY-FOUR

"Miss Strickland?" inquired Dallington innocently.

She paused for a moment and then burst into laughter. "An excellent attempt, Lord John," she said. "We've only been in the same room thirty or forty times, after all."

Dallington smiled, too, beaten. "Are you really she?"

"The very same. Please, come sit. Letitia, now that you've made the catastrophic error of admitting these two gentlemen without my permission, you may as well bring them a cup of tea. Mr. Lenox, please, you sit, too."

Lenox came to the sofa, his gloves in one hand, his face no doubt betraying his consternation. "Are you really Miss Strickland?" he asked.

"Did you think it was Anixter here?" asked Polly Buchanan in turn.

Lenox smiled. "I admit that I thought the name was a blind, used by some ex-member of the Yard looking to attract women as clients. If there was a Miss Strickland at all I assumed she would be . . . I don't quite know. An actress, perhaps."

"No, it was my idea—it's been my money, my advertisements. I couldn't use my own name, of course. It is scarcely respectable in you two gentlemen to pursue a career in detection, but it would be ruinous for a woman."

All at once Lenox realized what had been happening in Hyde Park. "You asked Thomas McConnell to work for you," he said.

For the first time Polly's charming face lost its lightness. "He told you that?"

"No," said Lenox.

"You will grow more accustomed to these sudden insights if you spend time with Lenox," said Dallington.

"I did ask Dr. McConnell to come work for the agency," said Polly. "There are very few men in London with an aptitude for criminal medicine, and certainly he is one of their number. He declined, though he put me in the way of a gentleman in Fulham of whom I have high hopes. I mean to modernize this business of yours, you know."

Dallington looked delighted at the news. "Yes, we heard about the charcoal portraits. In fact, we were full of admiration for everything you did on Miss Ammons's behalf, before we knew who you were. Now we're forced to withdraw that admiration, I'm sorry to say. Hard cheese."

Dallington could smile if he liked; Lenox could not. He felt as if, without her knowledge, he had wronged Polly Buchanan. He also felt irritated. "There are no successful female detectives of whom I'm aware."

"We can deliver milk, and for that matter babies," said Polly. Tea came in, and with all the appropriate and feminine grace of her birth, she began to serve it to them, her elegance in stark contrast to Anixter's silent, glowering East End bulk. "There aren't two more difficult tasks than that, physically. As for brains—I prefer Miss Gaskell or Mrs. Humphrey Ward to any of your male novelists. Well, possibly excepting Trollope. I have a terrible weakness for Planty Pall."

"Not Burgo?" asked Dallington, feigning disappointment.

She laughed. "I am too much Burgo myself. And with Alfred such a Glencora, too."

It was this kind of talk—rather daring, even flirtatious—that had earned Polly her reputation. She had a spark of originality in her voice and mien. Lenox had learned when he ran for Parliament that people didn't like one to do anything *new*—they sat upon their lily pads, and knew which lily pad belonged to everyone else, and preferred no change. It made them uneasy, perhaps envious. Polly was always doing something new. Here was an example. People hated her for it.

Once the tea and biscuits had been distributed, Polly began to ask questions. She was sharp, no mistake about that, and as she drew more and more information about the Godwins out of them—determining to her own satisfaction, finally, that Grace Ammons was in all likelihood out of harm's way—Lenox half-forgot that she was such an unusual sort of detective. Then he thought, when his mind recalled the fact to him, why not? If Audley could maintain a practice, half-soused, why not this young woman? He worried about her physical safety—but then here was Anixter. Plainly she had solved that problem.

When her questions were concluded Lenox looked at his watch. He was due in Parliament soon for a meeting. "I hope to see you again soon, Miss Buchanan," he said, rising. "If you ever need professional advice I would be happy to offer it. Mr. Dallington can, too, of course."

He bowed slightly, a stuffy, uncertain gesture, and she inclined her head. "Thank you, Mr. Lenox."

"John, shall we be on our way?" asked Lenox.

"I might stay for another cup of tea, if you're going toward the Commons—and if it is not disagreeable to Miss Buchanan and Mr. Anixter, of course."

"Never in life," said Polly. "I have a whole raft of questions I should like to ask you about this business."

Anixter's consent was less graceful, but he nodded, stiffly. "Right."

So Lenox left his protégé there—with his own protégé, it might come to pass, albeit in a strange, distaff line.

He took his steps slowly, through Green Park, skirting near Buckingham Palace, and then down toward Whitehall. It was a long walk; on normal days he would have hailed a hansom cab, but he liked to have the time.

For the terrible day had come: He had to let Graham out of his employment.

He could have resisted his peers, the members

of his party, James Hilary, Lord Cabot, even his brother. Gladstone was a different matter. *The opinion of the world is set against Mr. Graham,* he had said, and threatened the back benches. Lenox hadn't come to Parliament to provide another sleepy vote, another desultory speech.

He reached his office twenty minutes after leaving Polly Buchanan's house. Graham and Frabbs were in deep conversation, and both looked up to greet him, briefly, before returning to the memorandum upon which they were collaborating.

Lenox's early afternoon was filled with meetings. General Bott wanted more armaments allocated to the Blues and Royals, Lord Monck bethought an alliance they might make on Ireland between the Commons and the Lords, and so on and so forth.

At last at three, Lenox had a moment to himself. "Graham," he called out to the outer office.

"Sir?" said Graham, appearing at the door.

Lenox looked at his face and saw that there were wrinkles around his secretary's eyes, a slight sallowness in his complexion. Of course, if Lenox had heard the rumors about Graham, Graham himself had heard them two days earlier. Had he remained silent out of consideration? Reticence? Guilt?

No; not guilt. That was not possible.

Lenox's mind flashed to a day that now seemed

long in the past, nine or ten years before, when Lady Jane Grey had been merely his closest friend and confidant, and when his interest in politics had been a spectator's, unburdened by the reality of daily life in Parliament.

It had been the bleakest part of February, an icy rain harrying everyone indoors toward the fireside—except for Lenox, who was out upon a case. It was a matter of burglary, one shopkeeper stealing from another. Even now he could recall the details perfectly.

Lenox had arranged that morning to meet with one of the shopkeeper's clerks in St. James's Park. Anywhere would have been better—the arcades in Piccadilly nearby, whatever public house you cared to name—but the clerk had insisted upon this plan, as being most natural.

Unfortunately the lad was late in arriving. Lenox, seated miserably upon a bench in the empty park, watching the wind whip the branches from the trees, almost left after ten minutes. Then he saw a figure approaching.

It was not the clerk but Graham—at that time still Lenox's butler. He was carrying a parcel, apparently out upon some errand of his own for the household, tucked into a warm greatcoat and protected by a large umbrella.

"Hello, sir," he said, smiling faintly, as if they were meeting in the quiet halls of their own house.

Lenox smiled, too. "I liked the idea of a walk."

"A salubrious day for it, sir."

"It's for the case, I'm afraid—the dressmakers." For it was the feud of two successful and enterprising women, in this instance, that led to the burglary. "Waiting for that dratted Jacoby."

"I'll wait with you, sir," said Graham and sat down upon the bench.

"No, you must get along home."

"I've nowhere particular to be."

Lenox had insisted, but Graham, quietly imperturbable, had remained there with him nevertheless, parcel in hand, for another twenty minutes, until at last the dressmaker's clerk, fearful for his job, skulked into the park and exchanged what information he had for a few shillings from Lenox's pocket. Then the two men together made the short walk back to Hampden Lane.

He wondered what had become of Jacoby. Or his client, for that matter, Anna Armitage. Was she still making dresses?

Recalling all this, Lenox must have remained silent for a moment longer than he intended—for Graham said, prodding him out of his reflections in a tone of minor reproof, "Was there anything urgent, sir?"

Lenox shook his head. "Sorry, sorry. Mind was elsewhere. Yes, shut the door if you would, come sit."

Graham closed the door. "Is it about your luncheon with Coleridge tomorrow, sir?" he said.

"No, no," said Lenox. "In fact, you had better cancel that. The reason that I wished to speak with you is that I've decided it's time for me to leave Parliament."

CHAPTER FORTY-FIVE

Dallington was gone all weekend. Lenox stopped into Half Moon Street on Saturday morning and Sunday afternoon, but according to Mrs. Lucas her tenant still hadn't returned. He hadn't telegrammed for Lenox or Jenkins either, which was rather surprising.

Hopefully he would be back by Monday evening. Aside from Lenox's pure curiosity, the grand dinner they were throwing for the opening of the season was then, and Dallington was scheduled to come. Lady Jane had been in a whirl from noon to night, barely managing to dart out in the evenings to the parties, where she had a quick sherbet and a quicker glance at the dresses before leaving again. It was the most significant dinner they had yet thrown; and at the last minute, not two days before they would all sit down to dine, Princess Helena, one of Queen Victoria's daughters, had sent word that she meant to come after all.

Royalty would add a tremble of glamor to the

supper, of course—some people could barely look away when Princess Helena, or Princess Louise, was in the room, or even Prince Leopold, their unfortunate-looking brother—and for that, Jane was happy. However, it meant altering half of her carefully laid plans. The seating would have to change, the order of the toasts. Still: to have the Prime Minister and the Princess in Hampden Lane on one night! It felt like a zenith, a juncture in their lives.

Certainly it was a political zenith, a fact whose irony wasn't lost on Lenox. Returning home in the early evening Friday, he had thought that perhaps he might delay the news of his decision about Parliament until after the party, but when he saw Jane he realized he didn't want to keep a secret.

They were in the small study off of their bedroom, with its wide windows looking over their small back garden. Lenox was removing his cufflinks. "My dear, I have some news that will surprise you—not make you miserable, I hope, for you must believe I'm not miserable about it."

"What is it?" she asked, face concerned.

"I'm leaving Parliament."

She looked at him for a moment and then, smiling, said, "Thank goodness for that."

"The news doesn't upset you?"

"I think it's the best thing I've heard all day. Though I did get a joke from Duch, how did it go? Never mind, though, come, sit, tell me what made you decide that."

They discussed the decision for a few minutes, though Lenox spoke mostly in broad terms. ("Oh! I've got it!" she said, interjecting at one point. "When is the moon heaviest?" "When?" "When it's *full,*" she said and waited, expectantly, for his laughter. He rolled his eyes.) For her part she was glad that all of his late nights and taxing afternoons would come to an end.

Graham had been less complaisant, earlier in the day, when he heard the decision; his face had grown wary, and almost immediately he had said, "Now is the time to push on, if anything, sir. In fact, I was going to speak with you later in the week—it is time you had a more professionally experienced secretary, as you rise up in the party. That will make the work seem less daunting."

"We'll leave at the same time," Lenox said.

Graham was silent for a moment. "I wonder if you have heard my name recently in connection with Mr. Whirral or Mr. Peligo's, sir?"

Lenox refused to place Graham under any kind of moral obligation. "Certainly, inasmuch as I have met with them, and you told me when the meetings were, and wrote my questions down for them. Not otherwise. Why?"

"No reason," said Graham.

Their cagey conversation went on for another

325

few minutes. "What will become of Frabbs?" asked Graham. "Or Markson, for that matter? He has been doing well, young as he is."

"Frabbs can go work for Edmund. Markson will have a reference. I mean to serve out my last eight months, anyhow. I will go up and see Brick to tell him face-to-face—meet with the people of Stirrington, too—next week. I wish you'd come with me."

"You had better still take the meeting with Coleridge," said Graham. "In case you change your mind."

Lenox shook his head. "I've heard he's intolerably dry. It's precisely the sort of luncheon I shan't miss after I'm gone."

There were things he would miss, as his own sudden decision gradually bore in upon him. The cut and thrust of the Commons's debates, for instance, those evenings when suddenly the somnolent chamber burst into fire with a new idea or an angry speech. He would miss the lazy comfort of the quieter sessions, too, the oak-and-leather smell of the benches there, the discreet tactical evacuations to the Members' Bar for a glass of claret. It was everything in between—the meetings, the luncheons, the patient auditing of every man's pet idea—that he would enjoy leaving behind.

After Graham left the office, Lenox returned to work. He felt rather giddy with his own impulsiveness, and as a means of subduing himself set to reading the dry blue books and constituent letters and newspaper editorials that he had set to the side, scrupulously making sure that he gave them the same attention he would have the day before, and the day before that. Eight months was a long time; it was many votes.

On his way out of the building at eight o'clock he saw Willard Fremantle. "Season's on, eh, Lenox?" said the Marquess's son, jovial at the prospect of a weekend. "Are you going to Lord Rash's party tonight?"

"Oh, yes, very likely," said Lenox, smiling and donning his gloves.

They progressed through the large doors out toward Abingdon Street, returning the nods of the porters. "He wants his son to marry a woman—a young woman—named Fisker, whose father built a railroad to somewhere called Salt Lake City. Imagine! She'll be there."

"You must admit it's an evocative name," said Lenox. "A lake of salt."

"It sounds like one of the torments in Dante to me. Lakes are meant to have freshwater."

"Here is my carriage. I'll see you at Rash's, or if not there, one of a dozen other places, I don't doubt."

Fremantle's farewell was prophetic; this was the first weekend of the season, and Lenox had no case or parliamentary responsibilities, while Jane was extremely busy. As such he became her emissary and representative at a whole multitude of parties across London. It was a pleasant task—punch, catching up with friends one hadn't seen in some time, the crisp comeliness of young men and women dancing in their starched new clothes. Young love added an exhilaration to the air, so promiscuous and free-floating that even the dowagers seated upon the divans felt it, and knew themselves momentarily more youthful, freshened by the freshness around them. Then there was always the excellent music.

So Friday and Saturday passed, and Sunday, when the hour of churchgoing had come and gone, women began to make Sunday calls upon each other to discuss the week, the engagements, while men trickled back into their clubs on Pall Mall, where, though they pretended to disdain the season, the conversations were all the same as the womens'.

Finally, on Monday morning, Dallington returned.

He came directly to Hampden Lane from Charing Cross Station, tired, his collar wilting (it was a warm day), and his suit smudged with dirt. Altogether he looked a bit beneath his Plimsoll line. "I didn't realize how long I was going to stay in Hampshire," he said, preempting Lenox's question, "but it was worth it."

"The Godwins?"

"I know the whole history of the family—a

strange one, too. Shall we call on Jenkins? I don't doubt he would like to hear it."

"Yes, though I'm all curiousness to hear your story."

They went to Scotland Yard and found Jenkins in his office. A flash of hope came into his eye when Dallington said he had returned with a story, for it had been a difficult weekend spent trying to coax a word out of Hetty and Archibald. "In all honesty I'm on the verge of giving the job up. We have Archie dead to rights, of course, at least on breaking into the palace, but Henrietta we cannot find anything to charge with. Leaving her hotel with a bag full of suspicious items?"

"Owning an illegally acquired key to the palace?" suggested Lenox.

"She says it was slipped under her door, and she kept it in case it had some purpose, not knowing what it was. Or rather her barrister says that. For of course she's as talkative as a corpse."

"I'll tell you what I know," said Dallington. "I'm not sure if any of it will matter in a court of law—but it made an impression on me that I won't forget."

CHAPTER FORTY-SIX

They all sat down; Jenkins began to pack his pipe, with the dreamy, practiced air of a man who finds a separate and nearly equal pleasure in the small preliminary physical handiwork that prepares the real pleasure—the drinker uncorking his bottle, the horseman tightening his stirrups. "If you solve the case, Lord John, the Queen will make you a duke," he said and smiled to himself, carefully sliding a shred of stray tobacco back into place.

"I'd rather not be if it's all the same to her," said Dallington.

"Tell us what happened," said Lenox.

"To begin with, your friend Hughes was an absolute brick. He apparently got your telegram, because he met me at the station when my train arrived and insisted that I stay with him. That castle is falling half to pieces—but by God, it's beautiful, and I must say, they make their little corner of it very snug. He asked me to come again for the shooting."

"He's a wonderful shot," said Lenox. "Always was."

"He was also very concerned about Godwin—said that you hadn't let on in your first letter how seriously the man had gotten himself into trouble, for of course now the newspaper stories have landed in Hampshire, and nobody in those parts is talking of anything else. The steward at Raburn Lodge has had to let the dogs loose, apparently."

"I didn't know when I wrote to him how grim Godwin's plans were," said Lenox.

"No, quite."

Jenkins lit his pipe; the smell of fire and tobacco made the room feel closer, a small lamplit vessel afloat in the great unending gray of the day's weather. It would rain before long, Lenox suspected. Bad news for the party. "Was he able to help you?"

"Not directly, but he put me in touch with a chap named Fox—and that was the first link in the chain. I should go back a little way, however, and describe it all chronologically. That way I won't get my story confused.

"After Hughes installed me in their guest bedroom, I borrowed a horse from him and together we rode up to Raburn Lodge. Lovely place—a manor house, very square-fronted, redbrick with white windows, and four chimneys coming right up out of the center of the house in a row. I suppose you would call it Queen Anne style. Ersatz Wren. If you've seen Winslow Hall, in Buckinghamshire, you'll recognize the type.

"It's not on very much land, however—and that comes into the story. We rode nearly up to the front door. It can't be on more than five or six acres, all fenced in with a very high hedge for privacy, but Hughes took me to a place where I could take a look at it. Rather eerie, I can tell you.

"Next I went to see this fellow Fox, Gerald Fox. He was gamekeeper for two decades to Godwin's father, though I immediately had the sense that his memories of the time weren't fond, exactly. The elder Godwin liked to shoot, and therefore he was courteous with Fox, but they didn't have a friendship. Fox was willing to speak to me but didn't know much about the living family, the brother and sister. He said Archie had been raised to shoot but had given it up the moment his father died."

"Until last week, the knave," said Jenkins.

"Fox did offer me one interesting piece of information. He said that it was known in town—and had been widely discussed since the news appeared about the attempt on the Queen's life—that the Godwins had always had a quarrel with the monarchy."

"Republicans?" asked Lenox.

"Fox didn't know. He was, however, able to introduce me to someone who did, a man named Harry Forrest. He's the town's historian—a rather abrasive fellow, meek wife, few friends, but damned useful in the end. He asked if I could ride up to Raburn, and so I borrowed a horse from Hughes again, and we went to the same spot where Hughes had taken me.

"Well, I admit that I thought it was pretty poor

sport—I was tired and it was getting dark—but then Forrest told me something interesting. Behind Raburn Lodge is a great deal of rolling countryside, rather picturesque. At first I thought it was farmland, but he said that it simply lies there, fallow. Then he pointed to a church spire, about the farthest thing one could see on the horizon, really no more than a speck. 'D'you see that?' he asked, and I must have sounded irritated when I said that yes, I did, because he smirked and said he wasn't giving me the architectural tour of Hampshire—that until 1715, everything that reached as far as that church had been Godwin land. It fairly took my breath away. They must have been the largest landowners in the county, I said, and he answered that they were second, after the Duke of Bolton. Nearly a hundred thousand acres in all."

Jenkins frowned. "What happened?"

Lenox knew—that date, 1715. "George the First," he said. "Are the Godwins Catholic?"

"You're quicker than I am, Charles," said Dallington.

"No. Only older."

Walking into Buckingham Palace, one was supposed to feel the great immovable silver weight of the Queen's power, extending as far backward and forward into time as anyone could imagine.

In truth, of course, the rule of England had

always changed with the caprice of the wind on a spring afternoon. In 1714, Queen Anne had died. The first fifty-six men and women in line for the throne, every stripe of princeling and princess, earl and duke, were all of them, every single one, Catholic. By the 1701 Act of Settlement, they were therefore ineligible to assume the crown.

The fifty-seventh fellow in line was a Protestant; he was a mild German fellow with the unspectacular title of Elector of Hanover. He ruled over a small piece of northern Germany— and then added to that, when his distant cousin Anne died, the whole immense Kingdom of Great Britain and Ireland, trailing behind it every variety of colony and principality across the globe.

When he took the throne, he barely spoke English.

This was King George the First. Queen Victoria's great-great-grandfather. In truth all three men sitting in the office were probably more purely English than their own Queen was, by the common understanding of the word— though of course even Englishness wasn't permanent. If one was willing to venture back to 1066, they were likely all French. Or even if one came of a family that predated the Domesday Book, that family was likely Viking, unless somewhere in their veins lingered a drop of druid blood; and even then, even if one's family predated the Viking incursions, it had almost certainly come to these shores with one of two loose Germanic confederations: the Angles or the Saxons.

So that, like Victoria, they were all German in the end.

Jenkins knew this in faint outlines. Lenox and Dallington, of the aristocracy and educated at schools where the history of the ruling class mattered, knew every wrinkled piece of the history, and recalled it in alternation. "The Godwins were Jacobites, then?" asked Lenox.

Dallington shook his head. "Yes, and worse. They were assassins."

Jenkins lifted his eyebrows. "The papers will like that."

"Forrest had spent the days before I arrived in the archives. The town knew the Godwins had lost their land, but the reason had been successfully hidden away. Godwin's own great-great-grandfather had organized a ring of aristocrats who plotted to murder George the First, and use the subsequent confusion to place James Stuart on the throne."

"Treason," said Lenox. Stuart was Anne's half brother, a Catholic. He'd had, briefly, wide support, but then George the First had emerged as a competent, gentle king, not power-mad in the slightest—happy, in fact, to let Walpole, his Prime Minister, rule the country. It was the beginning of the long relinquishment of power that had led to Parliament, and not the palace, ruling England. "He was foiled, obviously."

"Betrayed by another member of his circle, who had gone along with the plan only to gather evidence." Dallington grinned. "You won't believe who it is."

"Who?"

"A fellow named Arthur Hughes. Your friend's great-great-grandfather. As thanks he was awarded Leck Castle and its environs. The King escheated Godwin's lands, and they've lain fallow, untenanted, ever since."

Jenkins looked back and forth between Lenox and Dallington, both of whom were now smiling, Lenox half in disbelief. "Did you tell Hughes?"

"He knew the history of the castle. He didn't know that it was a Godwin who had been the chief conspirator. According to Forrest, there were a great many Godwins in London and the Home Counties who were deeply apologetic, and very rich, and arranged to have the matter hushed up—and even to keep Raburn Lodge."

"How did Forrest discover that?"

"The document of forfeiture—of the Godwin lands. He went back in the files and found it for me, and it described the reasons. Apparently it never went farther than that. I had it copied out. It's here with me."

Jenkins shook his head. "It's quite a tale, but I

cannot see what any of it has to do with Leonard Wintering, or the Graves Hotel, or Henrietta Godwin. Surely they cannot have simply held a family grudge all this time?"

Dallington shook his head. "That's the next part of the story."

CHAPTER FORTY-SEVEN

After Dallington had spoken with Fox and Forrest he had returned to Leck Castle, eaten supper with Peter and Frances Hughes—they had a very good chef, unusual in a household with only three servants, because Frances loved food—and gone to sleep while there was still light in the sky, exhausted. The next morning he went to Raburn Lodge.

Before he had left for Hampshire, Dallington had acquired, jointly from Jenkins and Shackleton, a letter that introduced him as their representative and begged the cooperation of witnesses.

It induced no special awe among the people of Raburn Lodge, unfortunately.

"What happened?" asked Lenox.

"An old stooped white-haired fellow answered the door, looked at the letter, and then spat at my feet and told me to be on my way."

"What did you do then?"

"He had dogs on the leash, so I took his advice. I didn't leave altogether, though. I spent the morning watching the house. I had a little eyeglass and looked in the windows. Curtains were drawn over most of them, but I could see three people at one time or another moving about the place, as if they expected Hetty and Archie Godwin back imminently—the old butler, an equally old housemaid, and a footman who must have been brushing up near a hundred."

"Family retainers," said Jenkins.

"Yes, and loyal I thought, unlikely to tell me anything. Then I had a stroke of luck. Just before noon, when I thought perhaps I would leave, a woman rode up to the house in a beaten-up dogcart, tied off her horses, and walked around to the servants' quarters. She knocked on the door, and it opened, and then closed again, and she waited outside for some time. When the door opened again it was the footman. He gave her the laundry."

"Excellent," said Jenkins, smiling.

"How old was she?" asked Lenox.

"About fifty. Robust, though. Needless to say, I stopped her as she came back out to the road."

"And showed her the letter?" asked Jenkins.

Dallington laughed. "I did show her the letter, and she couldn't have been off quickly enough. Then I offered her money."

"That did it?"

"Not exactly. It made her pause, and at last she declined. She said she couldn't stand to lose the business of the lodge. As she was driving away, though, she said that everyone in town knew about the old man—old man Godwin—and that I only had to ask about the note."

"The note," said Lenox, furrowing his brow.

"I didn't understand either. Nor did Hughes. I had lunch in the village and made a few friends at the public house, and none of them could make sense of it. At last I had the idea to seek out the local constable."

"First thing you should have done," said Jenkins, with professional satisfaction.

"He was about eighteen, sadly, a poor young pup, and didn't know anything about the Godwins—or the note—but he gave me the name of the old constable, who had retired to Allington, one town over, and opened up a public house. The Godwin Arms, it was called, if you can credit that. It was there, you'll be elated to hear, Jenkins, that the letters of introduction you and Shackleton wrote finally came in handy."

"What did he say?"

"The old constable was a reedy fellow with big eyes, Jonathan Blaine. Always felt he was watching me too closely—an uneasy sort, you know. Kept his cards close to the vest, but sharp. Once he had examined the watermark on Shackleton's notepaper and looked at the seals with a magnifying glass, he poured me a pint of mild and told me about Henrietta and Archibald Godwin's father, Winthrop.

"Apparently Winthrop was a bit of a devil. He was litigious—suits against about thirty different people across Farnborough and Hampshire, from what I could gather—and it was widely known that he used his wife and children cruelly. His wife died not long after giving birth to Archibald. She fell down a flight of stairs."

Lenox recalled the words in Hughes's letter: *a vicious old fellow, according to my own pater. He was always in and out of court.* "He pushed her, you think?"

"It's difficult to say—bad people's wives take tumbles, too. It seemed enough to me that everyone in the village blamed him for her mishap. Anyhow, as I say, he was always at law, but the local cases, Blaine said, were only minor pleasures for him. His chief quarrel was with the government. He wanted to reclaim the lands of his ancestors."

Jenkins bit his pipe thoughtfully. "You think Archibald was acting out his father's wishes, then, for revenge?"

"The story's not over," said Dallington. He paused and took a long sip of water; he looked tired and energized at once. "Three years ago last Tuesday, Winthrop Godwin killed himself."

Lenox raised his eyebrows. "Did he, though."

"Blaine was still the town's constable then. The

340

household made the initial report of the death to him, and he went out to Raburn Lodge. Soon enough the Hampshire police took over, but not before Blaine saw Archibald and Henrietta's father hanging from the rafters of the great dining hall. It was the central room of the house."

"Is this where the note enters into the story?" asked Lenox.

Dallington nodded. "I'm coming to it. According to Blaine, Winthrop Godwin had received a letter from the courts the day he hanged himself. His final request for the restoration of the Godwin lands had been denied.

"Apparently his death was a matter of no great sorrow to the people round about Farnborough, for he was in suit with half of his neighbors and threatening the other half—he sued Peter Hughes because Hughes refused to repair a fence on his own property, Lenox—but there was a great deal of concern for Archibald and Henrietta Godwin."

"They were well liked?" asked Jenkins.

"Neither was well known in the town or the county. Archibald had just returned from Oxford and Tonbridge, so in all he must have been away eight years or so at the time of his father's death. Henrietta kept house for her father, but she didn't have much of an acquaintance. It was widely expected that after their initial period of mourning, the two would take their place in local society—dine with the bishop; hire more staff, for of course their fortune was known to the last farthing, as it always is in such places; join in the Hunt."

"The Beagles."

"Yes, precisely. The Beagles are lords of all they survey in the Clinkard Meon Valley; it was astonishing. At any rate—they did none of that. On the contrary, they dismissed all of the staff except for the three I mentioned, they stopped ordering from local shops, they refused all invitations. They built up the hedges around the house."

"There is something eerie in them, these two," Lenox said. "I have seen it before. There was a case in Lower Danforth some years ago. There were two sisters, twelve and thirteen. Their mother was dead. Their father was a terror, beating them, berating the household, losing servants every fortnight. The two sisters grew strangely close. They had their own language, their own gestures. They wouldn't speak to anyone except for each other. The walls of the room they shared were covered with an odd kind of cuneiform writing, you might call it. I've never wanted to leave a place as badly."

Jenkins nodded. "I remember the case. The Thompsons."

Dallington looked puzzled. "What was the crime?"

"They had killed their father," said Lenox, "and after that every servant in the house. We found the housekeeper facedown in the coal scuttle. Old Thompson's valet was in the bathtub with his throat slit. As for the father, he was dressed in his Sunday suit, sitting at the head of the table, where they had been eating for a week before anyone suspected that things had gone amiss. He had been stabbed dozens of times—before and after death."

Dallington shivered. "Charming story, Lenox. You ought to tell it at parties."

The older detective smiled. "Apologies."

"No, it's relevant. I don't think they had their own language, these two, but they were uncommonly close. They were sometimes seen walking arm in arm upon the moor, as lovers might, according to the landlord at the Godwin Arms."

"Do you think they killed their father?" asked Jenkins.

Dallington shook his head. "No. If anything, I think they were hoping to avenge him. Clearly there is some madness in the blood of that family. I would be curious to hear about Godwin at school, at Oxford. He already told us that he didn't have friends. He must have been an odd soul."

"You think they were attempting to avenge their father simply because of the timing of his suicide?" asked Lenox.

"No," said Dallington and smiled faintly. "There we come to the note. It was found in Winthrop Godwin's chest pocket. It was signed 'VR,' and Blaine said they interrogated a fellow named Victor Robertson, with whom Winthrop had quarreled, at length. Of course, I saw something else immediately, though I didn't tell Blaine as much."

"What?" asked Jenkins.

"Victoria Regina," said Lenox. "Queen Victoria. What did she write, John?"

Dallington took a sip of water. "She used the royal 'we,'" he told them. "The note said, "We forgive; we cannot forget.'"

CHAPTER FORTY-EIGHT

As Lenox walked home along Regent Street he passed a wandering onion man, who wore a crimson bowtie, muttonchop whiskers, and a long strand of braided onions around his neck, and chanted, in a singsong voice, "Here's your rope, to hang the Pope, and a penn'orth of cheese to choke him." Lenox smiled and, reminded of supper and of Disraeli's aversion, walked more quickly. There was much left to do that day.

None of it for him, however. When he arrived home and offered to throw himself into work, both Lady Jane and Kirk (the latter almost angrily) told him that he was underfoot and needed to absent himself from the sitting rooms and the dining room at all costs. There were men garlanding the walls with flowers, others moving furniture to Jane's specifications, and servants lining up silver tureens along the old marble hunting table in the hall. With humble haste Lenox made his way upstairs.

For half an hour he sat at the escritoire in the third-floor guest room—he sometimes liked to work in parts of the house he visited less often, a new view refreshing his mind, permitting him to work longer—reading blue books and parliamentary memorandums. Then, almost with the force of revelation, he realized he didn't need to know about American railroads any longer. He was leaving politics.

With a feeling of liberation he strolled about the upper corridors of the house. They were empty; the whole energy of the staff was concentrated downstairs. After a moment he realized that he had directed his footsteps, unthinkingly, toward the nursery. He knocked at the door.

Miss Emanuel was reading to Sophia, a book given to her a few months before by Toto. Lenox couldn't stand the book. It was about a horse that got lost. The horse, even by the low standards of his species, was incalculably stupid, capable of confusing a lamppost for his master or meandering onto an ocean liner at random. Lenox understood that this was meant to be funny, and it was, indeed, the kind of humor that went straight to Sophia's simple heart, but it irritated him. As Miss Emanuel went on reading, he determined to ignore the horse and thought instead about the Godwins.

There were questions that only they could answer, at this stage. Dallington's story had satisfied both Lenox and Jenkins as to the motivation of the brother and sister, a long cathectic hatred of Queen Victoria, bred into the bone by their ancestors and their father, and flourishing, perhaps, without the soft guidance of a mother. Still: How had they discovered Grace Ammons's history? Why had Godwin killed the homeless man, beyond the convenience of pinning it to Wintering?

Killing Wintering was more understandable—trouble and dissent among criminals was common in Lenox's line of work—but he still would have liked to know the details. Unfortunately neither of the Godwins seemed likely to offer them. It was unclear how much Henrietta knew at all, for that matter.

Sophia's book had finished ("Again!" she cried, to Lenox's distress), and he had begun to speak to her nurse about the possibility of a walk in the spring sunshine, when there was a knock on the door of the nursery.

It was Kirk; he couldn't say, "There you are, you fool," to Lenox in an exasperated tone, but his face approximated the effect of those words. What a mood he was in! "A visitor, in your study, sir."

"Probably the horse," said Lenox to Sophia, who giggled. He turned to Kirk. "Who is it?"

"A Mr. LeMaire, sir."

LeMaire was seated on one of Lenox's red armchairs, reading from a small volume in French. When Lenox came into his study the French detective put the book into the breast pocket of his coat and stood, smiling and bowing slightly. "I hope you will excuse the intrusion, Mr. Lenox."

"Not at all. Can I get you a drink?"

"Have you a brandy?"

"Of course." Lenox went to the small lacquered table where he kept his spirits in crystal decanters and poured the drink for LeMaire. He took a small quantity of whisky and a large one of soda for himself, and the two men touched glasses. "Please, sit," said Lenox.

"I have a piece of information that I think you wish to know," said LeMaire, his voice no less accented outside of his office.

"About the Godwin case?"

"Ah! No," said the Frenchman sadly. "There I think you need more help, but I cannot offer. It is about your other line of work. Your Parliament."

Lenox gave him a quizzical look. "A piece of information?"

"In these battles there is a great element of gossip—and of course gossip is my trade, Mr. Lenox."

Lenox suppressed a sigh, covering it with a sip from his glass. It would be about Graham—that Graham was embezzling money. He had yet to tell anyone other than Jane and Graham that he was leaving Parliament. His brother would be devastated, he feared. "How kind of you to come to me."

"I will not insult your intelligence by pretending you are unaware of the rumors concerning your secretary, Mr. Graham," said LeMaire. He set his glass down, and in his face Lenox saw, again, a sharp, darting intelligence. This was a formidable fellow. "What I have learned is their origin."

Here was a surprise. "Their origin? Have you really?"

"It was Mr. Disraeli."

There was a long pause. Lenox sat in silence, his gaze level upon the visitor. At last he said, "How did you hear that?"

"The day after you visited me, I heard your name at the house of one of my clients—a friend, now, I would venture to say. He sits in the House of Lords. A newer earldom. He sits on Mr. Disraeli's side of the benches. When I inquired about the trouble you were facing, he informed me of your secretary's predicament. I took it upon myself to discover the truth."

"May I ask why you so decided?"

LeMaire shrugged in that Gallic fashion that seems to contain all meanings and none at once, a shrug that acknowledges the absurdity, the inevitability, the comic disloyalty, of the world. "I was sorry not to help you—and I think it is more than coincidence, Mr. Lenox, to hear your name again so quickly. Your career in London is, before which I advance here to the city myself, an inspiration. The Mad Jack case appeared in the French papers the week I entered the Sûreté. A private detective, beating the police! Not in a memoir, like Vidocq, but in the newspaper, the proper newspaper."

"How did you discover that it was Disraeli?" Lenox asked.

LeMaire smiled. "The Frenchmen in this city must stick together."

Lenox was in no mood for evasion, however, or charm. "Can you be more precise?"

"The French consul here is in the confidence of many men in your government. I asked him to make inquiries. Apparently Mr. Disraeli called Mr. Graham 'the most inconvenient man in Parliament,' at a small meeting of leaders of this party, his party, and stated his determination to be rid of the trouble."

This surprised Lenox at first—but immediately he heard the ring of truth in it. That very morning Graham had come to him with a way to kill the naval bill, a small procedural step they might take. Lenox had passed it on in a memorandum to Edmund. "I see."

"I asked my friend why he did not try to discredit you, instead. According to Mr. Disraeli, it wouldn't have been gentlemanly." LeMaire smiled. "I thought my own country a rigid place, but class—it is the English disease, truly."

They sat for a moment or two, the Englishman indignant and unhappy, the Frenchman quiet—permitting Lenox time to absorb the news. At last, Lenox said, "I must thank you very much for the information, unwelcome though it is."

"I have a favor to request, in return."

"Oh?" Lenox's guard went up.

"I am in a battle with Mr. Audley. Your friend Lord John Dallington is off to the side—his own kind of detective; it is Audley with whom I am concerned. He is your countryman."

"He's a Scot."

"He is close enough to being your countryman. I know your influence within the Scotland Yard, among the detectives, with Lord Dallington."

"Lord John," corrected Lenox, absentmindedly.

"I would like a fair opinion from you if ever my name arises, sir." LeMaire stood and passed a card across. "This is my friend. He will verify the information for you, if you like—he has names, sources. I must beg you to be very discreet if you call upon him. You may be certain that he speaks the truth, or you may follow your own line of inquiry. Regardless you will arrive at Mr. Disraeli. Good day, Mr. Lenox."

CHAPTER FORTY-NINE

Each evening at six o'clock a chap named Mr. Bernard Rider came down Hampden Lane, always in the same colorful attire: blue trousers, yellow waistcoat ("veskit" by his pronunciation), checkered shirt, and pink coat, with a long, slender pipe clenched in his back teeth. An old but sturdy horse pulled his cart. The housemaids of some of Lenox's neighbors, hoping for a few flirtatious words, looked forward all day to his visits, making sure to finish their chores by five to the hour so they could lounge upon the top steps of the servants' entrances. Rider stopped at each house, collecting the kitchen leavings, flirting along the way. When his cart was full he sold the leavings—what people called the "wash"—to a mill outside of London, which turned them into food for pigs. Such was the origin of the word "hogwash."

Just after Rider passed down the street that evening, a pair of carriages followed, both far more distinguished, one with vermilion trim, the other with a driver in full evening dress, both with tall footmen standing on the doors and horses glossy, brisk, and superior, trotting as if they had chosen to. The first guests were here.

It was axiomatic to say that parties such as this one passed in a blur, but in fact as people began to come up into the house, shrugging off their spring jackets and cloaks, jewels sparkling, full of compliments and greetings for their hostess, Lenox found that he had time to enjoy the company of each person he met, each sip of champagne he took with them. It was the season, and there was a great deal to discuss, news to exchange. The pink and yellow drawing rooms both immediately began to fill. Their especial friends arrived early and prepared to loft onto their shoulders the greatest social encumbrance; McConnell cornered Edward Twinkleton, by common consent the most boring man in London, and positively insisted upon hearing every detail of his most recent speech in Parliament.

Just after seven o'clock the Prime Minister arrived. Lenox was at the door to greet him personally. "It is a very great honor to welcome you, Mr. Disraeli," he said.

"Eh? No, the pleasure's mine, the pleasure's mine. Lovely evening, isn't it, too. And I hear Princess Helena means to come."

"She informed us that we would be so honored, sir."

"Is that your brother? Take me to him, if you would—I'd like a quick word."

Soon the party, as parties do, took on its own vitality, its own parameters, quite out of the control of its nominal commanders. After guiding Disraeli to Edmund, Lenox returned to greet the next guest, and the next, and the next. After about an hour the noise in the house was roughly that of a medieval battlefield.

Finally he stepped away from the door and found a glass of champagne in the drawing room; he stopped there for a moment and looked around, the familiar paintings and surfaces enlivened by all the fresh eyes he saw glancing at them with subtle assessment.

In the corner of the room Toto and McConnell were speaking to Dallington, and for a moment Lenox shifted his watchfulness to them, trying to analyze what he saw. He hadn't spoken to Thomas. Jane had visited Toto that very morning, though, and reported that she seemed happier—and less inclined to confidence in her older cousin, quick to dismiss the subject of Polly Buchanan, as if her weeks of unhappiness had all been a simple miscalculation on her own part.

They looked happy, to be sure, but there had been so many moments in the past years when the two of them had seemed to achieve a lasting happiness, not least when their daughter, Georgianna, had been born. He studied them—and suddenly his skepticism vanished, and he did feel that something had changed in them, in their animated faces. It was a sensation, nothing logical. In the past he had seen goodwill and love between them, but never an ease of togetherness such as this, a sense of quiet accord, of quiet warmth. There were the beginnings of lines at Toto's eyes—she was past thirty now, though he would always think of her as so young—and Thomas's hair was more gray than dark. Yet in the happiness of their eyes he saw a renewal of youth. It was love.

He realized, with gratitude, what his own face must look like as he stood beside Lady Jane.

Dallington must have seen Lenox staring, for he begged out of the conversation with the McConnells and came over. "Do you have a moment to speak?" he asked. "I know it's not an ideal time."

Lenox looked at his pocket watch. "There are twenty minutes until dinner. Why?"

"I was busy today. I learned something new. It will only take a moment to tell you—but I would rather do it in your study. I could smoke a cigarette there, too."

"Yes, I'll follow you," said Lenox.

The study was dim, and a great deal of superfluous furniture had been shoved without ceremony into its various corners. Dallington sat upon the arm of a sofa that belonged more properly to the yellow drawing room and lit a match against the sole of his shoe, then touched it to the end of the cigarette in his mouth. "I saw Miss Buchanan today. She's been as busy as we have."

"What has she found?"

"She's quite ingenious, Lenox—she has lessons to teach me. It's a thoroughly modern outfit she's building. The moment a case comes in, she has a team of people, specialists in different tasks. One of them is a financial investigator. His only work is to look into the money. How many times have you and I tried to parse a bank record or a receipt without success?"

It was true. "Innovative."

"Yes, that's the word for it. Anyhow, she discovered something about the Godwin family that seems significant to me. It's about their mother."

"Paget, was she called?"

"Yes. Apparently Winthrop Godwin lost nearly all of his fortune by going to law. He was especially unfortunate in a suit he brought against his father's land agent. For the last years of his life, he was living on the interest of the money his wife had left behind—a substantial fortune."

"Did that money come to Archibald and Henrietta?"

"There's the rub. When she died, Abigail Paget—Abigail Godwin—hadn't predicted that her husband would squander his fortune, and she had left the money to the heirs of her heirs, in effect her grandchildren, in equal distribution. According to Miss Buchanan's financial expert, this was because the Godwin money and the Godwin land was entailed upon the male heirs."

Suddenly Lenox understood. "Shall I guess what else he discovered?" he said.

Dallington smiled. "Please."

"That by the terms of the will, all the money in trust was to be released to Henrietta upon Archibald's death, should he die without children."

"Close enough. The exact provision was that if her own children should live 'beyond child-bearing age,' defined as forty-five in a woman and seventy in a man, the money should come to them outright."

"How old is Henrietta Godwin?"

"She turned forty-six last year," said Dallington. "Archie, of course, has thirty-eight years to go until he turns seventy. Imagine that, a child at seventy! His mother had a higher opinion of his virility than I do, I must say."

Lenox shook his head. "Funny, how even in these crimes with the noblest purpose—revenge, regicide—there is so often an element of money."

"Polly—Miss Buchanan—also agreed with us, that the murder was a convenient snare with which Godwin could entrap Wintering. It served more than one purpose."

"We still don't know what happened between

Wintering and Godwin. Perhaps we never shall, quite."

Dallington pointed at the carriage clock on Lenox's desk, whose face was visible in the moonlight. "We had better go back."

"Yes. I want to see this Miss Buchanan—she seems an interesting young woman."

"Ever so interesting," said Dallington, then must have realized the ardor in his voice, because he laughed and said hurriedly, "and likely to take away all of my own business."

They emerged from the study just in time to see Kirk come to the doorway where the drawing rooms and the front hall met; there he rang the bell for supper.

Lady Jane, rather daringly, had decided not to proceed to the dining room in the usual way—couple by couple, in order of seniority, down to the very juniorest and most negligible souls in the room—but to lead the way out herself and invite all to follow. This she did, with Dallington's mother by her side.

Word had apparently spread that this unortho-doxy (soon to be fashion, no doubt) was to be practiced, and in pairs and threes the men and the women, their faces half-scornful but also rather excited, began to follow. In the middle of the pack, evidently believing it to be a great lark, was Disraeli, accompanied, unsurprisingly, by two of the most beautiful women in the room, Jemima

Faringdon and the Queen's cousin Lady Louise Dietz.

Some habits die hard; the last pair out of the room were Grace Ammons and George Ivory, late replacements for a couple that had canceled, suggested as guests by Lenox to Lady Jane. Lenox bowed to Miss Ammons as she passed, and shook hands with George Ivory, a tall, straight-backed, very handsome fellow, with wavy blond hair and gentle green eyes. His manners were beautiful, simple, and appropriate. Grace herself said thank you, too, though in an extremely formal voice.

There were several small round tables in the dining room. Disraeli and Princess Helena—who had just arrived, taking all the breath out of the room, lovely in a sapphire green gown—were at Lenox and Lady Jane's own table, along with the Duchess of Marchmain, Toto, McConnell, and a few others. As Lenox sat, he recalled Disraeli's friendly manner in Parliament a few weeks earlier, as together they passed the Dwellings Act without respect for their different party affiliations. What a sly fox! Yet there was a strange modicum of pride in the whole saga—pride in Graham his friend, pride in having ascended high enough to irritate a Prime Minister.

Lady Jane had felt no such pride; as they were dressing for supper, earlier that evening, he had told her about LeMaire's visit.

"Disraeli did that?" she asked, shocked.

"Apparently. I took fifteen minutes to call upon John Baltimore afterward, and he nodded his confirmation, though he didn't speak it out loud."

She had gone white with anger. "What an infamous thing to do."

"Such is political life. We cannot treat him differently tonight."

"No. Of course not."

Nevertheless, Jane, unlike the Godwins, would have her revenge. As they sat down in the dining room, Disraeli busy with Lady Dietz's whispering inquiries, she was in the kitchen. Footmen poured wine; the other tables stole glances of Princess Helena.

At last she came out, at the head of a long line of servants bearing dishes. She walked to the Prime Minister and, putting a hand on his shoulder, said, "I know you are a gourmand, Mr. Disraeli. This first dish is our chef's special favorite, and mine, too. You must tell us how you like it."

"Delighted, of course," said Disraeli, smiling— a smile that vanished when he saw, placed in front of him, a large plate, heaped uncommonly high with stewed onions.

CHAPTER FIFTY

The spring passed into the summer then, the gentle pitch of the days and the particular pleasantness of the weather making it one of the finest seasons anyone could recall. In April there were a dozen engagements a day announced in the *Times*. By June half of the couples were newly married already.

In July the Godwins went to trial.

Neither had spoken more than a few words in the intervening months, and though they hadn't seen each other neither believed for a moment, as Jenkins would pretend, that the other had betrayed them. Their bond was the stuff of newspaper natter; reporters had finally followed Dallington's footsteps across the west toward Hampshire and discovered at least some of what he had, as well as paying local men and women for stories about the Godwins, which, as time passed, grew more outlandish in dimension.

A small amount of real information did trickle in. Jenkins went up with a warrant to investigate Raburn Lodge and found Archibald Godwin's personal study suspiciously empty of papers and correspondence. Desperate, he brought in a team of constables who combed the house over— which they did with success. A locked wardrobe in the nursery proved to be, in fact, a concealed work desk, and it was evident that Godwin had used this place to plot his crimes. Among other things there were dossiers on several dozen members of the staff of Buckingham Palace: the footman who was having an affair, the cook who had stolen a chest of silver plate from his last employer and then concealed the fact, various points of pressure on the personal lives of people close to the Queen.

There was no file on Grace Ammons, unfortunately. Had he taken it with him, believing her to be the easiest member of the palace staff to compromise? Nor was there any link that Scotland Yard could find to Leonard Wintering. In the end it was impossible to charge Archibald Godwin with Wintering's murder, with the blackmail of Grace Ammons (for which she was grateful, in fact), or even, realistically, with the murder of Joseph Thayer, the vagrant. True, he had been in Godwin's room at the Graves; true, Arthur Whitstable would testify that he had seen Thayer in the company of Wintering and Godwin; true, Thayer was wearing a suit Godwin had ordered from Ede and Ravenscroft. None of this evidence was more than circumstantial.

They came to trial, therefore, upon weaker charges than Lenox would have liked. Archibald Godwin was charged with the offense of high treason, which had been defined by the Treason Act of 1351—he had "compassed or imagined" the death of the Queen. (To plot the death of the monarch's spouse, eldest son, or chief heir was the only other time this charge could be leveled.) Treason was exceedingly hard to prove, even under the law that had been updated in 1848. Lenox would have preferred—as would have Jenkins—a plain old charge of murder. The crown also charged Godwin with attempted murder and a host of smaller offenses, all the way down to breaking and entering. His barrister made it clear that he would contest them vigorously.

Henrietta Godwin's crimes were more vexing still to punish. What had she done? Had a mad brother? Carried a key that anyone might have placed in her purse? She had never been anywhere near Buckingham Palace. It wasn't illegal to carry a small pistol, though it was unusual. Nothing at Raburn Lodge implicated her in her brother's plans. Out of desperation the prosecutor charged her, too, with high treason. Jenkins wasn't hopeful.

The first day of the trial was, as it could not help but be, in such circumstances, a circus, with crowded galleries, milling press outside the doors, and an unusually large contingent of guards and officers on behalf of the Queen. (The Queen herself was visiting Wales.) Parliament had risen for the summer, and Lenox was free to attend the trial; he and Dallington sat several rows behind the defendants. Lenox appreciated the company, which was by no means a foregone matter—for Polly Buchanan was there also, not on the face of it as an interested party, merely as a spectator, for her guise as Miss Strickland remained intact. At the recesses Dallington would excuse himself and speak to her when he could.

"She has a sharper eye for legal matters than I do," he said once when he returned.

"Oh?"

"She told me what the word 'malice' means for the first time. It can be expressed or implied, do you know."

"How interesting."

Dallington missed the sarcasm in Lenox's voice. "Yes, isn't it! And then there's *mens rea*. She has a great deal of material on that, yards of the stuff."

Soon Lenox himself had the opportunity to know her better, too—for as the days passed, the ranks of the hot, dusty courtroom grew thinner, as fewer and fewer of the press and the public found themselves able to tolerate the lengthy disquisitions and inactions of a courtroom trial. Eventually the three—Polly, Dallington, Lenox—began to sit along the same particular bench each morning. Throughout the day messengers would come in with notes for Polly, which she would answer directly or fold into a pocket. Presumably they were to do with her detective agency.

Though these notes represented a direct competition to his own business, Dallington thought them very funny.

By the second week of the trial the Godwins still had yet to speak, and there were only a few dozen consistent attendants at the court.

One of them was an old, stooped, white-haired man in a clerical collar, extremely thin. His vestments were of thick black cloth, but he always sat, motionless, in the very first row of the courtroom, never leaving his seat even during a recess. "Who do you think he is?" whispered Polly to them one morning before the proceedings began.

"Father Time," said Dallington. "No, I'm not sure. Lenox?"

Lenox smiled sadly. "I've wondered myself for some days. I think if we introduced ourselves we might find that he is Wintering's father."

Dallington and Polly, both struck by the idea, in unison turned their heads to look at the man again. Then Polly stood up. "I'm going to speak to him," she said.

Before either man could respond she was walking toward the front row. "She's an unorthodox young woman," said Lenox.

"Yes, it's wonderful," said Dallington, his eyes following her. "Yesterday she told me women should be allowed to vote. Who knows, perhaps she's right."

"It won't happen in our lifetimes," said Lenox.

Polly had sat now beside the old man and was speaking with him, a hand upon his forearm. At one point she looked back toward them and nodded almost imperceptibly: Yes, it was Wintering. Lenox considered the curate's back, his small church near Stoke, his white hair. What pain fatherhood could bring! Families were so strange—the Godwins, with their gnarled sense of duty to one another, or the Winterings, a thousand winters upon the same land and now brought to this, their last heir dead, his father alone in a London courtroom.

Upon her return, Polly said, "He has agreed to have lunch with us." Then she added, whispering, "I think he is very poor, however. He is staying at a hostelry the Church of England owns in Camden and walks to the court each morning."

He was a funny old soul, exceedingly gentle, with a pleasure in anything mildly funny. Forty years before he himself had been to Wadham, and he and Lenox reminisced about Oxford together. When the subject turned to the trial, however, he was, while polite, almost wholly silent—impenetrable. Soon, uncomfortable, they directed the conversation elsewhere.

Most days thereafter they took him to lunch, always at the Oxford and Cambridge Club, so that no bill would appear; they told the elder Wintering that Scotland Yard paid for these entertainments, an explanation he seemed to accept.

What brought him to court each day? They wondered to each other. Even after Polly befriended him, Wintering sat alone in the front row. Was it forgiveness? Dallington speculated. Curiosity? Lenox, the only father in the group of three, thought he understood: It was, no matter how unhappy a situation, the curate's final chance of closeness to his son.

Somehow the old man's presence lent a moral force to the trial that it might not otherwise have had, if it were just about the attempt upon the life of the Queen. After all, she was alive, and Leonard Wintering had involved himself in the matter, taken his own risks. It was on the curate's behalf, more and more, that Lenox felt himself hoping that the Godwins be found guilty.

On the day when the verdicts came in, the courtroom again filled to capacity. The judge very quickly handed down his first ruling: Henrietta Godwin was innocent, and free to go.

There was a murmuring at this. It was expected, but still newsworthy. She had almost certainly been intending to murder the Queen, after all. The judge added that he could not reasonably preclude Miss Godwin from remaining in London, but that he advised close police observation of her comings and goings until such time as she returned to Hampshire.

Finally, at this, she stood and spoke. "I will return to Hampshire this afternoon, my lord," she said. "With my brother, if God is good."

God was not good—not by the lights of Hetty Godwin—for the next news that the judge delivered was of Archibald Godwin's guilt.

This, too, had seemed the most likely outcome. He had offered no plausible defense for his presence in the Queen's bedchamber, or for firing a gun at her. It was the sentencing that interested the pushing multitude of newspaper writers at the doors of the courtroom. The judge sighed and then spoke.

"The court views crimes such as Mr. Godwin's in a very, very grave light—yet we find, regrettably, that there is little precedent for harsh sentencing in cases such as this one. Mr. Rhodes, in '58, received just five years in prison. The majority of Her Majesty's would-be assassins have begged off of their charges on the plea of mental illness.

"We considered placing you into prison, Mr. Godwin, for a term of ten years." Henrietta Godwin made a terrified, involuntary little cry at this. "But that won't do—you are too well situated, too financially secure, for prison to be an uncomfortable experience. Sadly, in this country money can buy comfort even for those guilty of very heinous crimes. Nor can we transport you to Australia, as we might have chosen to do in older—some would say better—days.

"Fortunately, because the target of your attempted murder was no less a personage than Her Majesty, the Queen, we have other options, rooted in deeper, less usual law. Therefore the crown elects to mulct, from you, the house of your ancestors, Raburn Lodge, along with all of its associated lands, which will henceforth be the property of the Queen, to dispose of as she pleases. In consideration of her safety you will also be imprisoned for a term of no less than ten years—no matter how comfortable such an interment may prove. That is my ruling. Consider it final."

The judge—face impassive, as if he were unaware of the sensation his speech had caused in the courtroom, the rising voices—smacked his gavel and stood to walk away.

Polly's hand found Dallington's forearm, and she gripped it tight, shocked; Lenox kept his eyes fixed on Archibald Godwin, whose face had gone white as a ghost. There was a moment of strange silence, and then Henrietta Godwin, weeping and screaming, threw herself toward her brother. The bailiff of the court separated them as gently as he could and led Archie Godwin away, and Henrietta chased through the doors after them, stricken with grief.

CHAPTER FIFTY-ONE

That October, Lenox, sitting upon one of the back benches in Parliament one evening, raised his hand and caught the Speaker's eye. It was the first time this autumn that he had risen to speak—once a daily occurrence—and the Speaker looked surprised. Nevertheless he called on Lenox.

"The Honourable Member for Stirrington."

"Thank you, Mr. Speaker," said Lenox. Not long before, Disraeli had finished speaking, and Lenox looked down and across the green benches at him. "I rise to thank the Prime Minister, Mr. Speaker. He has expatiated for us at some length upon the dimensions of the proposed Factory Act, and has my full agreement upon its virtues. No ten-year-old child should work upon a factory floor. No woman should risk dismissal because she will not work an eighteen-hour day. These are facts that seem self-evident to me, and I am sorry that there are those within my party who would disagree."

From the front benches, Gladstone looked up. Edmund was at his side, and near them ranged most of the shadow cabinet.

"In two months' time I will leave this chamber," said Lenox. There was an audible reaction to this. Lenox, hands behind his back, waited patiently

369

for the voices that rose to quiet again. "I am pleased that before my departure I will be able to vote for one of the Prime Minister's bills, for the second time this year. I would encourage every Member seated in this chamber to do the same."

There were calls of "Hear him!" from the other side. Lenox's neighbors seemed disinclined to take the advice; they wanted stronger measures, but Aristotle had it right, that politics was the art of the possible.

"The Prime Minister does not have an easy job. He must please his friends, his family, the members of his party. Everyone has a quiet word for his ear. When he speaks, he speaks for England, at least so long as he is in office. His actions are England's actions. I am sincere when I offer him my congratulations for this act he wishes to pass."

There was an expectant silence in the room, a stray cough. Lenox paused, and then went on. "My own party's leader, Mr. Gladstone, has been unimpeachably kind and honest with me, and as I leave I offer him my thanks—but I do not want to omit my thanks for Mr. Disraeli, either, though he has been my opposition. He sees, as I do, that he speaks for England. That is how we know that he does not gossip, would never deceive, would never slander a good name, whether it belong to a vagrant, or Queen Victoria herself, or any random person in this body—my secretary, for instance, anyone at all." Here Lenox paused again and stared directly at Disraeli. There were titters in the House, as men explained the reference to each other in whispers. "Like all Prime Ministers his speech is his character, and his chief glory. He would never therefore utter a word that was to the detriment of his post's integrity. He has my thanks. As I leave I only ask that all of you, after my departure, seek to rise as high as the standard of honesty and decency that Mr. Disraeli has set—or, if you conceive it possible, even higher."

This time there were a few outright laughs; Lenox tried to keep the smile off of his face.

He went on for some time longer then, discussing his impressions of Parliament, his fond memories of the place, his particular friends James Hilary and Lord Cabot, his brother, his father. It was his final speech; in all he spoke for twelve minutes. When he was finished, the men all around him crowded in to shake his hand. He saw Edmund smile up from the front bench. Disraeli, his usually imperturbable face darkened, took the caesura in the proceedings to depart the chamber, his stride angry.

After declining many offers of a drink—he had two months still, after all, to lounge around the Members' Bar—Lenox fetched his valise from his office and then went toward the building's exit, deciding that he would walk home along the river.

"Wait!" called a voice as he left the building.

He turned and saw his brother, hurriedly putting on a cloak. "Edmund, there you are!"

"Will you not stay for the rest of the evening?"

"Jane is having a supper of some kind. Your wife is coming, as I recall."

Edmund, who had reached his younger brother now, smiled wanly. "That's right, I remember. Well, at any rate I can walk you back as far as Hampden Lane." He clapped a hand to Charles's shoulder and chuckled. "Had to stick it to Disraeli, did you? Between the two of us I thought it very funny."

"I don't think it will give him a second's pause."

"There you're wrong. Any man can stand to be disliked—no man can stand to be a joke."

It was a lovely evening, a last warmth of summer in the air. In the late evening pink they could see the dizzyingly high riggings of the ships, casting a shifting black lattice against the sky. Amazing to think that forty thousand ships came through London along the Thames every year, five or six thousand docked there at any given moment—bound for India, Africa, the Americas, everywhere—and the river so slender that in places a child could throw a rock across to the other side. Really, it was remarkable. Lenox said as much to his older brother.

"That reminds me—we've had a letter from Teddy, in Gibraltar. McEwan sends his regards and says there are no chicken eggs on the whole rock, only duck eggs, but he has managed to bake biscuits with 'em nevertheless, and they turned out, let me remember his phrasing . . . they turned out charming."

Lenox laughed. "Vital news to be transmitted halfway across the civilized world."

"That's why I like Teddy's letters, they never say anything at all interesting. It makes him seem much closer to home than if they were full of emotion. Still, Molly shall be glad to have him back in December, I can tell you that."

When they reached Grosvenor Square, Lenox suggested that his older brother get in a hansom back to Parliament, but Edmund thought he just had time to come into the house—which he did, kissing Sophia on her cheeks and Lady Jane on hers, though Jane, with supper to be served in less than a hour, received the favor with less enjoyment; certainly with less giggling.

Edmund stood over Sophia's bassinet for an added moment or two, making foolish faces, and then looked at his watch. "I suppose I had better go. You're still coming to the country this weekend, aren't you?"

"Of course."

"You must ride the new chestnut mare we picked out—a beautiful creature."

Lenox smiled. "Why don't we go up in the morning?"

Edmund laughed. "Yes, rub it in that I have to return to the House." He put his cloak on again and lifted a hand. "Tell Molly I'll see her later this evening."

"I will."

Supper that evening was of course far quieter than the one Lady Jane had thrown that spring—and more to Lenox's taste. (What a luxury to have his evenings back! Never to have to read another blue book!) The guests were the McConnells, Dallington, Polly Buchanan, Molly, the Duke and Duchess of Marchmain, and one or two others of Jane's particular friends, along with their husbands. They sat twelve, and stayed at the table, laughing and talking, for an hour after they should have left for home. Polly and Toto found each other's company deeply absorbing, and for his part, McConnell was full of stories of the hospital, one of which was perhaps too lifelike for the preferences of the Duchess, who, though a sporting soul, had to fan herself.

"The patient was quite all right," said McConnell, laughing.

"Then he can say more than I can," said the Duchess.

Dallington smiled. "I would have thought they made tougher hides than that out in the country, Mother, where you were raised. It's the Londoners, like Father and me, who are soft, isn't it? Polly, what do you think?"

There was nothing in the question, but for whatever reason, perhaps because he was including her in a conversation with his parents, it warmed Polly's cheeks a brighter pink, and she smiled at Dallington, momentarily lost, for the first time since Lenox had met her, for words. She composed herself and offered some clever answer, to which nobody paid attention—because the love between her and John Dallington was so obvious, so true, whether they had even said it to each other or not yet, that it was hard to look away from.

CHAPTER FIFTY-TWO

The next morning, slightly worn from late evening cigars and brandy, Lenox padded downstairs in his dressing gown and slippers, took a cup of coffee from the pot on the sideboard, and went to his study.

Graham was there, reading the *Times*. "Good morning, sir," he said.

"Any news this morning?" asked Lenox, looking through the letters on his desk.

"Little of consequence. The vote upon the Factory Act has been scheduled for nine days hence, pending debate. Both of the big trials will have their verdicts sent in this morning, Osgood and Mitchell—guilty in both cases, the papers think, and Mitchell will likely hang. Queen Victoria is back in Buckingham Palace after her trip to Germany. And you are retiring from Parliament."

Lenox looked up, surprised. "Has that made the papers?"

"First page of the *Times*, sir, though just below the fold."

Lenox smiled. "I will have to live with the indignity."

Only three people—before yesterday—had known of Lenox's plan to leave Parliament: Jane, Edmund, and Graham. Now that the news was out the congratulations and regrets began to come in, handfuls of telegrams every few minutes that morning. There were also visitors, many of them curious to hear who would be the next Junior Lord of the Treasury, many others curious to hear who would take his seat in Stirrington. Lenox said that he imagined his old opponent, the brewer Roodle, would stand on the Conservative platform. The Liberals didn't have a candidate yet.

Just after lunch a note came by hand from Dallington. Two notes under one cover, more precisely—one marked for Jane, which would be his thanks for the evening before, and one for Lenox.

A scrap of paper fell from Lenox's own letter when he opened it. He stooped to pick it up.

Lenox, Dallington, Strickland
Investigators

It had been printed very handsomely upon heavy card stock, its black letters still almost wet-looking, the curlicues of the font crisp and decisive. Lenox stared at it for a moment and then turned his attention to the note, which was written upon Dallington's writing paper.

October 11, 1875
Half Moon Street

Dear Lenox,

I had a thousand of these printed this morning, so really I think you are honor-bound to join in. Polly has agreed already. She says her name should be first, but I pointed out that you have been a Member of Parliament, and while God-fearing souls such as ourselves may hold that position in low esteem, there are heathens out in the metropolis who feel differently.

Please respond by next post, or in a few days, or come round, or send a pigeon. Until then I will be sleeping off last night, which was a pleasure.

John Dallington

PS: I only had the one printed, so we can adjust it to put my name first, if you insist.

Lenox held the card in his fingers, flexed it, and smiled. During the summer, when they were in London, he had done a fair bit of armchair consulting, for Dallington, for Jenkins, even for Polly Buchanan, who was very sharp but also inexperienced.

And for a fourth person, whose name he could envision joining theirs upon the card: LeMaire. He and the Frenchman had developed a friendship, based in large part on their fascination with the history and patterns of crime.

An agency. That would rout Audley, at any rate.

Of course, he had plans for the immediate months following his departure from the Commons. He slipped the card into his pocket. There was a great deal to do; he was scheduled to visit Leck the weekend after he stepped down, and the weekend following that they were due in Somerset, to visit his uncle Freddie and show off Sophia's new skills. (She could speak a few halting words, and understand even more—a positive Pericles, Lenox insisted in his letters to Plumbley.) It had also been a while since he had set foot outside of London. He would like to see the mountains of Italy again, and taste their strange, rather wonderful food. He wondered if the idea would appeal to Jane.

At teatime later that afternoon he was at the Commons, reading the evening newspapers as they came in. They all mentioned his speech, though only the *Evening Star* picked up on its oblique references to Disraeli's underhandedness. Several of them lauded his service, as the papers that morning had. Gratifying, of course. They also speculated about his replacement.

It was a line from the *Telegraph* that struck him: "Though the district has not yet favored Mr. Robert Roodle with the seat he has now sought three times, Mr. Lenox's retirement, and the lack of an obvious local candidate on the other side of the ticket, make his chances appear for the moment more favorable."

It gave Lenox an audacious idea. That evening when he arrived at home (the debate in the Commons had been quiet—rather enjoyable, now that their kind was numbered for him) he said to Jane, after giving her a kiss hello, "Do you want to travel to Stirrington with me tomorrow?"

"Not in the slightest. Why?"

"My dear!"

She laughed. "I do have appointments. But I'll go if you like. Why?"

When she heard his idea, she was immediately more willing, and so the next morning the two began the four-hour journey to Durham. When they arrived Lenox shook hands with the stationmaster (who had gotten so drunk the previous election day that he had forgotten to vote) and then with a succession of other locals, who stopped to ask if it was true, as the papers were reporting, that he was standing down. He felt rather guilty. England's system was so strange— that a man could represent a populace with which he had no association, or even, sometimes, affinity. Fortunately Lenox had grown truly fond of Stirrington's people; in most decisions he made he had tried to remember them, though sometimes the exigencies of London and her people, the great capital, predominated in his thoughts.

They took a brougham to the Queen's Arms, several streets away—a distinguished-looking public house, whitewashed and crossed with black beams, an old Tudor structure at the corner of two streets. Above the door was a bell that rang as they entered. A young woman was behind the bar, which was quiet at this time of day, two or three soft-voiced old men nursing their pints in amiable companionship.

"Nettie?" said Lenox.

"Mr. Lenox! How are you? We wondered whether we might hear from you."

Lenox went and gave her a kiss on the cheek. "You look lovely. It's not a month until your marriage, I believe?"

"Yes, three weeks. I'm awfully excited."

Nettie was the niece and ward of Edward Crook—the savvy, circumspect, overweight owner of the Queen's Arms, and Lenox's political agent in Stirrington. After she poured them each a glass of lemon squash she went upstairs to fetch Crook.

The publican was genuinely pleased to see them, in his reticent way, and, because it was nearing lunchtime, asked Nettie to run to the kitchens and order them all some food. He said he had read the speech in the papers and been surprised by it, but he seemed accustomed to the news already.

"Do you have a candidate yet?" Lenox asked.

Crook snorted. "What, in the last five hours? We don't. Old Stoke's grandson, the only logical candidate, wants no part of it—he's playing baccarat on the continent. It will be hard to beat Roodle."

"I have the man for you. He's a natural talent, Crook, really you have to see it to believe it."

"Who's that?"

"My secretary. Graham."

Crook laughed. "Your butler? That is your proposal?"

"He's not been my butler for many years now."

Lenox saw the skepticism in Crook's face.

"Have you informed him of your plan?"

"Not yet. You do not reckon him a worthy candidate?"

"Upon the contrary, he is one of the sharpest political minds I have known, and was your best surrogate here during your elections, but he was once your butler, Mr. Lenox."

"I cannot allow that it matters. He'll have the money. I'll stake him. I've brought Jane up to speak to the women of Stirrington—you recall what a bond they had—and I'll stay and campaign for a month, longer if I'd be useful. And Crook, you wouldn't believe how he could excel in Parliament. More than ever I could. Why, Disraeli—"

Here Lenox launched into the story of the spring, telling it very vividly. When he was part of the way through, Nettie came out of the kitchen, struggling under several plates of steaming food.

Jane went to help, and as she returned she heard Crook say, "We could give it a go, I suppose. It would be a long shot, mind."

"We can but try," Lenox answered immediately, his voice optimistic.

Hearing those words, seeing his face—flushed with excitement at his plan—Jane, still a few steps away, felt a tremendous burst of love for her husband. It was strange: She saw him, just for a brief instant, from a very great distance, as he sat there by the fireplace, an aging spaniel curled at the rug near his feet, a scent of fall in the air when the door opened and a new customer entered. What an astonishing world, she thought during the fleeting moment before she set the plates down and joined the conversation again. And what happiness to share it with someone.

Center Point Large Print
600 Brooks Road / PO Box 1
Thorndike ME 04986-0001 USA

(207) 568-3717

US & Canada:
1 800 929-9108
www.centerpointlargeprint.com